MW01598086

STORIES OF MY DINOSAUR LIFE

STORIES OF MY DINOSAUR LIFE

TAYLOR JAY FOX

STORIES OF MY DINOSAUR LIFE

© **2025** by **Taylor Jay Fox**. All rights reserved.
Debut Edition (Paperback) published May 17, 2025
ISBN: 978-1-0693417-3-0

No part of this book may be reproduced, distributed, or transmitted in any form or by any electronic or mechanical means, including information storage and retrieval systems, without prior written permission from the author, except in the case of brief quotations used in reviews or other uses permitted under Canadian or applicable local copyright laws.

The font MOONBLOSSOM designed by Crystal Kluge is used under license from Adobe Fonts.

Cover designed by:
@CodiAsFox
https://codiasfox.me/

Published by:
Vedla Creative Publishing Services
Ottawa, Canada
https://creative.vedla.ca/publishing

General Inquiries & Reader Feedback: hello@vedla.ca
Media, Licensing & Editorial Rights: creative@vedla.ca

A cataloguing record for this book is available from **Library and Archives Canada**.

❦ WRITTEN AND PUBLISHED IN CANADA

DISCLAIMER
This is a work of fiction, written in the style of a memoir. All names, characters, businesses, locations, events, and incidents are the product of the author's imagination. Any resemblance to actual persons, living or dead, businesses, or events is purely coincidental.

10 9 8 7 6 5 4 3 2 1

MAKING LITERATURE ACCESSIBLE TO ALL

Before we begin, I want to take a moment to acknowledge something close to my heart. As someone with a hidden disability, I understand the challenges some people face when reading. Personally, I find it difficult to keep text unless I'm reading it alongside an out loud voice.

I want to make sure my stories are accessible to everyone. If you've bought this book and require an alternative format—such as a synthesized (computer-read) version, a screen reader–friendly file, or an eBook in a different file type—please reach out to accessibility@vedla.ca.

I'll do my best to make those options available to you. However, I might not be able to fulfil every request—there may be limitations due to licensing, store policies, or, if you're reading this a hundred years from the publication date... I might not be around to check my emails.

Thank you for your time, your support, and your interest in my stories.

–Tay

DEDICATION

For those of us who feel like we don't quite fit in a world that often feels alien.
To Alex—thank you for accepting my quirks and letting me daydream about animal people.
And, of course, to my bro, Robin—thank you for fostering my creativity and encouraging my 'silly side' and wild dreams of writing about them.

Prologue:

WHO AM I?

Honestly, who am I? That three-word question has haunted me for years. Even now, after everything I've experienced, I still struggle with something I should have answered long ago.

First, you should know I never aspired to be a hero—even the word itself rubs me the wrong way. Hell, being a fox wasn't something I wanted, or even considered possible.

I was just another nobody—your average nerdy guy, the kind of person who fades into the background, and I was okay-ish with it, until everything shifted.

The world shattered in an instant, and I became... something else.

I remember it clearly—one of those days that sticks with you forever, etched into your brain like a scar.

May 17, 2015. 3:47 PM. Just another sunny spring Sunday, the kind where life hums along in its ordinary rhythm.

I was standing on the sidewalk, headphones in, scrolling through my phone, annoyed at some random crap in my life—when, out of nowhere, the sky changed.

The familiar blue shifted to an intense, pulsing green.

At first, most people barely reacted—some slowed down, confused, but life kept moving. Until they just stopped—mid-step, mid-sentence, mid-whatever— craning their necks to stare up, confusion etched across their faces.

The green hue grew brighter and brighter, and then the hum deepened into something you didn't just hear—you felt it, rattling your bones.

Then came the wind—powerful and all-consuming. People grabbed onto anything—lamp posts, cars, each other.

A deafening boom shook the ground beneath us, followed by a blinding white light.

Then... silence. Total, eerie silence.

My memory blurs here—most of it feels like a dream. Confused, I rubbed my eyes, and my hands felt strange, as if I were wearing fuzzy-lined gloves.

At first, the subtle changes made it seem like someone had rebooted the world. People started moving again, brushing themselves off. Until the screaming began.

People—just regular people—were changing. Their skin rippled and shifted, colours bleeding where none had been. Fur sprouted, ears grew, tails appeared.

Some transformations were subtle—a tuft of fur, whiskers, maybe a tail or fangs.

Others were... extreme. Like mine. I went full fox—fur, ears, tail, the works.

As expected, the world lost its collective shit. Emergency lines were jammed, hospitals overcrowded, law enforcement shattered. News stations scrambled to broadcast shaky videos and wild speculation.

Was it an attack? A divine reckoning? A freak accident? The 5G conspiracy? Nobody knew.

Only one thing was certain. The world had changed forever.

That day became known as *The Emergence.*

The following decade was anything but smooth.

Some called it evolution. Others, a curse. Some embraced their transformations and others feared them.

Aniforms—what people started calling us—found ourselves caught between fascination and fear.

What about me?

I continued doing what I'd always done. I tried to stay invisible and out of trouble.

I convinced myself I could coast through life unnoticed.

But well, life's a bitch with a twisted sense of humour. Wrong time, wrong place. You know the drill.

The interesting part of my story—and the reason you're probably reading this—happened ten years after the Emergence, when my quiet, insignificant life got shaken up again.

Choices were made. Alliances forged. And Mistakes? Well, I made plenty of those, too.

And now, years after my first visit to the *Global Unity for Interspecies Protection,* I'm still here trying to figure out what it all means.

I can't help but wonder—out of billions of people, why did I end up in the middle of all this?

Was it Fate? Perhaps destiny? Or just terrible luck? Your pick.

This isn't a story about how I became a hero. At its core, it's a narrative of survival—of breaking free from the shadows and seeking some kind of normalcy.

Or maybe it's about how I went from being a nobody delivery guy to a mid-tier international agent fighting for Aniforms everywhere. (Could be both?)

Because in the end, the real question isn't who I am. It's who I've had to become to get here.

But enough chit-chat.

Let's get into it, shall we?

Chapter 1

DELIVERING A HERO

During my career, I have been asked the same over and over: "Did you always know you wanted to be an agent?" I usually nod and say, "Yeah, I did." It's easier that way—no follow-up questions or awkward silences.

But if I'm being honest? The idea seemed so far-fetched; I couldn't even dream about it. Instead, I opted for a life that required less of me—just a simple existence where I could stay under the radar and out of trouble. I thought that was enough. But life, as always, had other plans.

So... how did I go from a mundane life to who I am today?

Well, it all began sixteen years ago—on a typical day that, ended with me falling from the tenth floor, surrounded by flames, busted office furniture, and a guy I'd just met.

Back then, I was just another delivery guy weaving through Mapleview's crowded streets on one of those rare, warm early-spring days in March. It was the kind of day that tricks you into believing everything might be okay.

The sun was out; the city buzzed with life, and everything felt... normal. Well, as normal as it gets when you're a 5'8" fox human hybrid in a world still figuring out how to deal with us.

By then, the term *aniform* had stuck—what people called us. But even ten years after the Emergence. The world wasn't sure what to do with us—or if it even wanted us here.

My appearance wasn't anything special—still isn't. Red, almost orange fur, accented with cream-coloured markings and chocolate-coloured paws (or hands, whatever you wanna call them; I use both), and a small earring in my left ear.

I wore plain Costco jeans, and a faded purple hoodie. Over my shoulder was a *Munch Munchy Bites* delivery bag, and my wireless earbuds that hummed some old song I can't even remember now.

The *Norforms*—as we used to call regular humans—didn't look at me, which was funny when you think about it. Like if they avoided eye contact long enough, I'd just poof out of existence. Subtle steps away, quick glances, an exaggerated we're-just-sharing-the-sidewalk-nothing-weird-here vibe. You get used to it... *Mostly.*

I remember noticing a billboard across the street celebrating the tenth anniversary of the Emergence. Someone had taken a black marker to it, adding a very... uh... *phallocentric* touch over the aniform's face.

Although the world had come a long way by then. It was still common to see faded "*Humans Only*" signs clinging to shop windows.

But it wasn't all bad. Some treated us with respect—like Fred.

Bear Fred's Pizza & Pasta wasn't far from the intersection, and I could smell the garlic and dough before I even opened the door.

Fred was an aniform, too. Bear features with golden fur, massive paws, and a voice that could soothe or scold you. He always wore this crooked purple chef's hat that made him look like some wizard—a wizard of carbs.

"Hey, SJ!" Fred boomed as I walked in. "What's the rush?"

"Hi Fred," I shot back, leaning against the counter. "Same old; Dodging traffic, pedestrians, the occasional cyclist..."

Fred chuckled, smoothly flipping the dough into the air. "Well, don't dodge too hard. You're late again."

"Oh, Freddy, what's life without a little last-minute adrenaline? It's cheaper than an eight-buck latte." I said with a grin.

Fred slid a pizza into the oven and shook his head, placing a paper bag on the counter. "Your order's ready. Just try not to get yourself hit by a bus, okay?"

"I'll try," I said, grabbing the bag and heading back outside. "Take care bud."

Enjoying Fred's easy banter always brought a sense of normalcy. Sadly, it didn't last. My good mood shattered when, across the street, I saw a norform shove a small cat-aniform out of their way.

"Move, freak!" the bastard said.

The kid ducked his head and shuffled off, clearly used to it. My tail twitched in frustration. Was this the moment my heroic journey began? Did I jump in and save the day? Ha. Nope!

Instead, I pulled my hood up, stared at the pavement, and kept walking. *Best not to get involved*, I told myself.

Believe me, I wanted to step in. But it's hard to fight for something when you don't even know if the cause is worth it.

By the time I made it back to my car, whatever energy Fred had given me was long gone.

I tapped my phone for directions to the next drop-off, and the robotic voice chimed, "Getting directions to GUIP Offices."

"Really, GUIP?" I muttered.

The *Global Unity for Interspecies Protection* wasn't a site you casually visited. A place straight out of news stories—agents in sharp uniforms protect both

Aniforms and Norforms. It seemed unreal, as if designed for those much cooler or braver than I was.

I shrugged, started the engine, and followed the GPS. It was just another regular delivery during a typical day, or so I thought.

I left my car outside GUIP's sleek, modern building, deliberately ignoring the *No Parking* sign. With a shrug, I flicked on my hazard lights, grabbed the food bag, and headed inside.

The lobby buzzed with activity—agents moved with purpose. Their sharp attires made me feel out of place in my hoodie and jeans. Not that anyone cared.

Posters lined the walls, showcasing heroic-looking Aniforms with bold slogans like *Beyond Borders, Beyond Species* and *Safeguarding Our Shared Home.* One, in particular, caught my eye:

Be The Hero The World Needs.

For a second, I let my mind wander—me, up on that poster, a medal around my neck, crowds chanting my name.

Until the receptionist's sharp, impatient voice yanked me back to reality.

"Next."

I stepped forward. "Uh, food delivery for... Agent Tay–uh...Tyrann?" I said, stumbling over the name.

"ID?"

The receptionist—a sleek, no-nonsense cougar-aniform with black fur and subtle blue highlights—barely looked up.

His name tag read *Kingston*, and his sharp, focused eyes stayed glued to his monitor as he swiped my driver's licence with practised efficiency.

"Tenth floor," he said. "Agent Tyrann is waiting for you."

He slid a visitor badge and my licence across the counter with a paw flick. "Put this on," gesturing toward the elevators without sparing me another glance.

"Thanks," I said. Clipping the badge to my hoodie and heading toward the elevators.

I walked away, my gaze swiping the unfamiliar place. When, I accidentally bumped into someone solid. I stumbled back, nearly dropping the food.

"Whoa there!" a firm voice said to me.

I looked up to see a lioness-aniform grinning down at me, her hand steadying my shoulder. Her warm eyes sparkled with amusement. "These hallways can seem like a jungle,"

"I'm so sorry!" I said. My face burning with embarrassment.

She waved it off with a friendly smile. "No worries, it happens to the best of us. You'll get the hang of it."

Surprised by her kindness, I managed a weak smile. "Thanks... I'm just here to deliver some food."

"Ah, keeping us running," she said with a wink. "That's an important job, too. And hey, who knows? Maybe someday you'll be walking these halls as one of us."

Before I could reply, she gave me a casual salute and walked off, leaving me wondering if she was serious.

Inside the elevator, I couldn't shake her words off my head. Me, an agent? The polished elevator doors reflected my image at me—unkempt fur, a ratty hoodie, a delivery bag slung over my shoulder. I didn't look like hero material. But as I stared at myself, the thought lingered.

It's possible I had more to myself than I had thought.

I felt a hint of excitement in my chest as I climbed to the 10th floor.

When the doors slid open, I took a steadying breath, pulling back my hood as I stepped into the reception area. My eyes scanned the room and landed on him— Tyrann.

He had that kind of presence that commanded attention without effort. Mid-forties, *mostly human*, but the sharp cat-like ears and flicking tail gave him away. The tail, a clear indicator of his emotions, swayed gently, hinting at his composed state.

He matched his impeccably tailored suit with a brown tie that conveyed both *I mean business* and *I'm approachable*.

"The food hero is here," I announced, grinning and holding the paper bag like a trophy.

Tyrann raised an eyebrow, smirking as he checked his phone. "Well, Mr. Food Hero, thanks for your..." he lowered his voice with mock seriousness, "late service."

"Heroically late," I shot back. "That's my style."

I tapped my phone to complete the order, and his phone pinged with the confirmation. *Mission accomplished.*

"Well, bud. Duty calls," I said with a wink, turning to leave.

Right before I could take another step. Alarms blared—loud, piercing, and unrelenting—drowning out every other sound. My ears flattened instinctively as the mood switched around us.

A mechanical voice echoed through the building: "*CODE E 6 21. ALL FORCES BE ALERT*."

Tyrann's complete demeanour shifted. His tail raised up, his ears nudging as his body tensed.

His previous calm and approachable demeanour faded away, giving way to a sharp, focused intensity.

"Stay here," Tyrann said. His voice leaving no room for argument.

"What is going on?" I called after him, but he was already sprinting down the hallway, his tie flapping behind him.

Agents darted out of their offices, shouting into radios, bolting toward the stairwells.

I stood there, clutching an empty bag, wondering what in the hell I'd just walked into.

The smart thing would've been to leave, but I'm not known for thinking before acting, so I followed Tyrann, weaving through the office as agents scrambled, their movements sharp and deliberate. My heart pounded as I tried to piece together what was happening.

I spotted something dropping from the ceiling—a strange-looking figure with what looked like a rocket launcher.

I didn't have time to think. I jumped, and yelled, "Dude, watch out!"

The explosion rocked the room. I barely tackled Tyrann under a desk before debris rained down on us. My ears rang, my thoughts scrambled, and the only thing I managed to say was, "Eight lives left, eh?"

Tyrann gave me a look that was equal parts shock and gratitude. "Thanks," he said as we crawled from under the desk. He dusted himself off, his tail flicking. "But you need to leave. Now."

Before I could argue, he grabbed the hood of my hoodie and yanked me toward the fire exit.

He kicked the door open, peered down the stairwell and shouted, "Clear! Now go!" Pointing downstairs.

"Alone? Are you fucking serious?" I planted my feet, resisting his shove.

He pushed me closer to the stairs. "I'll be right behind you. I need to grab something. Just move!" And with that, he disappeared into the smoke filled chaos of the office.

I hesitated, tail flicking. The idea of leaving didn't feel right, not when the guy better equipped to handle the situation was running towards the danger.

"No way am I going down alone," I muttered, spinning back to face the room.

"Uh... cat-guy?" I called, my voice barely audible over the wailing alarms and the distant rumble of another explosion. I forgot his name, but I scanned the wreckage, hoping to spot him.

I looked around the room. My eyes landed on a poster with bold letters stating, "It's Your Time..." *Wait, is it?* I thought. *Was it the sign from the universe I needed?* Maybe—if you believe in that sort of thing. My head was spinning too much to notice the rest of the ad that read "...for pies! GUIP Annual Pie Sale."

However, something clicked inside me, or maybe it was just the toxic fumes from the burning office furniture messing with my head.

It was a stupid decision; I know that, but I had to do something. I took a deep breath, sharply—perhaps too sharply—and immediately regretted it as black smoke seared my throat. "Ugh, this is such a bad idea," I said, coughing.

I pushed through the haze, dodging broken desks, shattered glass, and burning objects. My heart pounded, every instinct screaming for me to turn back, but my feet kept moving deeper.

Finally, I spotted him—Tyrann—emerging from a room marked *"Authorized Personnel Only"*. He was slipping something into a messenger bag when I stumbled into view. "There you are!" I called, relief and exasperation flooding my voice.

Tyrann's ears flattened, his expression a mix of annoyance and surprise. "Fox? Why are you still here?"

"You forgot to tip," I shot back with a smirk. "And it looks like you could use my help."

"This isn't a game," His tone sharp. "Get out. Now."

I crossed my arms, standing my ground. "Not without you."

We just stared at each other for a moment. His eyes narrowed, and I thought he might punch and drag me out by the scruff. But he just sighed, shoulders relaxing. "Fine" he said, "but stay close."

We rushed, Tyrann checking corners and clearing rooms as we went. The eerie silence made my fur stand on end. *Where was everyone? Wasn't this place supposed to be filled with agents?*

Tyrann seemed to have the same thought. "Damn, where is everyone?"

"Probably far away from trigger-happy aliens," I said, trying to lighten the mood or calm my nerves. "Looks like we're the only ones stupid enough to stick around."

Tyrann didn't respond, but the flick of his tail told me he didn't entirely disagree.

We turned a corner, and something in a cracked mirror caught my eye—a shadow moving behind us. I pulled Tyrann's sleeve. "Uh... Mr agent?"

"What now?" he said, clearly losing patience.

I pointed to the mirror. "Incoming baddie. Five o'clock."

Tyrann spun as a shadowy alien figure stepped out of the smoke, weapon raised. I hit the floor as a bolt of energy zipped past, striking a fire extinguisher. The explosion sent foam spraying everywhere, coating us in a thick layer of white.

My ears were ringing—again. I staggered to my feet, coughing and brushing away the foam. Tyrann was flat on his back, groaning as he tried to sit up.

"Great time for a nap, eh?" I said.

"Help me up," he murmured. His voice was annoyed and exhausted.

I crouched, hoisting him to his feet with an exaggerated grunt. "Oh, look who needs my help now."

He shot me a tired glare but didn't bother with a comeback. Instead, he pointed toward a fire exit across the conference room. "There's another way out through there. Move."

We were halfway across the room when something outside caught my attention—a chaotic view of the street below. Agents and police clashed with more of those strange, copper-plated creatures.

A small metallic object rolled into the room and stopped a short distance from us.

"Plasma grenade!" Tyrann said.

I snapped back to the moment, my eyes locking onto the blinking light.

All I have time to say was: "Oh shit"

A blinding flash and heat swallow everything. The force pushed us backward, our bodies shattering the floor-to-ceiling window. A fireball and glass shards rained around us as the world outside became a spinning, chaotic blur.

In that moment, nothing else mattered. Only one thought echoed in my mind: This is it. This is how I am going to die.

Chapter 2

DORKY FOX

Ten stories, about 30 metres or 100 feet for my American friends (give or take), approximately a 2.5-second drop. It might not seem like much, but believe me, a thousand things race through your mind at that time.

Was this it? People say your life flashes in front your eyes just before you die. For me? My only thought was how embarrassing was to die in a worn-out hoodie.

But instead of the pavement ending my existential crisis, we landed on a *conveniently placed* awning. It sagged dramatically under our combined weight, slowing our fall just enough to avoid certain death.

The landing was rough. We hit the ground with a loud thud that knocked the wind out of me. Dust and shards of glass covered us, and every part of my body ached. But hey—we were alive.

"Ugh," I said, dusting myself off. "Definitely not how I pictured my day going."

Tyrann leaned against a nearby wall, steadying himself. His face was a mix of exhaustion, gratitude, and frustration. "Thanks for jumping in, Fox," he said, his voice heavy. "But you've got to get out of here. I can handle the rest."

"What?" I asked, glancing at the surrounding destruction—burning vehicles, aliens, and sirens wailing in the distance. "After nearly dying twice today? No chance. I'm sticking with you." Not the smartest move, I'll admit, but hey, don't question my logic. I probably had a concussion.

Tyrann sighed. "You're relentless, you know that?"

I gave him a wry smile. "Relentless, annoying... I've been called worse."

We ducked behind my parked car for cover—still in mint condition. Well, as good as a *2014 blue Mazda 3* could be. As I crouched behind it, my eyes landed on a horrific sight.

"Oh, come on. Not again!" I groaned, snatching a parking ticket off the windshield.

"Move!" Tyrann barked, scanning for a safer path.

Before I could even shove the ticket in my pocket, a laser beam sliced through the air—straight into my car. It exploded in a flash of heat and metal, reduced to a smoking pile of ashes.

"My car!" I said, throwing my hands up. *Well... guess I don't have to pay the ticket now.*

Tyrann didn't even look at me. "Go."

We sprinted across the street, diving behind a dumpster. Smoke burned my lungs, my fur was singed, and I probably was bleeding from somewhere—but at least we had a second to catch our breath.

Tyrann's ears twitched as he turned to me, frustration boiling over. "Help me understand something, Fox. I told you to leave. Why were you still in there?"

I shifted, my tail twitching behind me. "I wasn't just gonna run with my tail between my legs," I said, then, lowering my voice, "And... I thought I could help. For once."

He was still annoyed. But his voice had a hint of curiosity. "So, your grand plan was to play hero? You're not trained for this."

"I don't know," I admitted, scratching the back of my neck and avoiding his gaze. My tail drooped, and my ears flattened. "I know I'm no hero. But if I'm stuck as a 'dorky fox,' I might as well be a useful one, right?"

For a moment, Tyrann just looked at me. His face was unreadable, but I swore I caught a flicker of something—respect, maybe? Whatever it was, he didn't let it linger long.

I peeked over the dumpster's edge, scanning the street. "Just out of curiosity... what's got those aliens so pissed off?"

"The Zenitharians."

I blinked. "Zenitha-what?"

"Zenitharians," he repeated, tone sharper. "Trust me, you don't want to be on their bad side."

Let's pause for a sec. *Who are these creatures?* You see, the *Zenitharians* are an intelligent, highly advanced species from the planet *Cosmarchea.* Tiny but powerful. These little bastards are more trouble than they look.

Cool, but what are they even doing here on Earth? The public—and official—story says their arrival was an accident. A navigation error during an interstellar battle.

In short? They had shit aim and caused the Emergence. *Do I know better now?* Yeah. But you'll just have to wait for that part.

"And right now, we're on their bad side?" I said, raising an eyebrow.

Tyrann nodded. "Yeah. Very bad."

I remained baffled, unsure about what was happening. "Okay, and why are they after us?"

"It's classified." Tyrann said, firm and without hesitation.

I couldn't take it any longer. My tail shot up, and my ears perked up. "Oh, come on, man!" I said, waving a paw in frustration. "I think I've earned the right to know why my fur's about to become an alien rug! And, by the way, you still owe me for not tipping."

I tried to hold my serious expression, but Tyrann just stared at me. For a moment, I thought he'd brush me off again. Then, with a sigh, "Alright." he said.

He reached into his bag, and pulled a small and glowing object. I instinctively leaned in, curiosity taking over. It was a strange-looking device—a sleek blue box that pulsed with an eerie light.

"Ooooh, pretty. So... what's that?" I said. My tail wagged.

Tyrann looked unimpressed. "It's an energy core," he said, slipping it back into his bag. "Powers their tech. We confiscated it during an operation at one of their bases last month. The location was classified." His expression darkened. "No idea how they found out where it was."

I could see the worry on his face. "We need to secure it. Fast."

"Okay, and how exactly do we do that?"

Tyrann scanned the streets, his eyes locking onto something in the distance. "We need to get to my cruiser," he said, pointing. "There's a proton laser in the trunk."

I perked up at that. "A proton laser? Now we're talking! Where is it?"

He nodded toward his car just as another laser blast ripped through the pavement nearby, sending chunks of asphalt flying. "Right there," he said.

I followed his gaze. I groaned when I saw the cruiser sitting smack in the middle of the fire. "Of course it is..." I said.

"We have to hurry. Move!" Tyrann said, taking off without waiting for a response. He darted between overturned cars and flaming wreckage, and I was right on his tail, adrenaline surging.

We were almost at the cruiser when another vehicle exploded, shaking the street. I fell hard, dust and smoke clouding my vision as I scrambled to my feet. Tyrann wasn't far off—the blast had thrown him back, slamming into a pile of rubble.

The core slipped from his bag and rolled across the pavement.

And well, one of the Zenitharians spotted it, hissing as it signalled to the others.

Tyrann lurched up and dove for the core. I rushed to help, but the Zenitharians were closing in, weapons ready.

"Forget me, Fox! Get to the cruiser!" Tyrann said.

I rolled my eyes. "I have a name, you know."

"Not the time. Go!"

I didn't argue. I rushed towards the vehicle and grabbed the handle. It was locked.

"Ugh... perfect," yanking the door again out of frustration. My eyes darted around until I spotted a metal rod on the ground. Grabbing it, I smashed the driver's side window. Glass scattered everywhere as I reached in to unlock the door.

I got inside and yanked the trunk release. The trunk popped open with a creak, revealing a heap of agency folders, emergency supplies, and random junk. And the proton laser.

I grabbed it, my heart pounding. The sleek weapon felt heavy and dangerous in my hands. The design looked simple enough, but there were no labels on the buttons.

On my way up, I noticed Tyrann in the distance, bound by a couple of Zenitharians. Behind them, a couple of ships loomed closer, engines whining.

I glanced down at the weapon, muttering, "Oh, come on!" as I pressed a random button. I waited—nothing. Pressed another—still nothing. Panic rising, I jabbed more buttons as the Zenitharians got closer. In pure frustration, I slammed my fist down on all the buttons at once.

The laser hummed to life with a high-pitched whine.

"Fuck yes!" I said. Feeling relief as a red light blinked on. That had to be the trigger. At least, I hoped it was.

I sprinted toward the descending Zenitharian ship. The wind from its engines whipped my hoodie and ears around. I planted my feet, and aimed the laser at it.

"Say hello to my little friend," I muttered, squeezing the trigger.

With a deafening roar, the weapon fired a massive beam of light, exploding the ship in a fireworks-like display.

A shockwave hit throwing everyone—Tyrann, the Zenitharians, and me off our feet. I hit the ground hard, skidding across the pavement. My wallet tumbled from my pocket and spun off into the distance, but I didn't care. For a few moments, I just lay there, staring at the fireball, grinning like an idiot as metal shards rained down around me.

I forced myself back up. My ears rang for the 3rd time that day, the tip of my tail was on fire, and my head spun like I'd just gotten off the world's worst rollercoaster. But I felt... alive.

I spotted Tyrann on the ground next to an immobile Zenitharian in the wreckage. Still clutching the proton laser, I staggered over to him.

"It's becoming a habit for me to save your tail, isn't it?" I teased, extending a hand to help him up.

Tyrann winced, brushing off some rubble as he took my hand. "Thanks,

Fox," he muttered, voice low. "That was brave... and incredibly stupid."

"Hey, stupid's what makes it fun," I shot back, helping him steady himself. "Now come on, we've still got some aliens to deal with."

We turned to face the remaining Zenitharians—only to see them retreating toward another ship in the distance.

"They're getting away!" Tyrann said, his eyes narrowing. "Shit, They've got the core!"

Grinning, I reached into my hoodie pocket, pulled out the glowing blue object, and held it up. "You mean this core?" I asked, trying to sound casual.

Tyrann froze mid-step, staring at me like I'd grown another tail. "How... how did you—?"

"Being part fox finally came in handy," I said with a wink. "When the explosion sent it flying, I snagged it before running to you."

The look on his face—half shock, half disbelief—was almost worth all the near-death experiences of the day.

As the Zenitharians' ship disappeared into the sky, we stood there in the aftermath; the tension easing. Tyrann let out a long breath, his shoulders relaxing for the first time all day. His burned and torn shirt revealed faint scars across his chest.

We just stood there in silence for a bit, taking a moment to breathe.

I tossed the core from one hand to another, playing with it like a ball. "So... now what?" I asked, glancing at Tyrann.

"We call it in," he said, his voice steady. "And we take the core to a secure location."

He chuckled, then winced in pain. "Come on, help me get to the car."

We picked our way through the wreckage, the sounds of sirens blending with the crackle of lingering flames in the distance. The surrounding chaos was fading, but my thoughts were the opposite.

Tyrann's voice broke through my reverie, steady but firm. "You are a natural for this. You know? We could use someone like you."

I raised an eyebrow, glancing over at him. "Me? An agent?" I let out a short, nervous laugh. "I don't know... This was more than enough craziness for one lifetime."

He stopped walking, turning to face me. "Think about it," he said. "You've got potential. More than you realize."

I looked away, unsure of how to respond. I considered ignoring his words, but I couldn't let it go. *Is he right? Can I have more than a simple existence?* I thought.

We reached the car, Tyrann lowered himself into the driver's seat, wincing.

As I climbed into the passenger seat, I spoke, breaking the silence. "I'll think about it," I said.

Tyrann gave a faint smile, starting the engine. "That's all I'm asking."

My mind was still spinning as we pulled away, a thousand questions and doubts swirling in my head. I stared out the window as the city rolled by. My reflection stared back at me—tired, dishevelled, and ash-covered. But beneath all of that, there was something else: a spark of potential.

Chapter 3:
YOU TOOK MINE; I TAKE YOURS

The drive to the secure station was quiet. Tyrann looked exhausted, though he'd never admit it. The streets were still a mess—emergency vehicles flashing, debris from the Zenitharian attack scattered everywhere—but it all felt distant, like a dream I hadn't woken up from.

It was just the engine's hum and the occasional clatter of the loose junk in the trunk for a while.

"You're awfully quiet for someone who just saved the day," Tyrann said, breaking the silence.

I kept my eyes on the road ahead. "Still processing," I said. "A few hours ago, my biggest worry was delivering food on time. Now? I'm jobless 'cause my car's been reduced to ashes, I've survived aliens trying to kill me, a ten-story free fall, and—oh yeah,—I'm probably partially responsible for millions of dollars in damages. So, yeah... just a lot to process."

Tyrann chuckled, though it sounded more like a grunt. "That's how it starts. One day, you're just a regular guy. The next, you're in the thick of it."

I glanced at him. "Is that what happened to you?"

"Not exactly," he admitted. "My fight was to make GUIP a reality."

That caught my attention. "Wait—seriously?" I gasped, my voice higher than I'd meant it to be.

"Yeah," he said, his voice quieter now. "Long story, but let's just say I know what it is to be thrown into something bigger than yourself. To wonder if you're up for it."

He stopped at a red light and turned to me, his gaze steady. "You've got what's needed for this fight, Fox."

I raised an eyebrow, half-laughing. "I didn't sign up to save the world."

"You already did," he said.

I opened my mouth to respond, but nothing came out. *What could have I said?* He wasn't wrong, but *was I ready for more?* That day might have unlocked something in me, sure. But committing to that life was a whole other level.

The silence stretched until we pulled up in front of an unmarked building. It was the kind of place that blended into the city, the kind you'd pass a hundred times without noticing. Tyrann killed the engine, letting the moment settle before speaking again.

"Come on," he said, pushing open the door and wincing as he stood. "Let's get this thing locked up."

I went inside, nodding, my mind still replaying his words.

The secure station was much more intense than I'd expected—cameras everywhere, high-tech security checkpoints, and more armed agents than I could count. This was the kind of place that practically screamed, *Clearance required.* Tyrann, though? He didn't even have to flash a badge.

"He's with me," Tyrann told one agent, a guy who hadn't blinked since I arrived. The agent gave me a once-over that lasted too long for comfort, then nodded us through without a word.

We moved down the corridors, and the air seemed to thicken with every step. Screens lined the walls, displaying live footage of the city. Somewhere in the background, the faint hum of the security system droned on, almost hypnotic.

We stopped before a thick steel door marked *Evidence Locker,* that looked like something straight out of a heist movie.

Inside, the room was dimly lit and eerily quiet. Glass cases lined the walls, each holding strange pieces of alien tech or artifacts. Some looked like they belonged in a sci-fi horror movie—half-melted machinery, a helmet fused with something organic, and other things I couldn't even describe. A few looked more alive than mechanical, and that thought alone made my fur bristle.

Tyrann stepped forward and placed the core into a secure case. The mechanism locked with a soft click, and it felt like we could finally relax for the first time all day. I stood to the side, wrapped in one of GUIP's scratchy emergency blankets, sipping from a paper cup.

The events of the day were finally catching up with me.

"Safe and sound," Tyrann said, wiping sweat from his brow. His tail flicked. He turned to me, his sharp demeanour softening. "Thanks again. You saved my neck out there, Fox."

I shrugged, uncomfortable under the praise. "Yeah, well... no biggie."

He let out a short laugh—tired but genuine. He pulled out a folded flyer from his pocket and held it out to me with a casual air that didn't match the serious look in his eyes.

"Here. Consider this your official invitation."

I unfolded the flyer; the bold words *Join the Global Unity for Interspecies Protection* staring back at me. It seemed heavier in my hands than the paper should have been.

"You're offering me a job?" I asked, lowering my ears as I glanced up at him.

"I'm offering you a shot," Tyrann corrected, his tone firm. "You've got a knack for this kind of work. Sure, the hours suck, and there's always the chance of getting blown up, but I promise you'll never be bored."

I stared at the flyer, my mind racing. Hours prior, my life was a mess of deliveries and horrible tips, and now there I was, being told I had potential. It didn't feel real.

I chuckled, trying to lighten the moment. "So, daily life-and-death situations or terrible tips delivering pizza? Tough choice."

Tyrann smirked. "Just think about it," he said, his voice dipping into a more serious tone. "You don't have to decide right now."

I nodded, folding the flyer and tucking it into my hoodie pocket. "I will," I said, though I wasn't sure if I had already made my decision to pass.

Tyrann clapped a hand on my shoulder. "Need a ride home?"

I shook my head, managing a small smile. "Nah, I'm close. I could use the walk to clear my head."

"Suit yourself," he said with a nod, walking me to the front door. "Take care, Fox. And take your time."

I lingered for a moment after he left, the dim streetlights casting long shadows across the floor. My eyes drifted back to the building—a stark reminder of how strange that day had been.

The cool night air snapped me back to reality, sharp, and cold against my fur. The city buzzed as always, but it felt distant.

My paws moved on autopilot as I walked down the street, my mind spinning. Part of me wanted to crumple the flyer and throw it in the trash, forget the whole insane day, and pretend none of it had ever happened. But another part of me— the part that couldn't stop thinking about Tyrann's offer—tugged at something deep inside, a nagging suspicion that he possibly was right.

Maybe there was more to me than I'd realized.

Crystal Beach had always been a quiet, tucked-away borough of the city. The kind of suburb where rows of similar-enough houses lined the streets. *What a day*, I thought as I turned into my street that was poorly lit by the city's neglected infrastructure.

At the time, I was still living with my parents and my younger brother. *Yeah, yeah, I know*—but don't judge me. They didn't seem to mind... though, now that I think about it, I never asked them.

Our house sat at the end of a small cul-de-sac, neat but unassuming—a single-story home (or two, if you count the finished basement where my room was, which I won after an intense fight with my brother). It was a simple brick house with just enough charm to suggest a comfortable life.

As I approached, I noticed the porch light was off. My dad usually turned it on for me, but wasn't unusual for him to forget. The front door, though? It was ajar. I froze mid-step. *Had I forgotten to lock it?* I didn't think so. Besides, both my parents' cars were in the driveway—they should've been home.

I reached for my phone, my fingers hovering over the screen. *Should've I call 9-1-1? Tyrann?* No, I didn't even have his number. My instincts screamed at me to turn back, but something stronger pulled me forward.

I pushed the door open wider.

The living room lay wrecked; someone had upturned the furniture, pulled out drawers, and torn apart family photos scattered across the floor. I felt a stomach churning twist, but it didn't prepare me for what I saw.

My parents and younger brother, Andy (all of them humans), had their mouths covered and hands tied.

And standing over them, holding my wallet—my ID halfway out in one hand and a weapon in the other—was a Zenitharian.

"About fucking time you showed up," the Zenitharian said, their robotic voice sharp, like an angry, distorted Siri.

Everything else—the explosions, the near-death—faded into the background. That was worse. So much worse.

"You took something valuable from us," the Zenitharian said, their voice low and deliberate. "It's only fair we take something in return."

When they were in attack mode, the Zenitharians wore some kind of exoskeleton—basically an armour designed to make them look taller, bulkier, and more intimidating than they really were. Metal plating housing, accented by glowing sections and random buttons that seemed more decorative than functional.

Without the suit? Quite the opposite—shorter, more compact frame, with an almost friendly look.

Think of them as some sort of anthropomorphic house cat, just with no tail, less fur and more colourful.

It took a moment for their words to sink in, and rage flared inside me when they did. I had clenched my fists so tightly that my claws dug into my palms. "Whatever you want, it's between us," I said, forcing my voice to stay steady. "Leave them out of this—they've got nothing to do with it!"

The Zenitharian tilted their head, cold and calculating. "Nothing to do with it?" They said, gesturing toward my family. "You involved them the moment you took the core."

"I didn't—" I stopped myself. Arguing wouldn't help. I had to think, but my mind was blank. "What do you want?"

"It's simple. Return what is ours."

I swallowed hard, my voice shaking. "How the fuck am I supposed to do that? I'm just a delivery guy. I don't have access to it."

The Zenitharian stepped closer, their gun aimed at my dad's head. "You seem clever enough. Find a way, or they pay the price."

"Wait—" My voice cracked, panic breaking through my façade. "I'll get you what you want, but you have to let them go. They're innocent! They've got nothing to do with this!"

"Innocent?" They tilted their head again, their glowing visor casting an eerie light over the wrecked room. "Funny. You think innocence matters?"

I took a shaky step forward, my hands raised in desperation. "I'm begging you... Please. Don't hurt them. Use me if you need leverage, but let them go."

They let out a sharp, bitter laugh. "Leverage? You're not worth enough for that." Their weapon lowered; the barrel was now trained on Andy. "But them? They will be your motivation."

"Stop!" I shouted, my claws digging deeper into my palms. "I'll get the core! And do whatever you want! I promise. Just let them go!"

The Zenitharian paused, their finger hovering over a button on their wrist. "Your promises mean nothing."

Before I could move, they pressed the button.

A blinding beam shot from the ceiling, engulfing my family.

"No!" I screamed, rushing toward them, but it was too late. The beam sent them flying, their terrified faces disappearing into the light as the ceiling shattered.

"Mom! Dad! Andy!" My voice was raw, my throat burning. "Hold on! I'll save you; I swear!"

The light disappeared as quickly as it came, leaving silence and destruction in its wake.

I stood there, numb, staring up at the gaping hole in the ceiling. My heart pounded in my ears, drowning out everything else. My legs gave out, and I sank to the floor, surrounded by debris. Tears blurred my vision as my chest heaved with shallow, ragged breaths.

I buried my face in my hands; the guilt killing me. If I hadn't gotten involved, if I hadn't tried to be something I wasn't, my family would still be there.

I wiped my eyes with the sleeve of my hoodie, my breath hitching as I tried to steady myself. The promise I'd made echoed in my head louder than my doubts. *I'll save you.*

My eyes swept over the wreckage until they landed on a crumpled piece of paper near the door. The flyer Tyrann had given me. The words *Join the Global Unity for Interspecies Protection* stared back at me. This had become far bigger than just a job.

I forced myself back up, legs trembling. A family photo, hanging askew on the wall, with cracked glass, caught my eye. I stepped forward, taking it in my hands. My mom, dad, Andy, and I were all smiling.

"I'll find you," my voice breaking.

I tucked the flyer into my pocket, squared my shoulders, and turned toward the door.

The 11-kilometre (about 7 miles) walk from home to GUIP headquarters was long. Three hours long. The buses had stopped running by then, and I wasn't in the mood for car shares. Taking one of my parents' car seemed inappropriate with them gone, and Andy was still saving for one of his own. So, I walked.

The city seemed different somehow—quieter, colder. Every step heavy, but I kept moving, driven by the echo of my promise: *I'll save you.*

I stopped in front of the glowing sign.

Global Unity for Interspecies Protection: North America Dinosaur Division.

Agents were still buzzing around the perimeter, cleaning up the aftermath of the Zenitharian attack. The faint hum of machinery working overtime filled the air.

My mind raced, thoughts tumbling over one another. *What had I gotten myself into? How was I supposed to save my family when I didn't even know where to start?* But one thing was obvious: I couldn't do it alone.

I stormed through the front doors, my footsteps echoing in the silent lobby. The dim lighting gave the place a hollow, almost surreal, atmosphere.

At the reception desk sat a young jackal night guard. He looked up from his screen, his unimpressed eyes locking on me as I charged toward him.

"I need to see Agent Tyrann," I said, slamming the recruitment flyer onto the counter. "Tell him I'm in."

The jackal raised an eyebrow, his tone as flat as his expression. "No, you are not," he said, barely glancing away from his computer. "It's three in the morning. Come back during business hours."

"Fine!" I said. Snatching the flyer and storming back outside.

I collapsed onto a bench, the cold metal biting through my fur. My breath fogged in the chilly air as my mind spiralled into chaos.

"Come back during business hours," I said, mocking the receptionist's robotic tone. I shook my head and stared out at the empty street.

I pulled out my phone, aimlessly scrolling through my photos. After a few swipes, I found the one I was looking for—a picture from last year, one of the rare times the whole family had been together.

Dad was holding the camera, his grin so big it almost cut off the top of his head. Mom stood beside him, mid-laugh. I was in the corner of the frame, wincing as Andy accidentally stepped on my tail. He swore it was an accident, but I didn't buy it.

I smiled at the memory, but the warmth it usually brought was absent. All I felt was the guilt crashing down my chest. There was a voice in my head that kept reminding me it was all my fault.

I tried to stay angry—it was easier that way. Anger was clean and sharp, giving me something to hold on to. But the harder I clung to it, the more it slipped away, leaving only sadness and frustration.

The tears came before I could stop them. I buried my face in my hands, my shoulders shaking as the emotions broke free. Alone in the cold, dark night.

By morning, I marched back into the building, my energy drained compared to the night before. Kingston, the cougar aniform, was back at the desk, his disinterested expression as unshakable as ever.

But this time, I wasn't giving him the chance to brush me off. I slapped the flyer on the counter with more force than necessary.

"I need to see Agent Tyrann," I said, my voice steady but trembling. "Now."

Kingston gave me an angry look, but before he could respond, a familiar voice called me.

"Fox?"

I turned, my breath catching as Tyrann stood behind me. His eyes locked on me, scanning my dishevelled appearance with concern. He took a few steps closer. "What's going on? Is everything okay?"

I opened my mouth, but the words wouldn't come at first. Then they burst out in a raw, desperate rush. "Fuck No! Everything's fucked, Tyrann."

His face hardened instantly, concern giving way to focus. "Tell me what happened."

"They took my family," my voice cracking. "The Zenitharians—they want the core. And now they have my parents and my brother." My words echoed through the open space louder than I'd intended. "I need in, Tyrann. I need to get them back. It's my fault, and I'm not waiting for someone else to fix it."

Tyrann said nothing. His expression was unreadable, his tail twitching with restrained tension. The silence was unbearable. He sighed and motioned for me to follow him.

"I'll handle this," he said to Kingston.

"Please do," Kingston said, barely glancing up.

Tyrann led me away from the desk. Once we were alone in a quieter hallway, he turned to face me, his tone firm but not unkind.

"Listen," he began. "I want you on the team. I believe you got potential. But this? This is too personal. And when things get personal, you make mistakes. I can't have you going out there recklessly. It's not safe—for us, for you, or for them."

His words stung, but I refused to back down. "I don't care, Tyrann," I said, my voice shaking. "This is my family. I have to get them back. And I will—with or without your help."

We locked eyes, tension high between us. Tyrann nodded, his shoulders relaxing slightly. "Come with me," he said, his voice softer now. "Tell me everything."

I explained everything I knew—my family's names, the Zenitharians' demands, and their threats. As we went deeper, the quiet hallways only amplified the knot tightening in my chest.

We stopped in front of a door marked *Recruitment*. Tyrann gestured for me to wait inside. "Stay here," he said. "I'll be back."

He left me alone for what felt like hours. (Later, he told me it was less than 30 minutes.)

When Tyrann returned, he held a stack of papers, a Starbucks cup, and a few booklets. He handed me the coffee, which I accepted with a tired, "Thanks."

He sat down across from me, his tone businesslike but not cold. "First things first," he began. "Your home? It's compromised. The Zenitharians know where you live, and we can't risk them coming back. You'll be temporarily placed in a secure GUIP accommodation until we sort this out."

"What? Do I just leave everything behind?"

"For now, yes," Tyrann said. "We'll make sure you have what you need. I'll be forming a team to search for your family, and we'll keep you updated as soon as we have something concrete."

Relief washed over me, but it was short-lived. "And what am I supposed to do in the meantime? Sit around and wait?" the frustration creeping back into my voice.

"Not quite," Tyrann assured me. "But before you can step into the field, you need training. Real training. I can't send you out there unprepared."

"How long will it take?"

"A couple of months, at least," Tyrann replied. His tone softened, almost reassuring. "It'll be intense, but it will prepare you for what's ahead. We will find your family. But you'll need to be at your best when that time comes."

I nodded. It wasn't the answer I wanted, but he was right. "Alright," I said, my voice steadier.

Tyrann gave a firm nod of approval. "Good. For now, you'll need to fill out these forms, head to medical for routine checks, and get your training gear from uniforms. Then you need to—"

He paused, looking at me. "Fox, when was the last time you slept?"

I blinked, trying to remember. "Uh... I don't know. Thirty hours ago? Maybe more?"

Tyrann sighed, shaking his head. "Right. Scrap that. You'll be put up in a hotel for the night. Eat something and get some sleep. You'll need a clear head for what's coming."

I managed a weak grin. "Yeah, yeah. Food, sleep. Got it."

"And the forms," Tyrann said, pointing at the stack. "Those need to be filled out before we can finalize your accommodations."

"Paperwork, food, sleep," I muttered, exhaustion finally catching up to me. "Got it. Totally doable. Maybe."

As I filled out and returned the forms, a sense of clarity settled over me. With unwavering determination, I pushed forward.

Ready to take the leap that changed my life forever.

Chapter 4:
GETTING SERIOUS

The following months were the most challenging of my life. Training was… let's call it, a *unique experience*. Not much happened that's worth a complete retelling, but there are some highlights—and don't worry, I'll keep it brief.

First, let's talk about structure. GUIP operates *largely independently*, free from the control of any single nation. It's governed by the terms of the *Interspecies Protection Treaty*, which was signed by 18 of the G20 member nations.

GUIP isn't about enforcing laws; its primary mission is to investigate and neutralize any threats that could destabilize Earth's fragile coexistence.

Second—and because you're probably wondering—*Why hasn't anyone asked for this fox's name yet?* Well, here's the thing: from day one, we learned that revealing your real name is a big no-no. *But why?*

The official reason is to present agents as unbiased, professional entities, all united by a single objective. Sounds respectable, right? You might think so, but of course, the real reason is a lot more complicated—and a lot less idealistic. I've got strong opinions about it, but that's a rant for another day.

Over time, you stop asking for anyone's name unless you absolutely have to. It's just easier that way—no awkward exchanges, and no one asking for yours in return.

So, how do we call each other then? With code names, of course.

Non-field personnel, such as our friendly receptionist Kingston, are named after host nation cities or regions. Field agents, though?

We get an animal or mythical creature's name depending on the location of the branch. The UK has the Griffin Division, named after the legendary beast. Japan has the Kitsune Division—because, well, what else would they pick? Mexico's got the Aztec Division, drawing from their own mythology. Australia? The Bunyip Division, which—if you've never heard of it—just be aware that it's very on-brand. And here in Canada, we've got the Dinosaur Division. Which. Fun fact, I guess. It was originally supposed to be in the U.S., but, well, politics happened, and they pulled out of the treaty.

Each division operates on its own, but they're all interconnected, forming a global network to counter terrestrial and extraterrestrial threats. The whole setup sounds noble—and, in concept, it is—but reality is more complicated than that.

Anyway, even rookies get code names as part of our training. It felt ridiculous at first, but you learn to roll with it.

My group was small—just six of us, all Aniforms—and our names were all based on mountains.

There was Blackcomb, a cheetah who outran us all during those brutal 6 a.m. sprints. Tremblant, a hyena whose antics got him kicked out of the program before we even hit month two. Orford, a German shepherd so rigid, that she appeared to have the rulebook tattooed on her soul. Mackenzie, a golden retriever with the uncanny ability to boost everyone's morale, even during the worst drills. And Thor, a lion who only ever grunted—unless you asked him a direct question.

And me? I was Whistler. You didn't get to choose your name; you just lived with it. Eventually, those names defined us. Honestly, when you're dodging laser fire, real names don't seem all that important.

So, how was the training? Let's break it down:

The Boring.

Protocol lessons! Imagine hours of someone droning on about rules, regulations, and enough paperwork to make your fur fall out. Vulcan, our instructor—a Doberman-aniform—was stiff.

She'd start every session with something like, "Section 37.1-E, Subsection J of the Official Guidelines dictates that interaction with civilians should be conducted as follows…" blah blah blah.

The gist? Don't be a jerk. Follow the rules, don't misuse your position, and… paperwork. Lots of paperwork.

Luckily, I met Mackenzie. The first time he cracked a joke during one of Vulcan's endless lectures, I knew we'd get along.

Vulcan was halfway through a rant about *the proper reporting of missing assets* when Mackenzie leaned over and whispered, "And what form do I need for my missing interest?"

I tried to hold it in, but a snort slipped out. Vulcan didn't find it nearly as funny as I did. I got reprimanded, of course, but it was worth it.

The Not-So-Boring.

Things got more interesting during combat training. Picture a room full of skilled agents who know precisely how to take you down. I was the punching bag from day one, but hey, I wasn't alone in taking hits.

Mackenzie was just as clumsy as I was. The guy had strength and boundless energy—*the perks of being twenty-two*; I guess—but his punches rarely landed where they were supposed to.

We were on the mats far more than standing during the initial weeks. However, the way Mackenzie never quit and always smiled, even when lying flat on his back, began to have an impact on me.

"Come on, Whistler!" Mackenzie shouted one day after I got knocked down for the fifth time. "Get back up! Or beers on you!"

We started training together, pushing each other through every drill. Slowly—but surely—we improved. Mackenzie's bright eyes and constantly wagging tail made everything appear less like punishment and more like a challenge.

And, of course, the beers afterward helped numb the bruises.

The WTF—Are You Serious?

Alright, here's where things got ridiculous: the obstacle course.

The team-building exercise included live-fire drills, laser drones, and what I believe was a giant lizard chasing us.

A bunch of rookies, tired, hungry, and bruised in every place (yes, every place), stumbling through the woods. Someone trips over a wire, and the next thing we know, we're dangling in a net tied up to a tree.

And then there was Tremblant. I'm 90% sure he was high when he blew up something that wasn't even part of the mission. We ended up wandering through some weird side corridor that led straight into a restricted area.

Not our finest moment.

The Fun.

After the WTF days, things clicked. We hit the simulation rooms, running through virtual missions designed to test teamwork. That's when I realized something about Mackenzie: the guy was nuts—in the best way possible.

One simulation had us sneaking into a hostile base. Was all about stealth until Mackenzie decided stealth wasn't his thing.

He charged in headfirst, barking orders, firing, and hurling anything he could grab at the enemy—chairs, rocks, you name it.

It was a mess. It seemed we were failing the mission spectacularly.

But somehow, we clocked the best time. The instructors tore into us for being reckless, but Mackenzie grinned and said, "Hey, at least we're memorable."

That's Mackenzie for you—always turning disasters into something laughable. He had a way of making things easier with his attitude.

Failures became games, frustrations turned into challenges, and no matter how bad things got, he made us smile.

By the time training wrapped up, we weren't just clueless rookies anymore. We were a team. And Mackenzie? He taught me that sometimes the only way through the mess is to laugh your way out.

I'm so glad I met him and can still call him my friend after all these years. He didn't just help me survive training; he gave me something more—a reason to push forward.

In a way, Mackenzie helped turn my worries about my family into determination.

The Graduation.

Twenty-two weeks had passed. And in that time, I'd grown a little wiser and with a whole new collection of bruises (thankfully, fur hides most of them).

Graduation day was the highlight of the season—at least for GUIP. It began at the painfully early hour of 7 a.m., and I arrived at the training facilities, experiencing a mix of pride, exhaustion, and disbelief.

Only three of us made it through the program, so the event promised to be quick and far from glamorous.

What happened to the others? Well, Tremblant got kicked for being caught multiple times smoking weed in the restroom. Orford, I can't say for legal reasons. And finally, someone caught Thor having sex with Tremblant in the general trainer's office... twice.

"Hey, Ty!" I called out, spotting Tyrann outside the dressing room. He looked sharp in a dark grey suit paired with a tie featuring tiny green dinosaurs—a tie he wore on special occasions.

"Morning, Rookie," he said, grinning. "Ready for the big day?"

I smirked. "As ready as I'll ever be. Honestly, didn't think I'd make it this far."

Tyrann chuckled, his grin softening a bit. "Surprised? You earned this. Trust me, I've seen plenty of recruits, and you've got the right stuff."

I nodded, unsure how to respond. Compliments like that always make me a little... uneasy. "Thanks, Ty. That means a lot."

"Don't get soft on me now," he said, clapping my shoulder. "Come on, go get ready. The ceremony is about to start."

I headed into the dressing room, where my pressed ceremonial uniform awaited me. The slick black suit with red stripes gave a strange sensation, as if I was stepping into someone else's life. Once I had it on, I couldn't help but admit—I didn't look bad in it.

When I stepped out, Mackenzie was bouncing around in his uniform, his tail wagging like the overexcited puppy he was. "Can you believe we made it?" he said, his enthusiasm nearly knocking me off balance. "We're agents now!"

I rolled my eyes, but a grin appeared on my face. "Yeah, somehow, we did."

"Rookies, to the stage," a voice called over the intercom. "Ceremony will start soon."

Mackenzie grabbed my arm. "Come on, we're late!"

"We're only five metres away," I said, allowing him to drag me along.

The room went silent the moment *Chief Allosaurus* entered. She had the kind of presence that commanded respect without raising her voice. A former *RCMP officer*, she'd built GUIP from the ground up. Her impressive resume alone made her exceptional; however, her status as one of the few humans within a *predominantly aniform* agency set her further apart. Yet no one questioned her authority. She was the definition of unshakable.

Beside her was *Deputy Pteranodon*, another human. A former member of Parliament, his political career had been a rollercoaster of controversy—often because of his *unique* perspectives.

Despite his turbulent reputation, he'd been a vocal advocate for aniform rights, reminding anyone who'd listened that he helped to shape the policies that mattered most. Subtlety wasn't his strong suit.

The two of them embodied a sharp contrast: Chief Allosaurus, with her quiet, unwavering leadership, and Deputy Pteranodon, with his flair for self-promotion. But there was no denying their combined impact on the agency.

As they approached the podium, the room's energy shifted. Chairs creaked as everyone took their seats. Chief Allo stood tall, her posture firm yet approachable. She didn't need notes.

"Today marks the start of a new chapter," she began. "Each of you has earned your place here. You've shown strength, resilience, and a commitment to something greater than yourselves."

Her sharp gaze swept across the room. "The Global Unity for Interspecies Protection wasn't created out of ambition," she continued. "It was born out of necessity. After the Emergence, our reality changed forever. Humans and animals merged into what we now call aniforms. Fear and uncertainty filled the air. We exist to protect and unite this fragile, blended world."

Her words lingered in the atmosphere. Even the Deputy, who habitually stole the spotlight, stood silently by her side, arms crossed, nodding in agreement.

"This is not an easy road," the Chief continued. "You will face challenges that test your limits—your patience, courage, even your belief in this cause. But know this: the work we do here matters. All lives we protect, all bridges we build, all steps we take toward unity, shape our future."

She stepped forward. "Our goal isn't only about defence. It's about harmony, about bridging the gaps between species, mediating conflicts, and ensuring peace where there's only been chaos. And today," her voice softened, "we welcome three new recruits into that mission."

She paused, letting her words settle before continuing. One by one, she called us forward.

"Cadet Blackcomb," she said, addressing the first recruit. "Your analytical skills and leadership make you an invaluable asset. Welcome, Agent Velociraptor."

Next, Mackenzie stepped forward, standing straighter than I'd ever seen him, clearly trying to keep his tail from moving too much. "Cadet Mackenzie. Your enthusiasm and teamwork are unmatched—though let's keep the explosions to a minimum in the future." The crowd chuckled. "Welcome, Agent Stegosaurus."

Finally, it was my turn. "Cadet Whistler," Allo said, her voice calm but firm. "Your resilience has set you apart. Welcome, Agent Baryonyx."

She pinned the badge on my chest. "Congratulations, Agent," she said. Her tone was soft.

The rest of the ceremony was brief, consisting of photos, a few speeches, and usual formalities. After that, a flurry of handshakes, paw shakes, and everything shakes in between filled the room.

Tyrann found Steg and me grinning as he came closer. "Congrats, rookies. Welcome to the team."

He turned to Steg. "Agent Stegosaurus, have you received your assignment yet?"

Steg's excitement bubbled over, his tail wagging. "Yes, sir! Technical operations with you, sir."

Tyrann chuckled. "Please, call me Tyrann."

"Yes, sir—I mean, yes, Tyrann. You can call me Co—uh, I mean, Steg."

Before Tyrann could say anything else, Chief Allo approached.

"Agent Baryonyx," she said, her voice steady. "Impressive work during your training. We've decided to pair you with Agent Tyrannosaurus. You two have already shown good synergy."

"Thank you, Chief," I said, standing slightly straighter.

Chief Allo turned to Steg, who was nervous and grabbing his tail, but still managed a smile.

"And welcome to the team, Agent Stegosaurus," she said. "We're counting on your skills and enthusiasm."

Steg nodded enthusiastically. "Thank you, ma'am... uh, Chief. I won't let you down."

I exchanged a pleased look with Tyrann and couldn't resist adding, "It looks like you're stuck with me a bit longer, Ty."

Tyrann grinned. "Hey, Nyx, I wouldn't have it any other way."

Chief Allo, amused but still authoritative, cut the moment short. "Yeah, yeah, very touching. You boys can hug in your free time. Now get to work."

Tyrann and I snapped to attention. "Yes, ma'am." We muttered simultaneously.

When the room emptied, my gaze landed on someone lingering by the wall—a wolf aniform, her white-and-grey fur striking against the dim backdrop. She leaned casually, arms crossed, with rebellious hair falling over one eye and a sly smirk that screamed trouble. But what really caught my attention, The ankle monitor peeking out from her pant leg.

"Tyrann," I said, nodding toward her, "who's that?"

Tyrann followed my gaze and let out a chuckle. "Ah. Let me introduce you."

The wolf noticed us, her ears twitching in amusement as Tyrann waved her over. She sauntered toward us; her steps light but deliberate, like someone who never rushed but always arrived exactly when she meant to.

"Nyx, Steg, meet Consultant Ankylosaurus," Tyrann said. "Cyber operations specialist. Been with us for almost a year. Part of a reduced sentence agreement."

The wolf—Kylo—grinned, her sharp canines glinting. "Alleged sentence," she corrected, her voice dripping with sarcasm.

Tyrann smirked. "Sure. Alleged. Like that very alleged ankle monitor."

Kylo tapped the device with her foot, the monitor giving a faint beep. "It's a fashion statement! Just like the crypto bros are doing it."

I exchanged glances with Steg, already sensing Kylo would make things... interesting.

Kylo smirked, enjoying the tension she'd created. "Anyway, welcome, boys. We'll be seeing each other around. Now, if you excuse me, I need a refill of GUIP's finest orange juice," she said, turning on her heel and heading back to the catering table.

Tyrann clapped his hands, bringing the moment to a close. "Alright, rookies. We've got work to do. Let's drive back to the office, and by the way, Nyx, you'll love how the rebuilt office looks."

He gave us a nod before walking off, leaving Steg and me standing there. Steg nudged me, his excitement barely contained. "So... ready to save the world, Mr. Agent Baryonyx?"

I smirked, shaking my head. "Guess we'll find out."

I took a deep breath. Feeling ready for the unknown was a strange sensation. Walking out together for the first time didn't seem so scary. I was ready to face whatever awaited us out there.

Chapter 5

ABNORMALLY NORMAL

The first weeks on duty were... not what I'd imagined. Steg and I spent most of our days slumped over our desks, buried under a mountain of paperwork that seemed to multiply every time I blinked. The phones rang, and keyboards clacking mixed with the occasional bark of my fellow agents.

"I swear," I grumbled, tossing my pen onto the desk with a dramatic flair, "if I have to fill out one more incident report, I will lose it. Is this what this job is all about, to draw ourselves in bureaucracy?"

Across from me, Steg's tail thumped against the side of his cubicle. He leaned back in his chair, his usual canine grin in place. "Ah, my foxy friend," he said, stretching his arms behind his head. "Every hero's journey begins with the mighty trial of doing the jobs no one else wants to do. It's a rite of passage. Don't worry, though—one day, you'll have your very own rookie to torture with paperwork."

"Rite of passage?" I said, rolling my eyes. "All I am is just a city fox..." despite my grumbling, I couldn't stop the smirk tugging at my muzzle.

"Aww, poor boy," Steg said, his eyes sparkling with mischief. "Tell you what—let's make it interesting. The first one to finish their stack gets lunch bought for them."

My competitive streak flared to life. "Oh, you're on, doggo."

We dove into our respective piles, laughter mixing with the office cacophony. It wasn't the adrenaline rush of fieldwork, but the camaraderie made it almost fun. *Almost.*

"Better pick up the pace, Nyx," Steg taunted without looking up. "I'm pulling ahead."

"Keep dreaming, pup," I shot back, fingers flying over the keyboard.

I glanced at him, his ears twitching as he scribbled on a form. Steg had this annoying ability to radiate positivity, even when buried under a mountain of boring crap.

Right before I could declare my victory, Tyrann's office door swung open with a loud bang. Tyrann strode out, his tail swished, and his eyes were sharp and focused.

"Nyx, Steg—gear up. We've got a situation," he said, his voice calm but commanding.

I jolted upright, nearly knocking over my tower of documents. "On it, sir!" Finally, some action. I tried to play it cool, but my traitorous tail twitched with anticipation.

As we scrambled to follow Tyrann out, I shot a quick jab at Steg. "Looks like I'll have to beat you another time." I said.

Steg grinned. "I wasn't losing anyway, so I'm fine with that."

Before long, we were piling into one of GUIP's patrol vehicles. We settled into the car; Tyrann driving, me in the passenger seat, and Steg in the back.

I glanced at Steg as the vehicle screeched out of the parking lot. His tail wagged as he looked around inside, a grin spreading across his face.

"You are really excited for action, aren't you?" I said, surprised by his overwhelming happiness.

"Are you kidding?" Steg said, practically bouncing in his seat. "I'm in the back of a real cop car! With sirens! This is awesome!"

I couldn't help but laugh, shaking my head. "You're such a puppy sometimes. Next thing you know, you'll be sticking your head out the window."

"If only the windows back here opened, I totally would," Steg said back with a mischievous grin.

"I wasn't anywhere near that thrilled when I was forced to be back there,"

Tyrann's ears perked up, a smug grin spreading across his face. "Really? And when were you arrested?" he said.

My ears flattened. "Uh—I..." My tail twitching anxiously. "So... uh, what's this case about?" I said, desperate to change the subject.

Tyrann's smirk widened as Steg snickered in the back. "Smooth," Steg said, barely containing his laughter.

Tyrann chuckled, but quickly returned to the task, his expression turning serious. "There's a jewellery store robbery, south of Parliament."

"A robbery? Aren't we supposed to handle, you know, the big stuff? This sounds like local police business," Steg said.

"The suspects are Aniforms," Tyrann replied.

Now, you may wonder—*why does that change things?* Well, here's the thing: GUIP doesn't handle your average civil or criminal cases. But the second an aniform is involved, we get called in for support. The idea is to ensure fairness and prevent... let's just say, overreactions. The federal government put that policy in place after a few unfortunate incidents with local PD. You can probably guess how well those went.

"Oh." Steg said.

Tyrann nodded. "Exactly. But this one's... unusual. No jewellery was stolen, just property damage. Millions of dollars in stock left untouched. Something about it doesn't make sense."

The place was swarming with Mapleview PD, their blue uniforms contrasting with the sleeker black-and-grey GUIP gear. I could feel their gaze on us as we exited the vehicle; their faces a mix of curiosity, annoyance, and hostility.

"Well, well," one officer said. You could taste the venom in his voice. "If it isn't the freak police."

I clenched my fists, anger rising. I noticed Steg stiffen beside me as well, his easygoing demeanour replaced by tense silence.

"Listen, you motherfu—" I started, ready to bite their head off, but a firm hand pressed against my chest.

"Not while on duty, Nyx," Tyrann said, his voice calm. His amber eyes bore into mine, and I knew better than to argue. "Be better. Don't let them get to you."

I sucked in a sharp breath, forcing my fur to lie flat and my fists to unclench. "Right," I said, plastering on a grin that probably looked more like a grimace. "Just here to help, officers. Mind if we take a look around?"

The cop who'd spoken snorted, smirking as if he'd just made the joke of the century. "Knock yourselves out. Maybe I'll give you one of our K9 treats if you actually find something." His buddies chuckled, their laughter pissing me off even more.

We ignored them, stepping past into the store. As the heavy glass door swung shut behind us, I couldn't help muttering, "Real lovely bunch, aren't they?"

Steg nudged me with his elbow. "Hey, at least they didn't try barking at us this time."

"Yeah, small victories."

The store was a wreck. Shattered glass crunched under our boots as we stepped inside, the air full with the smell of dust and stale adrenaline. The store had their display cases smashed, their contents glittering under the dim security lights, but nothing seemed out of place: no missing jewels, no signs of valuables gone.

We ventured further into the store, trying to make sense of the scene. *What kind of thief smashes up a jewellery store but doesn't steal the jewellery?*

"Watch your tail," I warned as Steg swung a little too close to a crystal figure perched precariously on a shelf. Before either of us could react, the figure tipped over and hit the ground—the title moving unexpectedly.

"Uh... what?" I crutched down. My paw brushed against the floor, and I felt a faint seam in the tiles. Curious, I pressed lightly. A soft hiss followed, and a hidden panel slid open, revealing a small compartment beneath.

"Steg, get over here," I said, my voice hushed, my heart pounding. I stared at the sleek metallic objects inside—definitely not diamonds. I didn't know what they were, but one thing was clear: they weren't supposed to be here.

"What the hell is that?" Steg said, leaning closer.

"I don't know," I said, shifting to examine the objects' base. My finger grazed over a small button embedded in the compartment. I tried a gentle push; nothing. "Something's here," I muttered, pushing harder. A hidden chamber appeared when a wall section slid open after a soft click.

"Holy fuck," Steg said beside me, his ears perked and tail wagged a little. "This just got good."

I fumbled for my radio. "Hey, Ty, can you come here for a second?"

"On my way." Tyrann said back.

The hidden room contained sleek, otherworldly gadgets. Glowing panels lined the walls, casting an eerie light over the space, and strange devices hummed with low, rhythmic energy. At the centre, a pulsating blue cylindrical cube glowed.

"Is that...?" I asked, voice lower.

"An energy core." Tyrann said, joining us, his expression dark as his gaze swept over the room. "And other Zenitharian tech,"

I stared at the alien equipment. We weren't dealing with a simple robbery. This was far more complicated than we expected.

"Don't touch anything," Tyrann said sharply, as he pulled out his phone. "Chief? We've got a situation. Forensics are needed at the scene and let MVPD know we're taking over this investigation. Possible Zenitharian involvement. Yes, Chief... two suspects are in custody. No evidence of stolen property... Understood."

He pocketed his phone, his expression fixed. "We secure the area until forensics arrives," he said, turning to Steg and me. "Take the suspects into custody; then return to HQ to prepare them for questioning. I'll deal with our friends outside to make sure they understand we're in charge now."

"On it, boss," I said, straightening up and heading toward the curb where the two suspects sat, handcuffed and looking anything but remorseful.

One was a red panda aniform with pink-and-blue-dyed fur, swaying and giggling under her breath—she reeked of cheap vodka.

With multiple piercings in one ear, the fennec fox had a dreamy, distant expression while staring at the sky. She was on a mid-edible trip.

The red panda giggled as I approached, giving me a lopsided grin. "Hey there, cutie officer," she said, swaying closer. "How about this—you let me go, and I let you take me out for a drink? Deal?"

I froze for half a second, caught by the unexpected interaction. I let out a deep breath. "I'll pass, thanks," I said, trying to sound neutral. "Not my type."

She pouted dramatically, her ears twitching as she leaned back. "Your loss, officer cutie," she said with a giggle. As I helped her up of curb. "I'd have shown you a real good time."

"I doubt you could," I said, gripping her arm, leading her to her feet and guiding her toward the patrol car. My tail flicked irritably as she stumbled along, still grinning like she'd just won a game.

The local cops muttered some other intolerant nonsense at us, but I kept my head up. And then... it happened. The red panda lurched forward, and before I could react, she emptied the contents of her stomach all over me.

"Oh, come on!" I said, my ears flattening as the acrid smell assaulted my sensitive nose. Chunks of something I didn't even want to identify matted my fur. "Seriously? Fuck me!"

We loaded the suspects into the vehicle. Behind me, Steg's uncontrollable laughter filled the air. "Hey, Nyx, I guess you could say this case is getting a bit... messy!"

I shot him a withering glare, my tail flicking in irritation. "Oh, you think this is funny, eh? You want a hug, don't you? Come here, Steg. I insist."

Steg doubled over, clutching his sides. "No thanks! I think I'll pass, officer cutie."

I groaned, scrubbing my face with one paw. Yep. It was definitely going to be a long day.

Back at GUIP, I barely had time to clean up before Tyrann cornered me.

"Nyx, can you file the report while I interrogate the suspects?"

"Can't say no, can I?" I sighed, grabbing the paperwork. "On it, boss."

Before heading into the interrogation room, Tyrann handed Kylo the suspects' phones. "Do you think you can get anything useful from these?"

Kylo smirked, snatching the devices. "Oh, please. Let me work my magic."

Steg and I headed back to our desks. I started filling out the tedious forms when a new email notification pinged on my screen.

"Oh, shit," I muttered.

"Everything okay?" Steg asked, his expressive eyes flicking toward me with concern.

"Yeah... kinda," I said, making vague circles in the air. "With training and all this, I kinda forgot my temporary housing is up at the end of the month."

"Oh no!" Steg said, grinning mischievously. "Whatever will you do?"

"Not funny," I grumbled, my ears flattening.

"Lucky for you, I have a solution," Steg added, his tail wagging.

I raised an eyebrow. "Do you?"

"Yeah. My roommate Jack's moving out, so you could take his room in if you're interested." Steg said.

"Are you sure? Seems a *little convenient.* I mean, I don't want to impose."

"Of course, I'm sure! It'd would be great having you around. Plus, carpool!"

"Carpool? Don't you live a few blocks from here?"

"Yeah, like a 20-minute walk, But I was not going to refuse free parking downtown."

I shook my head and chuckled. "Alright, I'll come check it out tonight. I just need to go home and change first. Cool?"

"Works for me," Steg said. "12B-180 Metcalfe. Bring beer, and we'll hang out."

"Beer and pizza," I said, tail wagging. "And I'll finally get to meet Jack."

"It's about time you two meet." Steg said.

"Can't wait then," I said. Getting back into my not beloved paperwork.

Afterward, we met in Tyrann's office. I leaned in, curious to know more. "So, what did they say?"

Tyrann let out a smirk. "Not much, except one of them kept asking for the officer cutie's number."

"Oh, please, no," I said, covering my face.

Tyrann let out a chuckle. "Nothing admissible yet. They're still too out of it to give us anything solid."

Right on queue, Kylo strolled in, holding the suspects' phones. "Thought you boys might want an update," she said, twirling the device.

"Found anything good?" Tyrann said.

"Oh, you're gonna love this." Kylo's claws clacked against her keyboard, pulling up a series of encrypted messages. "Our little thieves? They are not exactly criminal masterminds. They heard through the grapevine about someone interested in the tech you confiscated today. Their brilliant plan was to steal it and sell it back to this group for a quick payday."

"Wait," I said, my tail bristling. "What group?"

Kylo leaned back in her chair, a smirk curling on her lips. "Did a little digging with some—let's say 'friends of a friend.'" She added air quotes for emphasis. "Word is there's an anti-aniform group interested in some underground Zenitharian tech. Black market, dark web, you name it."

Tyrann's expression darkened. "Can you trace it?"

"Not without raising some flags," Kylo admitted. "I need more time to dig without making myself a target."

"Thanks, Kylo," Tyrann said, his voice grave. "We need to put everything we've got into shutting this down before it's too late. Who knows how much of this is already on the streets?"

"Let's hope it's not too late already," Steg said.

I nodded as the room fell silent. Tyrann's keen eyes examined us one by one, his tail's deliberate movements hinting at the multitude of plans already swirling in his head.

"Alright," Tyrann said. "We've got work to do. Steg, Nyx, finish your reports. Kylo, keep digging—quietly. Please keep me updated about anything you find."

We all nodded. The meeting continued with nothing exciting happening; when we left Tyrann's office, Steg nudged me with his elbow. "So much for easing into this job, huh?"

I snorted. "Yeah, still beats the paperwork, though."

He grinned, his tail wagging slightly. "And the best part? We'll have a front-row seat when it all goes to hell."

"Comforting," I muttered, but his optimism was infectious.

As I sat back at my desk, staring at the half-finished report in front of me, my mind kept drifting to Kylo's words. An anti-aniform group. The idea of people plotting against us wasn't new, but this felt different.

Steg gave me a quick glance. "We'll figure it out, you know."

I met his gaze, forcing a small smile. "Yeah. I just hope we figure it out in time."

The sounds of typing and ringing phones filled the air again. I picked up my pen, determined to finish the reports. Hoping I'd be ready for whatever was coming.

Spoiler alert: I wasn't.

Chapter 6:
CHASING TAILS

For six months, I hopped between hotel rooms, GUIP training facilities, and even a safe house on the opposite side of the city. So, the possibility of finally moving into a more permanent place was, well, pretty damn appealing.

After my shift ended, I went to my hotel room to recharge.

By the time I headed out again, the sun had dipped below the horizon, painting Mapleview in streaks of gold and purple. And me? I was just glad to smell like myself again. A hot shower and a clean hoodie had worked wonders after the day I'd had. Small victories, right?

I adjusted my hood against the breeze that ruffled my fur and let out a sigh. "Hell of a day."

Then my phone buzzed, flashing a reminder: *Beer run for Steg.*

"Right!" I muttered, heading off down the street.

The city was quieting, rush hour giving way to the softer hum of evening life. My paws padded against the cold pavement.

At the time, some aniforms had ditched shoes altogether, especially in the summer, letting their foot pads do the work.

Steg swore it was the best thing ever—apparently, there was less pressure on the claws. I tried it that night, though part of me wasn't quite ready to be that adventurous.

The LCBO was as unremarkable as ever. I grabbed two six-packs of Steg's favourite lager and approached the counter.

"Long day?" the cashier asked with a friendly nod.

I offered a faint smile. "You could say that."

As I tapped my card, my thoughts wandered. *Moving in with Steg wasn't a big deal, was it?* Just crashing with a friend. But somehow, it felt like a huge milestone. Maybe it was the normalcy of it—buying beer, planning a move. It felt... grounding. A rare moment of stability in a life of chaos and existential crises.

"Thanks, bud," I said, tucking the beer under my arm. "Have a good one, eh?"

After a quick pizza stop, I arrived at Steg's apartment building—*Metcalfe Luxury Apartments*. A modern glass structure built atop a historic building, it blended into the quiet street, surrounded by rows of townhouses, small businesses, and other apartments.

The intercom buzzed as I scrolled through the painfully slow electronic directory.

"Who dares disturb the lair of the mighty Stegosaurus?" Steg's voice crackled through, barely masking his laughter.

I smirked, fighting the urge to roll my eyes. "Munch Munchy Bites delivery, sir. Let me in before I drop your beer."

"Ooh, magic words!" Steg said, as the door buzzed open. "Come on up, foxy!"

A strange sense of comfort settled over me as I made my way down the hallway. Quirky art decorated the minimalistic walls—abstract prints, a poster of a taco riding a bus—little touches that grounded and welcomed me to the space. My tail swished behind me, betraying my mood.

The elevator dinged, and as it carried me up, a thought lingered: This place could be home. It reminded me of how I imagined moving out of my parents' house—me and a buddy splitting a place, doing all the *guy stuff*. You know, dancing around in our underwear, eating pizza in our underwear, and, if we got lucky, maybe losing the underwear with a date once or twice a year (not all three of us at the same time, of course... *unless*... well, never mind).

But that old fantasy hadn't survived the Emergence. Most of my so-called "*friends*" ghosted me the moment I turned into what I am. *How about dating?* That hadn't even been an option. Staying with my parents had been the easy choice—a safe but stifling comfort. And now, even that was gone.

The thought of my family crushed that brief glimmer of hope. I wished I'd moved out under different circumstances—on my own terms, with my parents still in my life.

I shook the thought away as I reached Steg's door. A moment later, it swung open, revealing a cheerful dingo aniform I didn't recognize. Ginger and white fur, bright eyes, and—what caught my attention—mismatched socks: one fire-engine red, the other neon green.

"You must be Nyx!" he said, flashing a grin. "I'm Jack, Steg's soon-to-be former roommate. Come on in!"

I blinked, surprised by his energy. "Uh, yeah, nice to meet you," I said, stepping inside.

"You can leave your shoes there," Jack added, gesturing to a small rack by the door. Then his gaze dropped to my bare paws. "Oh, nice! How's the experience of going bare paw?"

"Satisfyingly dangerous," I said with a grin. "Though, uh, should I clean my paws before stepping in?"

"Yeah, Steg uses this–" he said, grabbing a pack of wet wipes from the counter and handing them to me.

"Thanks," I said, crouching to wipe off my feet. As I stood back up, my eyes lingered on his socks. He noticed and wiggled his toes. "And yeah, don't mind the socks. Life's too short to match them. Gotta keep things interesting."

"Sure... if by 'interesting,' you mean 'losing half your socks constantly,'" Steg teased from the other room.

Jack rolled his eyes, grinning. "It's a choice, not a problem, bro."

I relaxed as Jack ushered me further into the apartment. It could have been the casual vibe or the promise of beer, but the tension I'd carried all day eased.

"Where should I put these?" I asked, holding up the six-packs.

Steg bounded over, his tail wagging. "Perfect timing, Nyx! Let's get those in the fridge."

We settled into the living room, and I turned to Jack. "So, Steg told me you're heading to Toronto. Got a new gig?"

Jack leaned back, propping his mismatched socks on the coffee table like a man completely at ease with his life choices. "Yep. Starting next month. Got a sweet job offer I couldn't pass up."

"Toronto, eh?" I raised an eyebrow. "Big change."

Jack nodded, his grin softening. "Yeah, it's gonna be an adventure. But man, I'm gonna miss this place. Remember that time we tried to host a dinner party, Steg?"

Steg snorted, nearly spilling his beer. "Oh, yeah! We almost set the kitchen on fire."

"It wasn't that bad," Jack countered, but his laugh said otherwise.

Listening to their banter, a smile unconsciously touched my lips. No life-or-death decisions—just normal people, sharing normal moments. It was... nice.

"Hey, Nyx," Steg said, snapping me out of my thoughts. "Want the grand tour?"

"Sure," I replied, grateful for something to do.

As we walked through the apartment, I couldn't help but notice the little details. The city lights poured in through large windows, casting a warm glow over the space. Books sat in messy stacks on shelves, a couple of potted plants added life to the corners, and the furniture—all mismatched and well-loved—spoke of years of comfort and use. It wasn't fancy, but it felt real.

"So, what do you think?" Steg asked, his tail swishing. "Think you could see yourself here?"

I hesitated, my hand trailing over the back of an armchair. *Could I?* The idea of having a place to call my own, somewhere stable amidst the mess of my life... it was tempting.

"Yeah," I said, surprised by the certainty in my voice. "Yeah, I think I could. Next month work for you?"

"Absolutely! Welcome home, roomie!" Steg said, relieved.

Back in the living room, we cracked open more beers, letting ourselves get on the relaxed evening. Jack launched into a story about their high school misadventures, his animated gestures making Steg laugh so hard, his tail knocked over a lamp.

As the night wore on, I let myself loosen up.

Eventually, Jack stood to leave. "Early shift tomorrow," he said, stretching. "Nice meeting you, Nyx."

With Jack gone, the apartment went quieter. Steg and I settled back on the couch.

I stared at the beer in my hand. "You know," I began, my voice low, "sometimes I wonder if I'm cut out for all this."

Steg's ears perked up, but he didn't interrupt, his silence inviting me to continue.

"It's just..." I trailed off, fumbling for the right words. "Sometimes it feels like I'm one mistake away from letting everyone down." I'd never said it out loud before—maybe it was the beer, or maybe it was just Steg.

He leaned forward, his tone calm but reassuring. "Nyx, we all have those fears. Heck, half the time, I'm worried I'll blow something up with my tail."

I chuckled. "You often do."

He grinned, but his voice softened as he continued. "You're not alone in this. We all have our struggles, but we've got each other's backs. You don't have to carry it all by yourself."

Something shifted inside me. The weight didn't disappear, but it appeared lighter.

"Thanks, man," I said, meaning it more than he probably realized. "I guess we're all in this together, eh?"

Steg's tail thumped against the couch, his grin returning. "You bet your fuzzy ass we are. Now, how about another beer? I promise not to set anything on fire this time."

I laughed, the sound genuine and unguarded. "I'll hold you to that, buddy."

The next morning, I entered GUIP HQ refreshed, considering last night's beer. That buzz of energy carried me through the halls—right up until I entered the briefing room.

Kylo stood at the front, her wolf features set in a grim mask. I slid into my seat, fidgeting with a small gadget in my pocket—a nervous habit I'd never quite outgrown.

"Alright, team," Tyrann's voice cut through the silence. "We've got a situation brewing. Kylo found the organization we believe is behind the jewellery store."

Kylo tapped the screen behind her, dimming the lights. The monitor flickered to life, displaying a crowd of desperate-looking Aniforms gathered under a logo that made me uneasy: a human silhouette emerging from an animal shadow.

"Meet 'Chasing Tails,'" Kylo said, "They're an extremist group promising Aniforms a way to become human again."

"But... isn't that—" I said.

"Impossible? Yeah," Tyrann snapped. "But when you're offering hope to the hopeless, logic doesn't matter."

"There's more," Kylo continued. "The intel suggests they've got access to some Zenitharian tech. Still unclear what they want to do with it,"

"So, what's the plan?" I asked, surprised at how steady my voice sounded despite my nerves.

Tyrann stepped forward. "We're going undercover. There's a recruitment event tonight, and we need eyes and ears on the inside."

As Tyrann laid out the details of the op, excitement grew in my chest. This was a chance to do something for our kind. I glanced at the team, Steg's words from last night echoing in my mind: We've got each other's backs.

"Nyx," Tyrann's voice snapped me out of my thoughts. "You'll be going undercover. Think you can handle it?"

I met his gaze, trying to hide my doubts. "Sure. But... why me?"

Tyrann's expression softened. He crossed his arms. "Well, Steg's not exactly known for his poker face. No offense," he added, glancing at Steg.

"Nah, you got a point," Steg said, grinning.

"And I can't exactly blend in with this thing on my ankle," Kylo quipped, tapping her tracker with a smirk. "Unless, of course, Tyrann, you'd like to remove it?"

Tyrann shot her a pointed look. "I'll pass, Kylo. Thanks."

He turned back to me. "And I'm too recognizable. Some of them know me from previous arrests. So, you're our guy. If you're up for it."

I nodded, trying to sound confident. "I'm in. But how do we even get me in the door?"

Kylo grinned, her sharp teeth catching the light. "The event's invite-only, but thanks to my amazing hacking skills, you're already on the list."

Tyrann raised an eyebrow. "Hacking?"

"Okay, fine," she admitted. "They used an unprotected Google Doc. But still, you're in."

"Just say you're Jean Leduc," Tyrann said, tossing a sleek fake ID card. I caught it mid-air, glancing at the name. "And don't worry. I'll be in your earpiece the whole time. If things go south, we'll be there in seconds."

As we broke to prepare, a sense of purpose settled over me. I couldn't shake the feeling I was exactly where I needed to be.

The warehouse was an unremarkable grey block lost in the industrial sprawl. I tugged at the stiff collar of my borrowed jacket I wore on top of my hoodie, trying to steady my breathing. My ears twitched beneath the baseball cap I'd crammed them into.

I approached the door, eyes locked on a woman in a faded Humans Will Rise t-shirt. Her sharp gaze raked over me, assessing, dissecting, like she could sniff out a lie.

"Who are you?" she asked, her voice flat.

For a moment, I froze. Not because of her—though she was intimidating—but because the question hit too close to home. *Who am I? SJ? Agent Baryonyx? Or* just the guy who still can't figure out his place in all this. The lines blurred more every day, and I wasn't sure which version of me was real anymore.

But this wasn't the time for an existential crisis. "Jean," I said, almost whispering before I found my voice. "Jean Leduc." I said louder. The fake name felt clumsy in my mouth, but it had to work.

Her eyes narrowed. "Have an ID?"

I handed her the fake card, my fingers barely steady. She scanned it, then me. She stepped aside. "Go ahead."

The warehouse was poorly lit, shadows pooling in every corner. The crowd— a restless mix of Aniforms—huddled in groups, their faces painted with equal parts hope and desperation.

"Nyx? Is everything okay?" Tyrann's voice crackled in my earpiece.

"Yeah," I muttered, careful not to draw attention. "All good."

"Copy that," he replied, his calm tone steadying me.

I moved cautiously, my ears swivelling to catch snippets of hushed conversations. Around me, the atmosphere buzzed with an almost religious fervour. These weren't just people looking for answers—they were believers, clinging to the promise of salvation.

"Brothers and sisters!" A booming voice shattered the murmurs. The crowd shifted, pulling me with them as they surged toward the makeshift stage. At its centre stood Seb, the white wolf aniform, a member of Chasing Tails. Broad-shouldered and commanding.

"We stand on the brink of a revolution! We have been cast aside, forced to live as shadows of our true selves. But no more!" Seb said.

The crowd leaned in, their faces alight with something close to fanaticism. Honestly, they looked like a cult. Well... they kinda were.

"They have the power to bring you back, but they refuse to use it," Seb growled, his voice dripping with indignation. "They want us to accept this evil curse,"

He didn't say it outright, but it was obvious who *they* were: GUIP.

I forced myself to stay calm. A raccoon aniform next to me clutched his chest, shaking as he whispered, "Finally... someone's doing something."

Seb's voice rose, his passion electrifying the room. "But we—we—will take back what is rightfully ours. Through our efforts, we have secured advanced Zenitharian technology. With it, we can take those bastards down and reverse this curse and bring back humanity!"

"Join our fight!" Seb bellowed; his fist raised high. "Together, we will reclaim what was stolen from us. Together, we will end this nightmare and return to the good times!"

The crowd erupted in cheers, a wave of sound that vibrated through the warehouse. I joined in, faking enthusiasm as I edged closer to the stage, ears tuned to every word. My mind raced, piecing together the implications of what I was hearing. They weren't just selling false hope—they were weaponizing pain, building an army out of desperation.

Seb scanned the crowd, his sharp eyes darting over faces as if he were memorizing them. I froze when his gaze landed on me, lingering for just a moment too long.

"You!" he called, pointing at me. "Fuck," I muttered as all eyes in the room turned toward me. Even the raccoon next to me stumbled back in surprise.

"Uh... me?" I said, forcing a sheepish grin. My voice cracked slightly, betraying my nerves.

Seb grinned, beckoning me forward. "What's your name, brother?"

"Jean," I blurted out, the name slipping out before I could overthink it.

"Jean," Seb repeated, his tone warm yet piercing. "You've got the look of someone who's been through hell. Am I wrong?"

I hesitated, my ears flicking. "It's one way to put it."

Seb nodded, his grin widening. "Well, Jean, let me tell you something. You're not alone. None of us are. Together, we can fight back. Together, we can restore what we lost."

The crowd erupted in cheers. I nodded along, faking enthusiasm, all the while hoping this interaction would end soon.

Seb stepped down from the stage, his presence larger than life. My instincts screamed at me to run, but I stood my ground, forcing myself to appear calm.

"You've got the fire in you, Jean," Seb said, clapping a heavy paw on my shoulder. His grip was firm, almost possessive. "I can see it."

"Uh, thanks?" I replied, my voice trailing off.

Seb's grin didn't falter. "Don't thank me yet, son! Together, we can recover everything we've lost. What do you think?" He pointed the microphone to my muzzle, his eyes daring me to say the wrong thing.

"That I'm probably older than you to be your son," I said, managing a smirk. The crowd chuckled, a ripple of approval that seemed to amuse Seb.

"Ha! Smart mouth, Jean! I like you already," Seb said, his laughter booming through the room. "So, are you ready to join the fight?"

I forced a smile, my stomach churning. "Sure, dad," I replied, the words tasting like ash in my mouth.

Seb's grin sharpened, almost predatory. "Good. Registration's at the back. Make it official, brother."

He turned back to the crowd, raising his voice to a roar. "This is our moment! Be like Jean—stand up and join the fight for your future!"

The crowd roared back, their cheers vibrating through the walls. I kept my face neutral, forcing a wide, fake grin as if I were swept up in the fervour.

Toward the back of the room, a line of aniforms had formed behind a battered foldable table with a misspelled "*Regestration*" sign scrawled in black marker.

The energy in the warehouse was suffocating—a strange mix of desperation and excitement that clung to the air. I drifted through the crowd, keeping my head down but my ears perked, catching snippets of conversations. Some were whispers of hope; others were grim murmurs of vengeance. Either way, it was clear these people weren't here for casual chit-chat.

I let myself wander, staying toward the edges of the room. My curiosity tugged me further until I spotted a door slightly ajar near the back of the warehouse. It was unassuming, almost easy to miss. Glancing around to make sure no one was watching, I crept closer.

Peering through the crack, I saw a cluttered desk covered in papers. Blueprints, diagrams, and something that looked like a Zenitharian device were scattered across its surface. My heart raced as I tried to make sense of it all.

"What are you doing back here?" A voice made me jump.

I spun around to find Seb standing behind me, his sharp eyes boring into mine. He was close—too close—and his sudden appearance made me uncomfortable.

"I—uh…" My mind scrambled for an excuse. "I thought this was the washroom."

Seb raised an eyebrow, his expression unreadable. "The washroom, eh?" he repeated, his voice low and skeptical.

"Yeah," I said, forcing a sheepish grin. "Weird layout you've got here."

He didn't look convinced, but his grin returned, sharp and knowing. "So, Jean. Did you fill out your registration yet?"

"Oh, uh… no," I said, trying to sound casual. "Couldn't find it. But I did find your 'Regestration' table." I threw in a grin.

Seb chuckled, his gaze softening just slightly. "I like you, Jean. You're a smartass. Come on, let's fix that."

Before I could protest, he grabbed my arm—not roughly, but firm enough to make it clear I wasn't going to get out of this. He led me back toward the front of the room, weaving through the crowd like he owned the place. The line at the table was still long, filled with aniforms eager to join. Seb ignored it.

"Step aside," he barked, his voice carrying authority. The Aniforms at the front shuffled back, not eager to challenge him. Seb pulled me to the table, where a weary-looking wolverine aniform was struggling to keep up with the influx of applicants.

"This one's priority," Seb said, his grin never fading as he gestured toward me. "Get him signed up."

The wolverine blinked, then nodded, shoving a clipboard and pen in my direction. I hesitated, glancing back at Seb, who watched me like a hawk.

"Go ahead, Jean," he said. "You made the right choice coming here."

I scribbled some fake information on the form. The wolverine took it back, nodding in approval as they added my name—or, well, Jean's—to their records.

Seb clapped me on the shoulder, his grin widening. "Welcome to the fight, brother. You won't regret this." He leaned in slightly, his voice dropping to a conspiratorial whisper. "Stick around. Things are about to get interesting."

Before I could respond, he straightened, his attention shifting to another part of the room. "Now, if you'll excuse me." And just like that, he disappeared into the crowd, leaving me standing there, feeling like I'd avoided stepping on a landmine.

I glanced at the wolverine, who had already moved on to the next recruit. Taking a slow step back, I scanned the room for the nearest exit. My heart pounded as I slipped away from the table, weaving through the crowd until I reached the door. This time, I didn't stop to look back.

As I walked away from the warehouse, I pulled out my phone, snapping a few stealthy photos of the building and the crowd before slipping into the shadows. Whatever Chasing Tails was planning, it wasn't just misguided—it was dangerous. And we had to stop them before it was too late.

The cold air outside hit me, clearing my head. I exhaled, the tension finally loosening from my shoulders. That was way too close.

Back at GUIP HQ, I paced the briefing room, my tail swishing. The team gathered around; the air was heavy as we replayed the voice recordings from the night before. Each time Seb's words echoed through the speakers, my fur bristled anew.

"They're not just some fringe group," I said, my voice tight. "They've got real power. And those people—they believe every single lie he puked."

Tyrann's eyes narrowed. "You're certain?"

"Oh, I'm certain," I replied, my tone sharper than I intended. "The way those Aniforms reacted... they're desperate, and they're clinging to every word. It's terrifying."

Steg leaned forward with a rare look of seriousness. "How many are we talking, Nyx?"

I hesitated, swallowing hard before answering. "Hundreds. Possibly more. And that's just from one recruitment event."

A heavy silence fell over the room. My mind flashed back to the faces I'd seen—hopeful, desperate, and vulnerable. These weren't criminals or extremists at heart (yet). They were people looking for a way out, a way back, and *Chasing Tails* exploited that.

Tyrann broke the silence. "We need to act on this. Every day we wait, more Aniforms fall into their trap."

"I agree," said Kylo, though her sharp grin couldn't quite hide the weight of the moment. "Alright, dogs and... cat, let's break this down. We need a plan."

The corner of my mouth twitched despite myself, and a weak chuckle rippled through the team. It wasn't much, but in the face of everything, it was something.

We huddled together, tossing out ideas and piecing together the intel. Strategies formed and shifted as we pooled our thoughts. The tension in the room didn't lift, but there was something else now—a shared determination. Despite the looming danger, despite my own doubts, I knew we were in this together. And somehow, that made the impossible feel just a little more achievable.

"We've got this," I said, allowing myself a small, confident grin. "Chasing Tails won't know what hit them."

Chapter 7:
REVEALING CONSEQUENCES

Wanna know about one of the worst days of my life? Yeah, looking back, it was so stupid. But at the time? Felt like my life was ending.

We were trapped inside a meeting room for hours. Tyrann yapped about the latest shit from our "friends" at CT (that's Chasing Tails, for those not keeping up). Chief Allo's eyes were all over us. Tyrann had leaned in his chair, arms crossed, looking like he was about to bite our heads off. Nyx had that laser-focus thing going on, his eyes glued to the screen, while Kylo was drumming her claws on the table like she was trying to invent a new beat.

The rest of the agents? Mixed bag. Some looked like they were ready to jump into action. Others? Eh, not so much—simply shifting uneasily, probably wishing they were elsewhere.

I was some kind of both, unable to sit still. My golden fur was up, my energy was... well, also up. I was pacing the room like a damn caged dog, my brain screaming. And, when I get like that... let's say thinking before speaking isn't my strong suit. Not like it has ever been tho.

So, yeah, I slammed my fist down on the table. "Those Chasing Tails bastards can't intimidate us." I barked. "They will learn what Cooper Mills is cap—"

Oh. Shit. Fuck. Shitty fuck. Fucking shit. I froze mid-rant. My mouth snapped shut so fast I might've chipped a tooth. The room went dead silent. It was so quiet, you'd hear a pin drop. My brain screamed at me, *You messed up, dude. Big time.*

Here's the thing: I've always been the guy who pushes buttons, and maybe causes a little more trouble than necessary. *But that time?* Oh no, it was different. I had fucked up on a whole new level.

Everyone froze. My eyes widened as the horror of what I'd done settled in. Silence. Thick, fucking suffocating silence.

I'm sure Nyx has told you by now about revealing our real names. That's a big no. Like, number one rule. Hammered into us from day one. And I had blurted mine out like an idiot.

"I—I mean, Steg!" I said, my floppy ears flattening as if that'd somehow make me invisible. But it didn't. The damage was done.

"He broke protocol! That's grounds for immediate dismissal!" An agent said, pointing a finger at me like I had set fire to the place... *again*.

The room erupted into shoutings—everyone talked over each other, some demanding discipline, others begging for dismissal. I swear, someone muttered something about a public execution. Any sense of unity we'd had seconds prior? *Gone. Dead. Buried.*

"Hold up! Procedure dictates an inquiry before any decisions are made," Tyrann said.

"Protocol?" Deputy Pteranodon said. "He broke the most important rule we have! Do you even understand how dangerous this is? An experienced agent like myself would never make such a reckless mistake." Self-righteous asshole—I never liked him.

That's when my bro Nyx stood up. That guy always had my back. "Everyone, stop!" He said. "We can't let one mistake tear us apart. Chasing Tails is the real threat here, *not my super-handsome friend Steg!*" I swear he said the last part.

Tyrann nodded, backing him up. "Nyx is right. We'll deal with this later. We have more serious issues to address first."

The shouting lowered down, but I could still feel the judgment. Clenched jaws, furrowed brows, tails flicking—yeah, it wasn't over. Not by a long shot.

I was crushed. My tail hung limp, my shoulders slumped, and I was unable to meet anyone's gaze. I'd fucked up, and no one was going to let me forget it.

I have no idea how the rest of the briefing went. My eyes were locked on the floor, though at one point I caught Tyrann's eye. He gave me a subtle and reassuring nod.

"Alright, team, let's table this for now," Tyrann said. "Chasing Tails isn't going to wait while we sort out our problems."

A few grumbles echoed around the room—someone muttered something about throwing me into the river—but eventually, everyone settled down, refocusing on the mission.

I felt small. It was the sort of shame that you couldn't escape.

I looked at Tyrann, who was as calm and composed as ever. *Did he ever feel that way?* The constant worry that one wrong move might send everything crashing down.

I shook the thoughts away. It wasn't the time to lose myself in my own head.

When the meeting finally ended. Nyx gave me a small nod—a silent *I've got your back*—his worry was impossible to miss.

I walked around the building with nowhere to go. When I spotted Nyx, he leaned casually against the wall, chilling like if my career wasn't about to go to shit.

"You okay?" He asked and immediately shook his head. "Stupid question, sorry."

"Yeah... I'm fine," I said, trying to sound confident. "They can't fire me. I'm too adorable." Even I didn't believe that.

Nyx smiled faintly. "Mind if I...?" He gestured toward chief Allo's office door.

"Be my guest," I said, stepping aside as he knocked lightly.

"Come in," Allo called, her voice as sharp as ever.

Nyx disappeared inside, shutting the door behind him. I got curious, so I pressed an ear to the frosted glass.

"Agent Baryonyx," Allo's angry tone made me uncomfortable. "I assume you're here about Agent Stegosaurus?"

"Yes, Chief," Nyx said firmly. "With all due respect, firing Steg would be a mistake. He's been a loyal agent. One mistake shouldn't undo that."

"The anonymity rule exists for a reason, Agent," she shot back. "It's for your protection."

"I understand that," Nyx replied,. "But does it make sense to throw him out over one slip? We all make mistakes."

"Agent. Actions have consequences," Allo snapped. She was pissed, no doubt about it.

"Look," Nyx said, and I could tell he was trying to keep his cool. "I'm not trying to be an unruly asshole. I think if we really understood the stakes, maybe we'd all take the rule more seriously. We risk our lives every day, right? Facing down laser fire seems a bit more life threatening than saying, 'Hi, my name is S—'"

Fuck. He almost said his name. Part of me wished he had. First, because I was curious. Second, because it would've made me feel less alone.

"Careful, Agent," Allo snapped. "Or you'll join your friend in early retirement."

I froze. *Shit. I'm really getting fired.*

The room went quiet, and that silence. It was worse than the yelling. Then Allo's voice became gentler, a bit. "In GUIP's early days, we were less... careful. Some of our agents' identities leaked. It didn't end well. People used that information to target the agents, their families. The results were tragic."

"Shit," I muttered.

"That's why the anonymity rule is so strict now," she continued. "We can't afford to make the same mistakes."

Panic clawed at my chest. I needed air. So, I left and stepped outside. I didn't hear what came next, but Nyx later told me what he said to her:

"Steg deserves a second chance. He's one of us, and we don't abandon our own."

According to him, she replied, "I'll take your perspective into account, Agent Baryonyx. But remember, the final decision rests with me and the review board."

She concluded by saying, "You're a good friend to Steg. He's lucky to have you in his corner."

Whether she actually said that, or Nyx only wanted to make me feel better. I'll never know.

I leaned against the GUIP building in a narrow alley. My tail hung limp, and my energy was drained. I never smoke, but the moment felt like it would've been cooler with a cigarette.

About thirty minutes later, Nyx came out. His face relaxed a little when he spotted me slumped there.

"Hey, bud," he said softly, sliding down to sit next to me. "How are you holding up?"

I met his gaze, and it made me feel so vulnerable that I almost looked away. "Not great, Nyx," I admitted. "I really fucked up this time."

He bumped my shoulder lightly. "We've all had close calls. It so happened yours was a bit closer than most."

I let out a hollow chuckle. "Yeah, well, most agents don't go blurting out their real names in the middle of a briefing."

Nyx raised an eyebrow, and he gave me a genuine smile. "Cooper Mills, huh? Honestly, I pegged you as more of a 'Jake' or a 'Kyle.'"

I grinned a little. Could I be a Jake? Sounded like a jock name, so yeah, maybe. "Jake Mills. Has a ring to it," I said.

Nyx held out a hand with a small grin. "Well, Mr. Mills, nice to meet you. I'm—"

"Don't," I cut him off, wincing. "It's not safe. I don't want you getting in trouble because of me."

Nyx's smile softened. "Hey," he said gently. "Talk to me, Steg."

I stayed quiet for a long moment. Words weren't coming easily. "I joined GUIP to get away from all the expectations, you know?" I said.

"What do you mean?"

This wasn't something I'd ever admitted—not out loud, not even to myself. "My parents," I said, my voice low. "They're good people, but they had my whole life planned out for me. The Mills—highly decorated criminal lawyers and... well, kinda a big deal at the University of Toronto law school."

"So, what were you supposed to be? Doctor Mills? Professor Mills?"

My mouth twitched into a half-smile. "Yeah, something like that. They mapped out my entire future before I was able to spell my own name."

Nyx leaned back against the wall. "And instead, you joined GUIP? That's a pretty big detour."

I let out a long breath. "I believe in what we do. But... I also thought joining GUIP would prove I was capable of being something different—on my own, away from their success. But now... I don't even know who I am anymore. What if I've just been pretending this whole time?"

"You're not pretending, Steg," Nyx said. "You've earned your place here."

"Maybe," I muttered, shrugging. "But when I slipped up... the entire act shattered. Like I was only Cooper Mills again. The kid who was never enough. The one who'll never live up to his parents expectations."

"Listen," Nyx said. "None of us are here because we're perfect. What you did wasn't about failing; it was an accident. And it doesn't erase everything else you've done."

"It's...ugh... my parents always said never let anyone see your weaknesses. That's what unsuccessful people do. And, well... that's exactly what I did, Nyx. I let everyone see."

"Maybe that's not such a bad thing," he replied. "Letting people see that you're human—or part human, anyway—doesn't make you weak. It makes you real. And it doesn't change what you've done for GUIP."

I gave him a small, tentative smile. "You really think the review board will see it that way?"

"I'm gonna make sure they do," he said. "You've got people in your corner, Steg. You're not alone in this."

"Thanks, bud. I needed that."

He stood, brushing the dirt off his jeans. "That's what friends are for. But, uh, you might wanna come back inside soon before Tyrann sends out a search party."

"Yeah," I said, watching as he walked back into the building. But I remained, needing a bit more time.

I leaned my head back against the wall, staring at the grey sky.

I started to doubt about GUIP's priorities. Why were the rules so rigid, so unforgiving? And why did it always seem like we aniforms were the ones making the biggest sacrifices?

I couldn't shake the feeling that GUIP's way of doing things wasn't as solid as I'd once believed.

I spent the next week preparing for my hearing like it was the trial of the century. My dad used to drag me to his mock trials, so I figured I was able to channel some of that energy. I even bought an expensive suit to look the part—not that I felt it.

When the day finally came, I stepped into the hearing room with Nyx by my side. The place was a mix of cold professionalism and suffocating bureaucracy. A panel of senior GUIP officials stared us down from across the table, with Chief Allo seated dead centre. Her icy blue eyes scanned the room, offering zero clues about which way this was going to swing.

I sat down, my tail twitched, and my claws drummed against the table. I've always been hyperactive, but that day. I was hyper-hyperactive. Then it began.

"Agent Stegosaurus," Deputy Pteran started, his voice dripping with disapproval. "Your breach of protocol is extremely serious. As an organization, we must maintain the highest standards. Today, we must determine whether this... lapse... indicates a deeper issue of trustworthiness."

I clenched my fists under the table, already fighting the urge to snap. Trustworthiness? They were questioning my loyalty over one slip-up?

"Agent Stegosaurus," Allo said, her tone sharp and precise. "Do you understand the severity of revealing your real name?"

"Uh..." I stammered, my ears drooping. "Yes, but... I didn't mean to—"

"That's exactly the problem," Deputy Pteran interrupted. "This lapse raises serious concerns about your judgment."

Voices chimed in from the panel, cold and judgmental. "Intentions are irrelevant."

I wanted to scream. To tell them how absurd this was.

"Can we all take a fucking breath?" Nyx said, standing up, his voice loud and very angry. Every head turned toward him, including Chief Allo's.

"It was a slip-up, not a conspiracy," Nyx continued. "You're acting like he leaked classified invasion plans or tried to assassinate the prime minister."

"Agent Baryonyx—" Allo started, pissed, but Nyx wasn't done.

"With all due respect, if you think Steg isn't trustworthy, then you've clearly got your head up your ass," He said.

Oh shit. He is definitely getting fired, too.

The room erupted in gasps, and I swear someone muttered, "Oh my god, he's dead."

Nyx raised his hands but kept going. "Steg's mistake wasn't a betrayal. It was a moment of humanity—or, uh, aniformity, whatever. If anything, it shows how much he cares about what we do here. He's invested in the mission, maybe more than some of us in this room."

Chief Allo's glare could've melted steel. "Your argument is noted, Agent Baryonyx, but—"

"But nothing!" Nyx interrupted. "If we throw each other under the bus for every mistake, we're doomed. Chasing Tails is the real threat, not him." He pointed at me.

Kylo, who'd been leaning against the back wall looking bored, kicked off and stepped forward. "Look," she said, her voice sharp. "Rules are rules, but they're not sacred. Sometimes they just get in the way."

The ass of Deputy Pteran shut her down. "Ms. Kylo, may I remind you that as a consultant—and a former convict—your input on this matter is hardly—"

"Hardly what Pteran?" Nyx interrupted, his ears pinned back and his tail lashing like he was ready to fight. "Valuable? Kylo's intel is the only reason we even know Chasing Tails exists! How about you give her a little respect?"

The room erupted into a mess of shouting voices and clashing opinions. I stayed frozen in my seat, my tail limp, my heart pounding. Tyrann's voice cut through the noise, steady, and firm.

"Listen," he said. The room quieted. "Chief Allo," he continued, his eyes steady on her, "Real leadership means knowing when to adapt the rules for the greater good. Agent Stegosaurus made a mistake, yes. But his contributions far outweigh this one incident."

The room fell silent. Even Pteran looked like he wanted to argue, but couldn't come up with anything, that or he was pissed off with Nyx.

Chief Allo's icy gaze swept across the room. "Enough," she said. "The panel will convene privately to make its decision."

The wait outside the hearing room was pure torture. I paced the cramped hallway, casting anxious glances at Nyx, Kylo, and Tyrann. None of them said much, but their presence alone kept me from unraveling.

The door creaked open, and Chief Allo stepped out, her expression unreadable. "The panel has reached a decision," she announced.

Inside, by the table's head, she stood, voice cold. "Agent Stegosaurus's transgression is severe and cannot go unpunished."

I braced myself.

"However," she continued, "in light of his exemplary service record and the unique circumstances of this case, the panel has decided on an alternative to termination."

Nyx shot me a quick glance. For once, I let myself believe it wasn't over.

"Agent Stegosaurus will be placed on probation," Allo declared. "He will undergo additional training in operational security and will be required to wear a body camera at all times while on duty."

It wasn't great—I was on a leash—but it was better than losing my job. I let out a shaky breath; my tail rose a bit.

"Understand," Allo added, her gaze cutting through me, "this is an exception, not a precedent."

As we filed out, Nyx clapped me on the back. "See? Told you we've got your back."

"Thanks, man," I muttered.

Tacos and an excessive amount of margaritas were the highlight of that night, and damn, it was worth it.

See? Told you, it was one of my worst days. It was all so stupid. But at the time, it felt like the end of the world.

Nyx told me I should close this chapter on a positive note, so here it is:

Even if that day had ended with me getting fired, losing my dream career, one thing would've stayed the same—I had friends who had my back. And no disciplinary committee could ever take that away from me.

And if you're wondering, I wore the body cam for, what, maybe a month? Before I "accidentally" let it fall during a mission. Could I get in trouble for me telling you that? Nah. It was so long ago that no one cares anymore.

Chapter 8:
SHEEP IN WOLF'S CLOTHING

One secret you have to understand about this type of work: *it's not for the faint of heart*. It twists your trust and flips your world upside down. You start questioning everyone—your allies, your friends. Hell, sometimes even yourself.

It started in a dim room with shadows that stretched across the interrogation table. Steg sat at one end, arms crossed, his usual cheerful demeanour nowhere to be found. His eyes had a colder look.

Across from him, Kylo slouched in her chair, unreadable as ever. Her ears twitched a little—so subtle you'd miss it if you weren't paying attention.

"Let's try this again," Steg said, voice low, deliberate. The kind of tone that made you sit up straight, whether you wanted to. He leaned in, locking eyes with Kylo. "It's clear you've been holding out on us."

Kylo's smirk widened as she cocked her head. "I don't know what you're talking about, Steggy boy."

Steg slammed his fists onto the table, the sharp metallic clang making even me flinch on the other side of the mirror. "Cut the crap, Kylo," he said, his mock authority dripping with exaggerated drama. "The clock's ticking, and Mr. Nice Guy just walked out that door."

Kylo leaned back in her chair, tail wagging lazily. "Oh no," she said, voice thick with sarcasm. "Fine. I'd talk, but come closer."

Steg narrowed his eyes but leaned in, his floppy ear brushing near her muzzle.

Kylo whispered, slowly and deliberately. "Go. Suck. A. Lemon."

Steg's fur bristled, his ears standing upright as anger filled his eyes.

"Fuck Kylo! So, this is how you wanna play, eh? Fine. This isn't over."

Steg stormed out of the room, shoulders squared, leaving Kylo grinning behind him.

He met me in the observation room, looking defeated.

"I have no idea what else I could try," he said. "She won't talk."

I sighed, running a hand through my fur. "Time for drastic measures," I said, picking up a small envelope from the desk. "Time to bring out the secret weapon."

Steg's ears perked up. "You're really gonna do it?"

"Whatever it takes." I said, heading into the interrogation room.

Kylo's ears flicked toward me as I entered. "Save it, Fox," she said, her tone sharp but amused. "If dog boy was unable to break me, you have no chance."

"Are you sure about that?" I asked, placing the envelope on the table and sliding its contents into view.

Kylo's smirk faltered, her tail going still. "You wouldn't."

I leaned in, my voice low and deadly serious. "Tell us what we want to know, and this original Fireburr Pokemors card is yours."

Her eyes narrowed as she stared at the holographic card, her resolve visibly crumbling. The room went silent. She sighed, her ears flattening.

"Fine. I'll tell you everything."

Minutes later, I bursted into Tyrann's office, barely able to catch my breath. Steg was already there, tail and ears drooped in defeat.

"Guys!" I said. "I got it! I know where she gets those sandwiches! But we've gotta move—lunchtime's almost over!"

Steg perked up instantly, his tail wagging, and we both bolted toward the door.

Just as we reached it, Kylo strolled in, casually munching on one of the sandwiches we'd been chasing.

She arched an eyebrow, her tail flicking lazily. "You're such dorks."

"Never denied it," Steg shot back with a grin as we rushed past her.

Lunch turned into a rare moment of camaraderie — the kind of simple joy that made the pressure of our work feel a little less crushing. Even Tyrann cracked a smile as he wiped mustard off his tie after giving us a quick lecture about using official facilities for personal stuff (which, honestly, I don't regret — that sandwich was so worth it).

I'm kind of a slow eater, so by the time Steg and Tyrann had finished their lunch, I still had half a sandwich left. Lunch hour was over, and they went back, leaving me alone in the restaurant. Naturally, I pulled out my phone to scroll mindlessly while finishing my food.

My ears twitched, scanning the room without turning my head. That nagging feeling of being watched crept in. But when I glanced around, the restaurant seemed normal—just the usual noise of clinking plates and murmured conversations.

I shook it off and went back to my phone.

Someone sat down across from me, the chair scraping loudly against the tiled floor. A voice followed, low and disturbingly familiar.

"Fancy seeing you here, Jean, isn't it?"

I froze, my ears swivelling toward the sound before I looked up. It took me a second to place him.

Seb. The white wolf from last week's Chasing Tails meeting.

It wasn't just the voice; it was the way he leaned forward, arms resting casually on the table, his eyes sharp and fixed on me. GUIP gear was heavy and uncomfortable, so I'd left it at the office. All I had on was a white hoodie and jeans, my badge, and the card key clipped to my waistband—thankfully hidden from view under the table.

"Oh, hi, Seb," I said flatly, forcing my voice to stay calm as I lowered a paw, unclipping the badge and slipping it into my hoodie pocket. "What... are you doing here?"

His grin widened, smug and self-assured. "Just lunch, you know. But seeing you here? Well, what are the odds, right?"

I tried to play it casual. "Uh, yeah. Small world."

Seb stood, brushing imaginary dust off his jacket. "Lovely. Well, I've gotta run. Enjoy your lunch. I'll be seeing you soon."

The casual tone in his voice made me uneasy. *He wasn't here by accident, was he?*

I grabbed my sandwich and left the shop, my pace casual despite the adrenaline. I didn't look back, but I could feel him following me. My tail flicked nervously as I took a deliberately winding route, weaving through crowded streets.

Without hesitating, I hopped onto the LRT at Parliament Station, even though the office was only a few blocks away. Blending into the commuting crowd was just the quickest way I could think to throw him off. The last thing I needed was him figuring out where I worked—or worse, following me in.

When I finally approached the GUIP's secure entrance, I swiped my card with practiced ease. The glass doors slid open with that familiar mechanical hum, and I stepped inside, heart still pounding.

But at least I was safe.

"Everything okay, Agent?" Kingston asked, giving me an odd look. My breathing must've been more laboured than I realized.

"Yeah, all good, sweet, perfect," I said, flashing what I hoped was a convincing smile.

Kingston didn't look convinced. "Uh-huh." His skeptical tone followed me as I headed toward the elevators.

I leaned against the cool metal wall as the elevator doors slid shut, my thoughts racing. I should have felt safer now, inside HQ, but I didn't. My mind replayed the encounter with Seb—his smug grin, his calculated words "I'll be seeing you soon."

Even a rookie like me understood that was a threat. *But was it?*

Did he know I was an agent? Maybe he saw Tyrann and Steg at the restaurant too. *But he couldn't have followed me... right?* GUIP's clearance protocols were strict. No badge, no entry. That was the rule.

Right? Fuck. Right?

Then it hit me, and panic set in. Back when I was just a delivery guy, I came inside without clearance. *What stopped Seb from getting in as easily as I did?* I should have warned Kingston, but first, I needed to talk to Tyrann.

The elevator dinged, snapping me out of my thoughts. The doors slid open, revealing the familiar 10th floor.

Our office space was on the north side of the building, past administrative offices, conference rooms, utility closets, and meeting rooms. I walked fast, nerves on edge and thoughts racing.

I was halfway to Tyrann's corner office when it happened.

Someone shoved me hard out of nowhere. My body slammed into a cleaning closet, the door shutting behind me with a dull thud. I stumbled, disoriented, as the sudden darkness made it hard to focus.

"Aaaah, what the fuck?" I snapped, instinctively reaching for the wall to steady myself.

"About time you showed up. Nice place you've got up here."

The speaker turned on the light and stepped closer.

"Didn't peg you for the law-abiding type, Jean,"

I straightened, my ears twitching. "Shit, Seb," I said, keeping my voice low and steady. "You're not supposed to be here."

He smirked, leaning casually against the wall. "Neither should you, right?" His grin widened. "And yet, here we are."

"What do you want?"

Seb leaned back, casually inspecting a mop. "What do I want?" he said, his tone light but laced with something darker. "Let's call it... a friendly chat."

I pressed my back against the shelves behind me. "Friendly? You shoved me into a fucking closet, Seb. That's not exactly screaming 'friendly.'"

His grin widened, showing just a hint of teeth. "Fair point. But desperate times call for desperate measures, don't they? I figured you wouldn't willingly talk to me otherwise."

"You're right, I wouldn't; So why don't you say your shit and leave me alone?"

70

Seb stepped closer, his sharp eyes locked onto mine. The cramped space felt even smaller with him invading my personal bubble.

"Alright, Jean—or whatever your real name is—here's the thing. My boss says you are good. Better than most of the idiots we've come across. The only problem? You're playing for the wrong side."

I blinked, taken aback. "Your boss? The fuck are you talking about?"

"You heard me," he said, calm as ever, as though he were stating an obvious fact. "GUIP isn't the saviour you think it is. It's just another cog in a broken machine, pretending to care about you while it grinds you down."

I laughed, trying to mask the unease in me. "And you think your little hate group is better? You're out there trafficking alien tech and recruiting desperate aniforms with promises you can't keep."

Seb tilted his head, his grin faltering slightly. "You really believe that, don't you? That we're the bad guys. But have you ever stopped to question why GUIP exists in the first place? Who they're really protecting?"

I hesitated, but my voice stayed firm. "I don't have time for your conspiracy theories, Seb. GUIP isn't perfect, but at least we're trying to help."

"Oh, is that what you think?" he said with a laugh, sharp and mocking. "Tell me this—if GUIP's goal is to help Aniforms, then why are things still shit for our kind? Why are we still treated like second-class citizens?"

"I—We..." I stammered, my words faltering. The answer I wanted to give didn't come, because deep down, I wasn't sure I had one.

Seb's smirk widened, but his voice grew colder, more calculated. He leaned in, close enough that I could feel the heat of his breath against my fur. "You can ignore me all you want, but deep down, you know I'm right. Why do you think the Zenitharians are still here? Why do you think GUIP only hires aniforms? You really believe they're protecting you? Or are they just using you to do their dirty work?"

I glared at him, trying to not react, but doubt was seeping in. "What's your point?"

"My point," he said, his voice dropping to a growl, "is that GUIP doesn't care about you, me or anyone like us. They care about covering the truth. The Emergence? The Zenitharians? You honestly believe it was an accident?"

"It was an accident," I shot back, my voice full of frustration. "The Zenitharians made a mistake, and we got in the way."

Seb's laugh was harsh and humourless. "An accident? Is that what they've been spoon-feeding you? That some aliens just tripped over a wire and turned a chunk of the world into freaks like us? Wake up, Jean. The Emergence wasn't a mistake—it was planned. Every last bit of it."

"You're lying,"

"Am I?" Seb's grin turned sharp, his eyes locked on mine. "Think about it. If it was an accident, why are the Zenitharians still here? Why hasn't anyone fixed what they 'accidentally' broke? You think GUIP doesn't know the real story? They're in on it, fox. They've been from the start."

I clenched my fists, my claws digging into my palms. "Shut up. You're just trying to get in my head."

Seb chuckled, stepping back toward the door. "Maybe I am. Or maybe I'm the only one telling you the truth. Think about it, Jean. If you want answers, you won't find them here."

"I'm going to enjoy throwing you in a fucking cell," I said, but before I could make a move, Seb's fist connected with my gut, knocking the wind out of me.

I doubled over, gasping for air as pain shot through my torso.

Seb leaned in one last time, whispering in my ear. "I'll be seeing you soon. And next time, I hope you've picked the right side."

With that, he slipped out, leaving me slumped on the floor of the closet, trying to catch my breath. My body ached, but it was nothing compared to the storm raging in my mind. His words echoed, taunting me.

Twenty minutes later, after finally regaining my breath and composure, I sat at my desk, staring blankly at my half-finished report. I should've gone straight to Tyrann, reported Seb, and let him handle it. But instead, I sat there, seething. Fuck Seb. He had no right to plant doubt in my head. And yet... it was growing, anyway.

My mind wouldn't stop spinning. *What if everything I thought I knew was just... wrong?*

I slammed my paw down on the desk; the sound startling a few agents nearby. I didn't care. I needed answers. I spotted Steg and Kylo chatting by the coffee station. I grabbed them by the arms, and yanked them into one of the smaller briefing rooms. I shut the door behind us, locking out the world for a moment.

"Guys, I need to ask you something," I said, pacing as they exchanged confused glances. I spoke with more tension than intended. "What do you know about the Emergence? Like... really know?"

Steg blinked. "Uh... I mean, what they taught us in training. Zenitharians miscalculated. We got in the way by accident, and—boom—Aniforms."

Kylo frowned, leaning against the table. "What's this about, Nyx? You're acting weird." She paused, narrowing her eyes. "Weirder than usual."

I stopped pacing, turning to them with a mix of frustration and desperation. "Remember Seb?—the guy I told you about from the Chasing Tails recruitment meeting? He cornered me. Here. And he... he said some things."

Steg's tail wagged nervously. "What kind of things? Wait. Here? Like around here, or here here? Like inside here?"

I hesitated, my ears flattening. "In the broom closet next to the copier. Here."

Kylo blinked. "The copier closet? That's like two feet wide. Not much room to corner someone."

"Next to it! Focus, Kylo," I snapped. "Listen, he said stuff that made me wonder if we've been told the whole truth. About the Zenitharians. About GUIP. About everything."

Kylo's eyes narrowed. "Nyx, you can't seriously be taking what some Chasing Tails lunatic said at face value."

"I'm not. Or—I don't think I am," I said, though my voice wavered. "But I hate the uncertainty. What if he's not entirely wrong? What if there's more to the Emergence than we know? Don't you think it's weird that—"

"Stop," Kylo said, holding up a paw. "Just stop. You're going crazy."

Steg stepped closer. "Look, bud, if this is eating at you that much, why don't we check the archives? If anyone has the full story, it's gotta be in there."

I hesitated, my tail flicking behind me. The archives. Of course. Why hadn't I thought of that?

"Wait. Don't we need extra clearance for that?" I asked, still uncertain.

"Yes. But not really," Kylo said with a shrug. "The archive is a mess. And Banff, who's supposed to manage access and keep it organized, doesn't really care enough to do their job. So getting in should be easy."

"Are you sure?"

"Yeah," Kylo said. "I've been in there before, and I'm not even allowed to—" She stopped mid-sentence, then cleared her throat. "I mean... someone told me. Hypothetically."

"Yeah... someone," I said, though my voice felt steadier now. "Well, let's go."

Steg glanced between us, his tail flicking. "Oh, this is definitely going to end well." His tone was sarcastic.

"You can sit this one out, Steg," I muttered, already heading for the door.

"What? And miss out on the fun? Not a chance." He grinned, falling into step beside me. "Besides, if we get caught, I'm telling them it was your idea."

I shot him a look, deadpan. "Thanks, bud. You're a great friend."

"Always," he said, his tail wagging like this was some kind of game.

Kylo sighed. "Let's just not get caught, okay? I don't want to spend my summer back in prison."

We made our way to the archive storage on the 6th floor. Only agents with clearance could access the room. Everyone else was supposed to submit a formal request, so Banff, the archive manager, would retrieve the file for them—or at least, that's how it was *supposed* to work.

Instead, a pot plant propped open the door, and Banff sat inside, headphones on, staring at their phone.

They didn't even glance up, just gave us an annoyed hand gesture that clearly meant "get on with it."

The room had towering shelves, rows of endless boxes stuffed with classified files, agency secrets, and folders boldly stamped *Top Secret.*

Or it would have been, if my story had taken place in the 1980s.

In reality, it was just a handful of secure terminals hooked up to an isolated server. No shelves. No boxes. Just a sterile room running custom software that was supposedly impenetrable. Though, if you asked Kylo, *impenetrable* felt more like a polite suggestion than a fact.

We slipped into one of the terminal rooms, closing the door behind us. The space was dimly lit, the faint hum of servers filling the air. Kylo took the lead, settling in front of one of the terminals. Her claws danced across the keyboard as she navigated the system, muttering under her breath about its inefficiencies.

"What are you pulling up?" I asked, leaning over her shoulder.

"Files on the Emergence, internal memos... anything that mentions the Emergence or GUIP's formation," she replied, her eyes scanning the screen with practiced focus.

Steg hovered nearby, his tail twitching. "Are we sure this isn't going to get us fired? Or, I don't know... arrested?"

"Relax," Kylo said, not looking up. "Banff doesn't care. They didn't even glance up from their phone when we walked in. Besides, you're not doing anything illegal. Technically, I am."

"Comforting," Steg muttered, crossing his arms but staying put.

"You'll be fine," Kylo shot back, smirking as the terminal finally loaded a relevant file. The screen flickered for a moment before the first document popped up.

"Alright," she said, scrolling through the file. "Let's see what says about the Emergence."

I leaned in closer, my eyes narrowing as the words formed a picture—one that might finally answer the doubts in my mind. Or make them worse.

What did we find? What really happened? I'll tell you—with the very real risk of me getting arrested for revealing classified secrets. You're welcome.

Records show the Zenitharians arrived on Earth about fifteen years before the Emergence. How come no one noticed? Honestly, I have no clue. Sure, some YouTube videos surfaced, but most people wrote them off as a weird cat sighting or shitty CGI.

So, if they didn't arrive during the Emergence, what were they doing here? Easy: studying us. They learned our languages, watched our behaviour, analyzed our defensive tactics, and—most importantly—pinpointed our weaknesses. Basically, it was an alien reconnaissance mission.

But why? That's the tricky part. It's not like the Zenitharians are giving interviews. (And trust me, some people have tried.) From what we know, it boils down to resources—their goal was to take over the planet and strip it of anything valuable.

Now, you're probably thinking, *Cool story, but what does this have to do with the Emergence?* And, *Was GUIP lying to us?*

Well... it's complicated. Technically, GUIP didn't lie.

The Emergence *was an accident*. A big, messy accident that, ironically, worked out better for us than them. *Confused?* Yeah, me too. Let me break it down.

During those fifteen years of sneaky science, the Zenitharians focused on collecting DNA—predator DNA, to be exact. Wolves, foxes, lions... you get the picture. Oh, and humans too. *Why?* Bioengineering. They were trying to find weak points in the Earth's most dangerous species genetic code—anything to make wiping us out easier.

But they screwed up. Whatever big, shiny weapon they were cooking up, didn't work. No mass extinction, no global takeover. Hell, it was mostly harmless. No animals were reported affected. And only about 15% of humans experienced side effects (aniformism).

Why only 15%? No clue. Honestly, I don't even think the Zenitharians know.

So... why are they still here? No one knows for sure. If I had to guess, They're still trying to finish what they started.

And getting rid of them? Yeah... not exactly easy. Turns out they're a bunch of sneaky idiots. We still don't know how many are hiding on Earth—or where.

And what about GUIP's true mission? The archives didn't offer much—just some early mission statements and contradictory memos. Some made it seem like we were more for show than actually useful, while others highlighted our achievements. Nothing particularly helpful, really.

Was that a lot? Maybe. But hey, that's the condensed version of a multi-page report. *Again, you're welcome.*

Steg was the first to break the silence after reading the report. "I don't understand," he said, his ears twitching. "Why hide this? "

"Maybe they didn't want to cause mass panic," Kylo said, her tone skeptical as she scrolled through more pages. "Or maybe they didn't want people asking questions they couldn't answer."

"Wait—who signed off on this?" I asked, leaning closer to the screen.

Kylo's eyes scanned the bottom of the file. "It's signed by Agent R. Brian Moore," she said.

"Who?" Steg and I said in unison.

"No clue," Kylo replied, clicking on the name to pull up more information. "But I guess we've got someone to look for."

"No results found," Kylo said, frowning at the screen. "Well, at least there's one thing they manage to keep secret in this crappy system. All agents' identities are redacted."

"Can you print the report?" I asked, my voice firm.

Kylo hesitated, her claws hovering over the keyboard. "Nyx, I don't think that's a good idea," she said, glancing back at me. "This is classified. If someone finds out—"

"I know," I said, cutting her off. "But it's the only clue I have. Please."

She sighed, her ears flicking with reluctant frustration. "Okay, fine. I really hope you know what you're doing." With a few clicks, the printer in the corner whirred to life, spitting out the report.

"Thanks, Kylo," I said as she handed me the freshly printed pages.

"Hey, I'm leaving. I need to lock up, so get out," Banff's voice came through the closed door, flat and uninterested.

Kylo smirked, shutting down the terminal. "If there's one thing Banff care about, it's leaving on time."

I tucked the report into my hoodie pocket and nodded toward the door. "Let's go before they decide to actually care about their job."

Steg didn't need telling twice. "Finally," he muttered, following us as we slipped back into the hallway without a second glance.

We said little as we headed back to the 10th floor. Our heads were still spinning.

"But... we're still the good guys, right?" Steg broke the silence, his voice uncertain.

"Yeah," I said, but it came out too soft. I didn't actually know if we were.

"There you are." Tyrann's voice cut through the tension, making us all jump. He spotted us down the hall and strode over. "I thought you'd called it for the day."

"Yeah. Almost," I muttered, trying to sound casual.

Tyrann's sharp gaze flicked between us, lingering on me. "Nyx, I need a word."

Steg and Kylo exchanged a glance, but I just nodded. "Sure."

Inside his office, Tyrann leaned against his desk, arms relaxed. "Sorry I haven't checked with you. How are you doing?"

"I'm good. All perfect," I said, the words dripping with sarcasm. My tone was more annoyed than convincing.

"You seemed uneasy after returning from lunch," he said carefully. "Look, I know you're under pressure—"

"Under pressure?" I snapped, a dry laugh escaping before I could stop it. "My parents have been missing for seven months. Pressure's a goddamn understatement."

"I get it—"

"Do you?" The anger came out sharper than I intended. I rubbed my face, trying to pull myself back. "Sorry. I just... I don't know how much more of this waiting I can take."

He nodded. "I'd be lying if I said I understood completely. But I do know how loss and uncertainty can eat at you."

I leaned back against the wall, arms crossed. "It's more than that. I keep thinking... what if we're wasting time? What if GUIP isn't telling us everything?"

Tyrann's eyes narrowed. "Where this is coming from?"

I let out a loud sigh. "Fucking Seb. He knows I'm an agent."

"Why do you think that?" Tyrann asked.

"He followed me here, and well, he practically threatened me to switch sides." I gave him a quick rundown of the day, skipping the parts that would land Steg and Kylo in trouble. I pulled the report from my pocket, and give it to him.

"Where did you get this?" Tyrann scanned the contents, his expression unreadable. He sighed. "Is this what you three were up to?... You know what? Don't answer that."

I stared at him, anger unable to hold my anger. "So... is it true, then?" My voice edged with something I hated—vulnerability. "It just feels like GUIP is hiding the truth from us."

Tyrann stood, posture rigid. "Because it is."

"Seriously? Why not just tell us? Why keep us in the dark?"

His gaze didn't waver. "Because the truth could do more harm than good," he said, calm but firm. "At least, that's what the higher-ups believe."

"And what do you believe?" I asked.

He sighed, the tension in his shoulders softening just enough to show he wasn't as collected as he wanted to see. "I don't agree with everything they do, Nyx. But I know this much—GUIP isn't perfect, but it's the only chance we have."

"Is it?" I shot back, anger bubbling to the surface. "Because things are still pretty shitty for us. Feels like we're here to put on a show... or be disposable."

I took a step closer, eyes locked on Tyrann's. "Just tell me—why is it that only Aniforms work here?"

Tyrann's expression faltered, a hint of sadness on his face. "Because we're the only ones who care enough to fight for our rights and protection. We've tried recruiting Norforms... but no one enlisted."

That shouldn't have surprised me. It did anyway. My fists clenched at my sides as I exhaled, shaky and uneven. I dragged a paw through my fur. "I'm just... tired," I said, voice cracking. "Tired of pretending I'm fine."

Tyrann stepped closer, placing a steady hand on my shoulder. His touch wasn't comforting exactly—but it was grounding. "I know," he said. "You don't have to pretend—not with me."

I searched his face for any sign of doubt, some crack in that unshakable façade. Instead, I found something worse—exhaustion, guilt, and a quiet resolve that said he'd already made peace with things I was just starting to question.

"Tyrann," I said carefully, lowering my voice. "If GUIP isn't telling us everything... how do I know we're really on the right side?"

Silence stretched between us. He didn't break eye contact. Didn't fidget. Just let the question hang.

"You don't." He said. His tone was steady—resigned, but not cold. "Not completely. None of us do. We just have to believe that what we're doing is bigger than us... and do everything we can to make that belief a reality."

"I guess." I muttered, although the words felt hollow. I glanced away, trying to hide my guilt. "And... sorry,"

"For what?" Tyrann said. His voice was soft.

"I don't know... For doubting, I think."

He shook his head. "There's no need to apologize. Doubt keeps you sharp—and sometimes, it's the motivation you need to make a change. Just... next time? Come to me before allegedly committing a federal crime, okay?"

I chuckled. "Right. I will,"

"Good," he said, warmth creeping back into his tone. "Now go home, Nyx. Get some rest. We'll talk more tomorrow."

I lingered at the door. "What about Seb? Aren't we going to investigate how he got in?"

"We are." His gaze hardened, professional mode back into place. "But that's for tomorrow."

Reluctantly, I nodded and stepped out into the quiet hallway. The door clicked shut behind me.

As I walked, my mind churned with everything I'd learned—and everything I still didn't know. Seb's words stayed with me, his punch still leaving a lingering ache.

Was GUIP really the best we had? Or was I just following orders without question?

By the time I reached the elevator, I wasn't sure if I felt more confused or angry. Probably both.

Chapter 9:

FOXY FOCUS, ENGAGED

The mid-summer heat was relentless, and I was roasting under my dark orange hoodie—a weird choice to wear under my uniform, but I wasn't going to change. So I just tugged at the straps digging into my fur, trying to focus on Chief Allo's briefing.

She was talking about a raid planned at a Chasing Tails base, rambling on about security measures and potential threats, but I didn't listen. My mind kept drifting to the weird text I'd received.

The message had been brief, a set of coordinates and one line:

Come today at 2 PM alone if you want to see your family alive.

It arrived at 1:30 PM.

It had to be a trap, right? Someone hands me the location of my parents and brother after all that time? And the timing—right before we did a raid? It felt too perfect. Too convenient.

"Nyx, are you even listening?" Tyrann's nudge snapped me back to reality.

"Yeah, yeah. Heavily guarded, extremely armed, yada yada yada. Got it," I said, flashing a grin that probably looked faker than it felt.

Allo's eyes zeroed in on me. "This is serious, Agent Baryonyx. If we pull this off, it could deal a major blow to CT operations."

"I know, Chief. I'm focused, I swear." I straightened up, trying to look like the reliable agent I was supposed to be. But my mind wasn't in there.

How did we even got there? It all started the day before. Tyrann had dragged me into the operations room, where Kylo was already at a monitor, her fingers flying across the keyboard.

"Do we have any idea how Seb got in?" Tyrann asked, arms crossed, his tone sharp.

Kylo sighed, clearly annoyed. "Not quite," she muttered, pulling up multiple windows on the screen. "But I did find some interesting stuff."

She played the security footage, switching between clips, and spreadsheets filled with dates and data. On-screen, Seb strolled into HQ like he owned the place. The camera clearly caught him swiping a keycard at the main gate, entering just like any other agent.

Tyrann's ears twitched. "That's good, right? We can easily figure out who is it registered to."

"Well, I thought so," Kylo said, opening another window. "But all logs for that time have been wiped."

"Could it be a glitch?" I asked, leaning closer to the monitor.

"I doubt it. Look here," she said, pointing to the screen. She compared the logs to the security footage. "At 1:12, Steg and Tyrann return from lunch. Both entries are in the log. A few more agents come through—same thing, they're logged. But then Seb arrives at 1:26. He's clearly on the footage, but there's no entry in the log. Right after that, Nyx, you show up at 1:34, and your entry is there. So either his card didn't leave a record, which is highly unlikely, or someone manually removed it."

"At least I wasn't followed. The bastard already knew," I muttered, rubbing the back of my neck. "So let me get this straight. Somebody gave him a card, he made a copy, or he stole one. Either way, someone's helping him from the inside?"

"Looks like it," Kylo confirmed with a grim nod.

"Do we at least know who he is?" Tyrann asked, his tail swishing behind him.

Kylo grinned, a spark of satisfaction lighting her eyes. "Oh yes. His entire scheme was good—avoided looking directly at the cameras, careful not to be noticed. But," she said, drawing out the word, "he made one tiny mistake. He made a phone call."

I raised a brow. "A phone call? Who even calls these days?" I said, trying to sound serious.

"Exactly!" Kylo said, laughing. "But here's the thing—cell signal sucks in old buildings like this one. Thick concrete walls, outdated insulation, you know the deal. To fix that, GUIP installed cell boosters all over HQ. And those boosters? They log every connected device. I simply cross-referenced the logs with the time of his call."

She clicked on another window; the screen filling with data. "The number he dialled? A prepaid burner phone. It's offline now, so we can't locate who he called. But it wasn't a total bust. With his number, I ran a carrier lookup."

Kylo's smirk widened as she pulled up another file. "Meet Sebastian 'Seb' Lapointe Jr. He lives near the Uplands. Not exactly a model citizen. Three prior arrests—petty theft, vandalism, and, surprise, surprise, assault during an anti-aniform protest. Very on-brand."

She leaned back in her chair, her grin practically gleaming. "But here's where it gets really interesting. His dad, Sebastian Lapointe Sr., owns a warehouse by the airport. Turns out, Senior shares some similar feelings about our kind. And well, He's been letting Junior use the property as a Chasing Tails base."

Her eyes flicked to me. "And guess who's been spending a suspicious amount of time there? Your 'friend' Seb. Bet you'd love to return the favour with a 'friendly' visit."

Tyrann's posture stayed calm, but his tail wagged slightly, betraying his satisfaction. "Good work, Kylo. Let's assemble a team and bring it down."

Fast-forward to the next day, and we were gearing up for the raid. All agents were lined up and prepped. Chief Allo's voice cut through the tension, barking out orders: "All right, gear up and get to the transports. We roll out in five."

Agents bustled around, getting ready for action, but I stood there for a moment, staring at my phone. Tyrann noticed and shot me a sideways glance. "Hey, you good?"

"Yeah, just pre-mission jitters," I said, forcing a chuckle. But my mind was torn between the mission and the message. The mission mattered—it mattered a lot. But the message... what if it was my only chance?

Tyrann clapped a hand on my shoulder, his grip firm and reassuring. "Whatever it is, try to shake it off. We need that foxy focus of yours out there."

"Right. I can do that." I shoved the phone into my pocket and followed him to the transport, the weight of my decision pressing harder with every step.

But as I climbed into the vehicle, I couldn't help but glance back, that voice in the back of my head whispering, What if you're making the wrong choice?

Tyrann was watching me, his brow furrowed. "Nyx, seriously, what's going on? You're not yourself."

I hesitated, but couldn't keep it to myself. "I dunno..." I murmured, leaning closer so only he could hear. "I got a message. It's about my family—they might be nearby." I handed him the phone.

Tyrann's ears twitched as he read it. "Shit, Nyx. That's..." He paused, his tail flicking thoughtfully. "But the timing... it's suspicious as hell."

"I know," I said, dragging a paw down my face. "But what if it's real? What if this is my only chance to save them?"

Tyrann sighed, his expression softening. "If it were my family, I'd probably want to dump everything and run toward it. But think about it—first Seb ambushed you here. Then you got this message right when we're about to strike. It's just too many coincidences not to be planned."

His words hit hard. I knew he was right, but it didn't make the choice any easier. My heart felt like it was being ripped in two directions.

"I just... I don't know if I can live with myself if I don't try," I whispered, my voice barely holding steady.

Tyrann's hand tightened on my shoulder. "And I don't know if I could live with myself if I let you go off alone and something happened to you. We're a team, Nyx. We stick together. We'll find your family—I promise."

I closed my eyes, letting his words settle in. The mission. The team. The greater good. It was a heavy burden, but it was the right thing to do.

"Okay," I said finally, meeting his gaze. "Let's do this."

Relief flickered in his eyes, though worry lingered. "That's the spirit. Channel that foxy focus, yeah?"

"Yeah. Foxy focus, engaged," I said, managing a small smile.

The weight of my decision pressed down harder. I hoped that when everything calmed down and the sun came up, I wouldn't be filled with regrets. *(Yes, I can be pretentious with my writing sometimes.)*

Mapleview EZ Storage, Boxes, and CarWash—a weird combination that made no sense but somehow didn't surprise me. According to intel, Chasing Tails was using it as a storage facility. The lacklustre industrial complex looked unremarkable, except for the unusually tight security—way more than your average storage business would ever need.

As we disembarked, I couldn't shake the feeling that we were—okay, let's pause for a second. There's something that has been bothering me all these years that I need to let out. Can we talk about how stupid the name "Chasing Tails" is?

I mean, I get it. They're trying to be edgy and clever with their wordplay, but have you ever actually seen a dog chasing its own tail? It's not intimidating—it's pathetic. Cute and sometimes funny, sure, but still. Just spinning in circles, getting nowhere. There, I said it!

Anyway, back to what you probably care about—I couldn't shake the feeling that we were walking into a trap. Tyrann's voice broke through my thoughts, grounding me back in the moment. "Stick to the plan," he murmured, barely audible over the hum of nearby machinery. "Get in, get the job done, and get out."

"Roger that," I muttered, adjusting my grip on my weapon as we moved toward the perimeter.

The team spread out to assume their positions. "I've got eyes on the entry point," Steg's voice crackled over comms. "Two guards. Armed. I can take them out on your signal."

"Copy that," I whispered, my gaze fixed on the dimly lit door. The faint hum of distant machinery buzzed in my ears as I adjusted my grip on the weapon.

"On my mark." Tyrann said. "Three, two, one..."

Steg's shots were dead-on. And yeah, I'll admit it—I always felt a twinge of jealousy at his precision. In a good way, of course. The guards dropped without a sound, their weapons clattering softly against the concrete.

Gunfire filled the air, reverberating off the metal walls while shouts echoed in every direction. The sharp tang of gunpowder stung my nose, and the lights overhead cast jittery shadows that danced across the building. My heart hammered in my chest as we moved as a unit, clearing rooms.

"Clear!" Steg shouted from the left.

"Moving forward!" Tyrann said from behind.

During high-stakes moments like that, it's almost second nature to slip into autopilot. It has to be. You can't afford to let the rational part of your brain—the one screaming "Get the fuck out!" every time a bullet flies—take control. You shut it down, push it aside, and let instinct take over. My focus was sharp—had to be—but even then, a gnawing unease clung to me.

Then, in one of the larger storage areas, we found him—Seb. He was standing near a cluster of Chasing Tails members, barking orders in a voice edged with panic. Papers, computers, and other junk were strewn everywhere.

His sharp eyes locked onto mine the moment we stormed in, his expression faltering for just a second.

"Hello, Sebastian," I said, my voice steady despite the adrenaline coursing through me. A grin tugged at my muzzle as I approached him, keeping my weapon trained. "Lovely place you've got here."

"Jean? What are you doing here?" he said, confusion on his face.

"It's Agent Baryonyx, tho you probably already knew that," I said, letting my smirk grow wider. "I told you I was going to put you in a cell. And, well... I'm a fox of my word."

"Still playing for the wrong side, eh? I thought you were smarter than this," Seb said with a smug grin.

I stepped forward, keeping my gun steady on him. "Nah, I'm as dumb as I look. Oh, by the way, you're under arrest. Don't even think about trying anything. I'd love an excuse to pay you back for that gut punch."

Seb chuckled, with a mocking tone. "You really think this changes anything? Chasing Tails is bigger than you, 'Agent.' Bigger than any of you."

"Yeah, yeah. Keep talking," I said, stepping closer, my patience wearing thin.

Seb made a weird growl, but didn't resist as Tyrann cuffed him. "This isn't over," he muttered, his voice low and vicious.

"We'll see about that," I shot back, biting back the urge to punch him. Although... someone might or might not have accidentally bumped his head on the door frame while loading him into the patrol. I— ugh I mean... someone regrets nothing.

Seb shot me a glare, but his smug grin didn't falter. Even in cuffs, he carried himself with an air of superiority, like he knew something we didn't. It was infuriating, and I just wanted to punch him, which I swear I didn't.

As we finished securing the area and loading the last of the detainees, we took a moment to glance at the scattered evidence, trying to make sense of it all. Papers, blueprints, and strange-looking tech—it was a mess, but it clearly pointed to something bigger. The adrenaline that had kept me sharp and focused during the fight began to fade, leaving a gnawing unease in its place.

The fight was over faster than I expected. As we moved toward the extraction point, my mind kept spinning over what we'd uncovered—not just the tech, though that was important, but the files. They held details about what our mission was originally supposed to be. And that didn't sit right with me.

Confused? Let me back up for a second.

The original plan was simple: infiltrate a warehouse across town based on intel we'd gathered. But something about it felt off—it was all too easy to uncover, almost like it was waiting for us to find it.

On the way there, Tyrann forwarded the message I'd received to Kylo. She did her usual tech wizardry, tracing its origin and digging deeper into its sender. What she found changed everything.

Turns out, Chasing Tails had planted evidence to lead us to the original base—basically a trap. While combing through one of their servers, Kylo uncovered traces of tampered documents. But she didn't stop there.

She dug deeper and found this place—a command centre they were clearly trying to keep hidden. Right then and there, we made the call to change course. And yeah, Seb's call wasn't a slip-up. He knew we'd trace it back to the fake intel.

And well, it worked. We found something big. But it also raised an even bigger question: *Who had access to plant the fake intel?* Not many. And that confirmed our suspicious—a traitor within GUIP.

Seb's capture should've felt like a win, but his demeanour unnerved me. Most people caught in a raid look panicked, desperate, or furious. Seb? He looked smug—like he knew something we didn't.

As the team huddled together, it was like we'd all become strangers. All having the same question: *Who can we trust?*

Tyrann stepped beside me, his voice low. "You don't look like a fox who just pulled off a successful op. What's on your mind, Nyx?"

I sighed, running a hand over my face. "You know what's on my mind, Ty. Seb, my family, the traitor—everything."

Tyrann studied me, his gaze steady. "It's a lot, I know. But we'll figure it out—all of it. And Seb? He's playing his game, but we'll stay one step ahead. You're not doing this alone."

We started boarding the vehicles to head back, but Tyrann kept glancing at me, his concern obvious. I shot him a quick nod—not because I felt okay, but because I needed to look like it.

"Focus, SJ, One crisis at a time. You can fall apart later." And I did.

Back at GUIP HQ, the team gathered in the debriefing room. Chief Allo sat across from me, flipping through the evidence we'd gathered.

"This is... significant," she said at last, her tone as neutral as her expression. "If this is accurate, we may have a serious security breach." Her eyes locking onto mine.

I nodded, my fur bristling. "We need to find out who's behind this," I said, sharper than I intended. "Before they can cause any more damage."

She leaned back. "Agreed. But we must proceed carefully. If there is a traitor, they'll be on high alert now. We can't risk tipping them off." Her voice dropped, cold and deliberate. "Agent, we have to keep this between us for now."

Something about her tone made me uneasy. The way she emphasized 'us'—so sharp, so deliberate—set off alarm bells in my head. I forced myself to hold her gaze. "With all due respect, Chief, the team deserves to know. They're the ones putting their lives on the line."

Her expression flickered—just for a second—a flash of irritation cracking her composed exterior. "I will decide when they need to be informed, Agent Baryonyx."

I opened my mouth to argue, but her glare shut me down before the words even formed. This wasn't a discussion.

I forced a nod, keeping my voice steady. "Understood."

"Good." She returned her attention to the files, her tone softening just enough to feel unsettling. "Now, you're dismissed, agent."

I hesitated, my ears twitching. There was something in her tone—something I couldn't place, and I didn't like it. "Yes, Chief."

As I stepped out of the room, my mind spun in a hundred directions. All of it pressed down on me. But now, a new thought clawed its way to the surface: *Can I trust the chief?*

I found myself on the rooftop of HQ, the cityscape of Mapleview stretching out before me. The sun was setting, streaking the sky with shades of orange and purple. It was probably beautiful, but my mind was too loud to notice.

"Figured you'd be up here," Tyrann said behind me, his voice calm. I didn't turn right away, letting the sound of his footsteps ground me.

"How'd the debrief go?" he asked, stepping up beside me.

I let out a long breath. "I dunno. Really strange."

Tyrann's ears twitched. "Strange how?"

I hesitated, searching for the right words. "Something about the Chief." I glanced at him, lowering my voice. "I don't know. I'm still pretty new here, but... how much can we trust her? Or anyone, really?"

Tyrann studied me, his expression thoughtful. "Nyx... you're not wrong to have doubts. But Allo's been in this game for a long time. She's tough, and she plays things close to the chest. That doesn't make her untrustworthy."

"Doesn't make her trustworthy, either," I countered. "If someone inside GUIP planted that intel, how do we know she's not part of it?"

Tyrann frowned, his tail swishing slowly. "We don't. But we can't afford to start turning on each other—not without proof. That's how we fall apart."

I turned to face him fully, my heart pounding. "I just can't help it. Everything seems to get worse every day."

Tyrann's gaze held mine for a long moment before he nodded slowly. "I get it," he said finally, his voice softer. "I've got questions too. But until we know more, we have to tread carefully. Deal?"

"Deal... I guess."

His smirk was faint, but the calm I'd always admired slid effortlessly back into place. "Look at you. Fully embracing the life. My little padawan."

I sighed loudly. "You're such a nerd," rolling my eyes.

"And you're not?" he said with a grin.

"Touché," I muttered, pulling out my phone. The message glared back at me.

I tightened my grip on the device. "We start with this. We find out more about who sent it, why they sent it, and what they know."

Tyrann nodded, his expression resolute. "Already on it. We'll get them back, Nyx. I promise."

A small but genuine smile broke through my frustration. "Thanks, Ty."

As we turned to head back inside, I glanced at him, a flicker of gratitude warming my worry. Whatever was coming, Tyrann would be there—and that meant everything.

Before leaving, I stopped by the holding cells. Seb sat inside, his posture annoyingly relaxed. When I entered, he looked up, a smirk tugging at his lips.

"Hey, you," he said smoothly, leaning back against the wall. "Come to tell me you're finally joining us? Fighting the good fight?"

"That's why I became an agent," I replied dryly, trying—and failing—to mask my annoyance.

"Ha! And here I thought you weren't an idiot, Jean."

I folded my arms, fixing him with a steady glare. "Really? Still holding on to the fake name?"

He chuckled, the sound low and grating. "Oh yeah. I'm not about to let GUIP rewrite who you are by stripping away your identity with their methods. Call it... a form of resistance. But if Jean bothers you, you could just tell me your real name?"

"Pass."

Seb tilted his head, his grin growing wider. "If I had to guess, you look like a Tyler. Or maybe a Cody? No? I could always go by calling you sheep."

"Whatever," I snapped, stepping closer, my patience thinning. "And for the record, I'd be more eager to share my name if you weren't such a condescending ass."

Seb's smirk widened, unbothered by my tone. "Your loss." He leaned forward slightly, resting his elbows on his knees, looking too comfortable for a man in a cell. "So, to what do I owe the pleasure?"

"You know why I'm here."

"Oh, do I?" His eyebrow arched, his tone dripping with mock innocence. "Please, enlighten me."

My claws curled into my palms, but I kept my voice level. "Who gave you the card to access HQ? Who's helping you?"

Seb tilted his head, his expression oozing mockery. "And why would I tell you that?"

"If you don't," I said, my voice sharp and icy, "I'll make your time here unforgettable—and not in a good way."

For a moment, his smirk faltered, but it was back before I could take satisfaction in it. "You've got fire, I'll give you that. But threats? Not your style, Sheep. You're too soft."

I clenched my fists, biting back the urge to wipe that smug grin off his face. "You're not going to win, Seb. Whatever you and your hateful friends are planning, we'll stop it."

His grin widened, and it made my fur bristle. "We'll see," he said, his voice dripping with confidence.

He leaned forward, lowering his voice to a conspiratorial whisper. "But you might want to move fast. I'm not staying long. Just a little overnight visit. My boss likes to keep me... mobile. He's letting me out first thing in the morning."

My stomach twisted, but I forced myself to stay calm. "You're not going anywhere," I said flatly. I glanced at my phone. I saw a message from Steg asking if I wanted pizza for dinner. "Well, I have better things to do," I added, turning toward the door. "Enjoy your cell, Seb."

His laugh followed me as I left, grating against my nerves.

As I stepped outside, the weight of everything pressed down on me harder than ever. Seb's words, the traitor, the mystery of my family—it all churned in my mind, a relentless storm I couldn't escape.

But one point was clear. I would not stop until I had the answers—even if it meant burning the entire city down to get them. *And yes, I'm being pretentious again.*

Chapter 10:
FAMILY PORTRAIT

I'd consider myself the kind of guy who sees the glass half full. Not an optimist exactly, but more of a positive realist. If that makes sense.

I try to focus on the good while keeping my expectations in check. But by that point? It was getting harder. The positive mindset was slipping away, replaced by something closer to *pessimistic cynicism*.

That morning, the soft chime of my phone broke through the quiet of my room. "Ugh... I hate that sound so much," I groaned, fumbling to silence the alarm. My paw brushed against the screen, and the noise cut off.

I lay there for a moment, staring at the ceiling. My thoughts pressed down on me. With a sigh, I swung my legs over the side of the bed, wincing as my feet hit the cold floor.

"Come on," I muttered. "Time to save the world. Or at least try to not screw it up too badly."

My muscles protested as I shuffled to the bathroom, each step feeling heavier than the last. The bathroom mirror greeted me with a sorry sight—bloodshot green eyes stared back from a face framed by matted reddish-orange fur. I looked like I'd been hit by a truck. A truck carrying a load of exhaustion and poor decisions.

"Well, you look like shit, Agent Baryonyx," I said to my reflection, running a paw through my messy fur. "Ready to save the world looking like you crawled out of a dumpster?"

Splashing cold water on my face did little to shake off the thoughts. My mind drifted to the message about my family and the eight months of uncertainty. Not knowing if they were alive or... I shook my head, scattering droplets across the mirror. "Stop it, SJ," I told myself. "Don't go there."

I shuffled out of the bathroom, my ears perking up at the sound of Steg's cheerful humming drifting through his door.

"Ugh. How can anyone be that happy this early?" I muttered, fumbling with the buttons on my pants.

As I geared up, I slipped into my usual civilian attire—dark jeans and a fitted t-shirt. I pulled my favourite dark hoodie. A badge clipped to the collar added a touch of authority.

I strapped on my belt, which held various gadgets and tools.

"Great," I muttered, adjusting my gear. "Now I look like a professional disaster rather than a typical one."

I gave myself one last glance in the mirror, trying to psych myself up. "Alright. You've got this. For them." But the words that used to lift me up now felt increasingly empty.

I headed to the kitchen, where Steg was already bustling about, singing along to a song playing on his phone, his tail wagging as he poured coffee. "Morning, Coop," I greeted him.

"Morning, roomie!" Steg chirped; his Labrador features creased in a warm smile. "Late shift? I didn't hear you come in last night." He studied my face, trying to gauge how I was holding up. "Fun or rough night. No. I know! It was both right?" he asked.

I grunted, reaching for the coffeepot. "Fun? I don't know that word."

"Seriously, man, you okay?" Steg's eyes narrowed with concern. "If you want to talk, we can call in sick, order some junk food, cheap beers, and chat about whatever or whoever is bringing you down."

I forced a weak smile, avoiding his gaze. "It's fine. Just been a rough week, you know? Nothing industrial levels of coffee can't fix."

As I sipped the reviving liquid, I couldn't help but wonder how I would make it through the day when I could barely make it through breakfast.

Living in Centretown meant that parking on the street after 7 AM wasn't an option unless you wanted to get towed. So even though our office was only a few blocks away, we took Steg's car each morning, where at least he could park for free.

"So, how was your night?" I asked, trying to divert my mind.

"It was good!" he replied, enthusiasm bubbling over. "Jack introduced me to this girl before he left, and well, we finally had a date last night. And man, let me tell you, it got wild!"

"Mm-hmm," I mumbled, though my thoughts kept drifting.

Steg, undeterred by my lack of engagement, "We went to the last drop last night, and we almost got kicked out!" he continued, his tail wagging against the seat. I wasn't really hearing "But then this guy—"

I forced a weak chuckle, my gaze fixed on the Parliament building passing by the window.

I had become an expert at hiding my feelings, but lately my brain refused to cooperate, and thoughts of guilt and sadness had taken centre stage.

"...turns out it wasn't just some random guy; he was her former math teacher. Wild, eh?" Steg's voice faded in and out of my consciousness.

"Yeah, wild," I muttered, unsure of what I was even agreed to.

As we entered GUIP headquarters, I got hit by the cacophony of a normal day. Phones rang, printers whirred, and agents shouted across the room.

"Nyx,"

On any other day, I'd be right in the middle of it, cracking jokes and diving into whatever conversation I overheard.

"Nyx!" I faintly heard.

But today? Why bother?

"Nyx!" Steg's voice cut through my haze. "You okay, bud?"

I blinked, realizing I'd been standing in the middle of the lobby, staring at nothing. "Yeah, sorry. Just... thinking."

Steg's eyes softened. "Look, if you need to talk—"

"I'm fine," I cut him off, perhaps a bit too sharply. "Let's just get to the briefing."

As we navigated through the controlled areas, I couldn't get rid of the feeling that I was drifting, untethered. The mission, my family, all... I wasn't sure how much longer I could keep pretending I belonged in that place.

When we entered the briefing room, I caught Tyrann's eye. His grin shifted into a subtle nod with hints of worry. I appreciated he didn't ask how I was feeling—though I was sure he knew.

Chief Allo's commanding presence filled the room as she strode to the front. "Listen up, agents. Today we have a highly sensitive situation," she said, her tone leaving no room for questions.

I tried to focus. Really, I did. But as she began outlining the mission parameters, my mind wandered.

"Following the raid at the Chasing Tails base," she continued, "...Kylo was able to decrypt....data points to the location of..."

Her words blurred together. Something about encrypted messages, coordinates, and other stuff that just wouldn't stick.

I couldn't shake the memory of my mom's frightened eyes the last time I saw her, or the thought that things might never have come to this if I hadn't tried to pretend I was someone I wasn't.

"Agent Baryonyx!" Chief Allo's sharp tone snapped me back to reality. "Do you think you can handle this? I'll understand if you want to stand down for this one."

Heat rose to my cheeks. I had no idea what she was referring to. "I... uh..."

I panicked and started scanning the screen, trying to gather as much information as possible about the mission, when I stumbled upon something I wasn't expecting.

MISSION BRIEFING

OPERATION:
EXTRACTION AND RESCUE OF OPERATIVE RELATIVES

TARGET PACKAGES:
- Female, 54: B., MELANIE
- Male, 51: B., ENRIQUE
- Male, 22: B., ANDREW JOSEPH

OBJECTIVE:
Secure and extract the target packages from
the Zenitharian stronghold. These individuals
are appointed as high-value assets, and their
well-being is of critical importance. Proceed
with caution—intelligence indicates a heavily
fortified guard presence and advanced security
systems.

It couldn't be a coincidence, could it? Those were my parents and my brother.

Tyrann stepped in, his voice steady. "We understand if this is overwhelming, Nyx. We've got your back, and we'll bring them home, okay?"

I took a deep breath. "I need to do this, Tyrann. I cannot sit back and let someone else handle it."

Chief Allo interjected, her eyes narrowing. "Every agent needs to be at one hundred per cent. Is that clear?"

"I'm ready for it," I said, my determination sharpening my tone. "I won't let anything stop me from bringing them back."

Tyrann glanced at me; concern etched on his face. "Nyx, we want to ensure you're in the correct mental state for this. It's going to be intense."

"Trust me, I can handle it," I insisted, trying to convince myself as much as him.

"Copy that," Chief Allo commanded, not letting the concern linger. "Agent Tyrannosaurus, please brief the tactical team. You'll be leaving at 1030."

Tyrann moved to the centre of the room as Allo exited. "Okay team," he said. "Now that we have Nyx's attention, this is how we're proceeding—"

As the briefing continued, I tried to push all my doubts away, focusing on the details the intel team had prepared for us.

As we began to gear up, the reality of what we were about to do settled over me. Whatever the outcome, this was going to change me forever.

On the way, I caught my reflection in a cruiser side mirror. "This is what you've been waiting for," I said to myself, gripping my tactical vest. "Your family needs you. No room for mistakes." Although all I saw back was a scared kid playing dress-up as a hero.

We arrived at the Zenitharian stronghold. An intergalactic fortress filled with looming shadows, strange alien rituals, and a few oversized tentacled beings lurking in the corners. The walls dripping with goo-like substances, bizarre devices buzzing with ominous energy, and an all-encompassing atmosphere of impending doom.

Or at least, that's what I was expecting. The truth? It was simply a decommissioned waste treatment plant. The only bizarre sight was a couple of *Amazon* packages at the door. Not exactly what horror movies had taught me over the years.

We gathered outside the building—Steg, Tyrann, and I were part of the breach group, accompanied by a dozen other agents as backup for the operation.

For a moment, everything went silent, the only sound being the distant rush of cars passing by the 416 highway.

A memory surfaced—my dad's confused expression when I'd first emerged from my room after the transformation.

It had started like any other day. I was a carefree eighteen-year-old.

I was waiting for the bus when it happened. You know the drill—the sky shifted to that eerie green hue, and then came the screams. It wasn't painful... or if it was; I don't remember.

I stood there, frozen, until I looked down and saw my hands. They... weren't hands anymore. They were more like paws.

Anyway, I bolted home. No one was there, so I locked myself in my basement room.

Hours passed—just me, and the confusion, and fear of whatever had just happened. I couldn't take the isolation any longer. I lurked into the living room, drawn by the sound of the TV. My parents were there, their eyes fixed on the news. I pulled my hood up, trying to hide my face—because, well, that felt safer.

As I stepped closer, my dad's voice broke the silence. "*Mijo?*" His voice hesitated. "Is that... you?"

After he just... hugged me. Not what I expected at all. I knew he was terrified—probably as much as I was—but his first instinct was to make sure I was okay.

I shook my head, trying to focus on the present.

"You okay there, Nyx?"

"Yeah, just..." I trailed off, unsure how to explain the jumble of emotions inside me.

Tyrann's tail twitched in what I'd come to recognize as a sympathetic gesture. "Ready for this?"

Another memory flashed— my mom arguing with my uncle Noah. « *Regardez-le, c'est un monstre !* » Noah shouted, pointing at me with disgust.

« *Un monstre ? Non, c'est mon fils,* » my mom retorted, her voice steady and fierce. "He's still the same boy I raised. If you can't accept him, you don't deserve to be in our lives." I'm paraphrasing here; My French isn't that good.

Noah scoffed, clearly unyielding in his judgment. "What kind of mother defends a freak?"

"Not a freak, Noah. And if you can't see that, *sors d'ici, bordel. Tabarnak !*" my mom snapped—basically telling him to fuck off.

Her eyes blazed with protective love, unwavering against his harsh words.

I swiped a paw across my face, pushing the memories away. With a deep breath, I braced myself for the task ahead.

"Green light. Breach in," Tyrann announced. The explosives planted at the door detonated, sending a shockwave through the corridor. We rushed inside, adrenaline surging.

We sprinted down the dimly lit halls, the air thick with tension and the smell of burnt ozone. I ducked as a bolt of energy whizzed past, narrowly missing my shoulder. "Ty, left!" I shouted, signalling him to take point.

Tyrann shifted his stance, his sharp eyes scanning for threats. He returned fire, the blaster in his hands glowing with lethal energy as he took down one of the Zenitharians. The body slumped to the floor, but we knew more were coming.

"Keep moving!" Steg said, falling back to cover our retreat. "I've got your six!"

With every step, my heart raced. I could feel the weight of the mission pressing down on me. The closer we got to my family, the more the fear grow in me. What if we were too late?

"Go, go, go!" Tyrann barked as we approached a junction. I pushed ahead, adrenaline drowning out the doubts.

As we rounded the corner, we came face-to-face with a squad of Zenitharian guards. Tyrann didn't hesitate—his shot rang out, clean and precise, dropping one instantly. I followed his lead, heart hammering as I fired, my pulse roaring in my ears. My target staggered, a perfect hit to the chest.

"On your left!" Steg warned.

I ducked just as a shot zipped past—close enough to feel the heat against my fur. I twisted, raising my weapon in a single motion. I fired. The guard dropped before he could react.

"Clear! Let's move!" Steg's voice cut through the adrenaline haze.

The fire didn't last long—or at least, it didn't feel like it. One by one, agents called out "Clear!" as the facility rooms were secured.

Tyrann and I pressed on, following a tangle of cables snaking along the floor. We kicked open the next door—and stopped cold.

"Fuck me, Tyrann," I whispered, dropping my weapon.

Three pods lined the far wall, their glass exteriors reflecting the cold, sterile glow of the overhead lights. Inside each one, a familiar figure lay still.

Zenitharian symbols flickered across the control panels, data scrolling too fast to process. We'd trained to decipher bits of their language, and I caught something that roughly translated to "suspended bio-element."

Tyrann stepped forward. "Requesting medical team," he said into his comm, voice steady.

Tyrann rested a steady hand on my shoulder. His voice was quiet but firm. "Nyx, reanimation after prolonged stasis can be... tricky. I need you to give the medical team some space. Whatever happens, we're here for you, okay?"

"Do what you have to." I said.

He began explaining the process, but my attention stayed locked on the pods. Through the frosted glass, I could see my parents' faces—still, unmoving. It felt wrong. Every instinct screamed at me to rush forward, to tear the pods open myself, but I clenched my fists and stayed put, forcing myself to listen.

"...and if anything goes wrong, we'll need to act fast," Tyrann continued. "You got all that?"

I nodded, not trusting myself to speak.

The medical team started the revival sequence. A dozen *what ifs* raced through my mind. What if something went wrong? What if they didn't wake up? What if they did, but they weren't themselves anymore?

An alarm blared that jolt me from my thoughts.

"Tyrann?" I asked, panic in my voice. "What the fuck is happening?"

His paws flew over the control panel. "Nothing for you to worry about."

But his face said the opposite.

I held my breath, watching the pods, willing them to open. "Come on, Andy, Mom, Dad. Wake up. Please."

The seconds stretched into an eternity.

A cloud of icy vapour filled the room as the pods hissed open. I rushed closer. I wanted nothing more than to wrap them in my arms and never let go. But I couldn't. Not yet.

Fear was taking control of me. I tried to hold my breath. We'd come so far, fought too hard for that moment. I closed my eyes, begging for a sign of life.

A soft whisper broke the painful silence. "SJ?" My mom's voice was fragile, hoarse.

"Mom!" I said. The word tumbled out, and for a moment, I wasn't Agent Baryonyx Nyx or Aniform—I was just... me. Her kid.

"Mom, Dad, Andy," I said, trying to keep my voice steady. "We're here to get you home."

Dad groaned. "Spence... where are we? What's going on?"

I pushed down the wave of emotions threatening to spill over. "I'll explain everything, I promise. Right now, we need to get you to safety. Trust me—it'll be over soon."

They nodded, dazed but willing. We helped them to their feet, their limbs unsteady after being motionless for so long. Relief flooded me, bittersweet and overwhelming.

After eight months of fear and uncertainty... and they were finally there. Alive.

"Dispatch, packages secured. Initiating extraction," Tyrann's voice cut through the moment. He turned to me. "Nyx, time to move."

"Nyx?" Andrew murmured, staring at me. "I like it. Fits you."

I ignored him.

"Yes, sir." I said and turned to my family. "Follow me. Stay close." Every fibre of me wanted to stop, to hold them and let the weight of everything fall away—but that had to wait.

Okay, I should probably back up a bit. You've been following me this whole time, and I just realized you don't even know my name. Good job, me—top-notch storytelling.

So, let me introduce myself. Hi. I'm Spencer James Baez—my friends call me SJ, though these days I'm officially known as Field Agent Baryonyx, or just Nyx for short. I'm a fox-aniform that join GUIP when I was twenty-eight.

I grew up in Mapleview, the kind of city where winters bite and summers cling to your skin. My mom, Melanie, is from Montreal. My dad, Enrique, moved here from Mexico City. And then there's my little brother, Andrew—or Andy. He's like me... just a bit less cool. (Don't tell him I said that.)

Anyway, that's all you were supposed to know ten chapters ago. You're welcome.

Now, let's get back to the story.

As we navigated the winding corridors, alarms blaring overhead, I couldn't help but wonder: Is this how it's always going to be? Running, hiding... never able to just be normal again?

Saving my family was all I'd wanted when I joined GUIP, but I realized saving them was just the beginning of my journey. I still had a lot to fight for.

The safe house was a nondescript two-story building on the outskirts of Mapleview, its bland exterior concealing state-of-the-art security systems.

"Home sweet... temp home!" I said, extending my arms to usher them inside. The living room was sparse but comfortable—less a sterile, cold chamber and more like an IKEA showroom.

Mom's eyes darted around, taking in every detail. "It's... cozy," she managed, her voice still weak.

I busied myself unpacking supplies. "So... the bathroom is down the hall, and inside the main bedroom, the kitchens fully stocked, including the best IPA for you, Dad. I think you only have basic cable, but the Wi-Fi is pretty solid. I already added my Netflix account to the TV. What else? Oh yeah! There's a panic button on each nightstand, as a precaution. Press it and we are here in minutes! Or if you want, I can crash on the couch. Uh... Are you hungry? I can go get takeout..." I couldn't stop my mouth from speaking, afraid of the emotions I bottled up for months that threatened to come out.

"Oh, just shut up," Andy interrupted, wrapping me in a hug. "I wanna say I missed you so much all this time, but I have no clue how long it was. I feel like I just took a nap." My tail wagged, in a way it hadn't in months.

Mom and Dad joined us for a group hug. "I'm so sorry," I said, my voice breaking as uncontrollable sobs wracked my body.

"No te preocupes, mijo. We're all good and happy to be together again," Dad replied, holding us tighter.

After a few minutes, we broke the hug, and Dad cleared his throat. "So, Spence... or should we call you Nyx now?"

I chuckled. "Uh, Spencer or SJ is fine. Nyx is just for... work stuff, and when I'm around other agents. It's a complicated mess I'd explain another day."

"So… Are you an agent now?" Mom asked, a mixture of pride and confusion in her voice. "It's all so…"

"Insane?" I said, a wry smile tugging at my muzzle. "Trust me, I'm still getting used to it myself."

Dad stepped closer. "We're so proud of you, son." He grinned. "You have to tell us everything."

"Thanks, Dad. I will." I hugged him again. "I'm so glad you're safe."

As I turned to adjust the thermostat—anything to keep my hands busy—I felt the façade I'd been clinging for months start to crumble. The pressure of the past eight months—the fear, the loneliness, the constant danger—all crashed down at once.

"I thought I'd lost you," I blurted out, my voice cracking. "Every day, I wondered if you were even alive. All while I was trying to do this job," I gestured at the logo on my vest, "I didn't know how to be me anymore."

Mom stepped forward, hesitating only a moment before wrapping her arms around me. "Oh, SJ," she murmured. "We're here now. And you're still you. You know we love you no matter what."

I closed my eyes, letting out a shaky breath. "But what if I'm not? What if all of this has changed me too much?"

Dad joined the hug, his presence solid and reassuring. "Change isn't always bad, son. Look at what you've accomplished. You are a hero."

I barked out a laugh, half-amused, half-bitter. "Some hero. I'm terrified most of the time. I don't know if I'm cut out for this."

They pulled back, concern on their faces. I sank onto the couch, exhausted. "I'm in way over my head," I admitted, voicing the fear that had been bothering me for months. "What if I screw up and someone who doesn't deserve it gets hurt?"

Dad sat down next to me, his hand resting on my shoulder. The familiar weight was comforting. "Spencer James Baez," he said, his voice low and steady, "the fact that you're worried about screwing up shows how much you care. That's strength, not weakness."

"Doesn't feel like strength," I muttered.

"Look at me, son," Dad insisted gently. I met his eyes, seeing a mix of pride and concern there. "You've carried this alone for too long. It's okay to let others help. Your mother and I might not understand everything about your new life, but we're here for you. Always."

A lump formed in my throat. I swallowed, fighting back the stinging in my eyes. "I… I really missed you guys so much," I whispered. "And maybe Andy too." I teased.

"Hey!" Andy protested, tossing a cushion at me.

Mom perched on my other side, her hand finding mine. "We missed you too, sweetheart. But look at what you've become—the person you are. You're brave, kind, and fighting for something bigger than yourself. We couldn't be prouder."

I finally broke. Tears streamed down my face, matting the fur on my cheeks. I let out a choked sob. All the pent-up fear and loneliness of the past months pouring out. My parents held me, murmuring soft words of comfort.

A knock at the door startled us. I wiped my eyes, trying to compose myself. "Come in," I called, my voice still rough.

Tyrann's imposing figure filled the doorway. "How is everything in here?" he asked, his deep voice softer than usual.

I nodded, managing a weak smile. "All good. Just catching up."

Tyrann turned to my parents, extending a paw. "Mr. and Mrs. Baez, I'm Agent Tyrannosaurus. Please call me Tyrann. It's an honour to meet you."

As they shook hands, I was amazed at how quickly my parents were adapting to all this. Tyrann continued, "I wanted personally assure you that GUIP would provide whatever support you need." He gave a card to my mom. "You can call me at anytime for whatever you need. We also have excellent mental health services available. Let me reassure you that your safety is our top priority."

Mom's eyes widened. "That's... very kind. Thank you."

Tyrann's gaze shifted to me. "And Agent Baryonyx here? He's one of our bravest. You should be incredibly proud."

I felt my ears flatten in embarrassment. "Ty, come on..."

"I mean it," he insisted. "What you've accomplished today, few could have managed. Don't sell yourself short, Nyx."

As Tyrann continued talking with my parents, I leaned back. The road ahead was still uncertain, but for the first time in months, I didn't feel alone. Maybe, I could face whatever came next.

I gazed out the safe house window, watching the sun dip below Mapleview's skyline. The city's night lights came to life. I let out a long breath, my tail swishing behind me.

"Penny for your thoughts, mijo?" Dad's voice pulled me back to the room.

I turned, a half-smile tugging at my muzzle. "Just thinking... it's weird, you know? I've dreamed of this moment for months, but now that it's here..."

Mom leaned forward, her eyes searching mine. "Are you okay, son?"

"I'm fine, Mom. Really." I fiddled with a loose thread on my hoodie. "It's just... I thought this was going to be the end... but there's still so much to do."

Tyrann's deep rumble cut the tension. "And that's why we have a team. Don't worry about it. Take a few weeks off with them. And that's an order."

I nodded. "Yes, sir." I gestured to my parents. "I think I can handle that." Then, lowering my voice, I added, "Thanks, Ty."

Tyrann gave a small nod before turning to my parents. "And don't worry. I'll make sure your son stays out of danger."

I grinned, unable to resist. "Out of danger? Me? Have you met me?"

Tyrann smirked. "Oh yeah, I forgot. The day I met you, we went flying out the office window—ten stories down."

"You what?" my mom shouted; her voice was sharp with alarm.

"Hey! It wasn't my fault a grenade—" I stopped mid-sentence, catching the horrified look on her face. "You know what? Story for another day."

The room filled with laughter, dispelling the last of the heavy atmosphere. As I looked around at my family and Tyrann, I felt a mix of emotions wash over me—relief, pride, and a renewed sense of purpose.

Chapter 11:
THE LAST DROP

I took a deep breath as I pushed through the gleaming glass doors of GUIP headquarters, the smell of antiseptic and coffee hitting my nostrils. The familiar buzz of Thursday activity washed over me, a stark contrast to the quiet comfort of my family's temporary home that I'd left behind hours earlier.

My fur bristled as I adjusted to the temperature-controlled air, a welcome change from the cooler autumn breeze outside.

"Well, well, look who finally came to work!" Deputy Pteranodon said as he welcomed me. I couldn't help but grin. Even when I doubted his remark was friendly, my tail swished behind me.

"Miss me that much, Pteran?" I shot back. He wasn't really thrilled with my comeback.

I made my way to my desk. I caught snippets of conversation—talk of weekend plans, mission reports, and the latest office gossip. It was like I'd never left.

"Hey, Nyx!," Kylo called out, her head poking up from behind her computer displays. "How was the family time?"

I leaned against her cubicle wall. "It was nice. Dad took some cooking lessons that resulted in a couple of visits from the firefighters. Mom is bored with doing nothing and she's itching to go to work, and my brother is back at university. Things are starting to feel pretty normal."

"Happy for you, dude. They seem to be doing well after everything that went down. And how about you? Ready to jump back into the ring?"

I hesitated, my ears twitching slightly. *Was I ready?* The past few weeks had been a cocoon of familial love, which I treasured, but as I looked around at the bustling office, I felt a thrill of excitement.

"You know what? I think I am," I said, surprising myself with the conviction in my voice. "Got anything that needs some good ass kicking?"

Kylo grinned. "Oh, you have no idea, Nyx. But I won't spoil anything; I'm sure your work dad," she said, referring to Tyrann, "would love to spill the details with you."

"Oh yeah, my daddy!" I said, then froze. "Fuck. That sounded creepy."

I spotted across the room Tyrann entering the briefing, his tail swishing with purpose as he flipped through a case folder. I walked over, unable to contain my enthusiasm.

"Hey boss!" I said, leaning against the desk with a casual grin. "Your favourite son is back! What's the scoop?"

"Son?" he asked. "You couldn't handle me as your dad. And for the record, I think Steg might be on the lead for that title," he teased. "Welcome back, Nyx! Couldn't stay away, could you?"

"What can I say? Danger is fun. So, catch me up."

"We got a lead on a potential weapons dealer," he said.

"Let me guess—involves our good friends at Chasing Tails?" I said, unable to contain my excitement.

"Bingo! Seems our furphobic buds are upping their game." He glanced around before continuing. "Kylo's been working her magic. She intercepted some encrypted chatter that suggests a meet-up between a dealer and some higher-up of CT."

The door swung open with a deliberate force, and Deputy Pteran strode in, his posture exuding the authority he loved to wield. Chief Allo and Kylo followed behind him, but Pteran barely acknowledged them, his gaze locking onto Tyrann like he'd caught him in the act of something illicit.

"Really, Field Agent Tyrannosaurus? Starting the briefing without us. A bit amateur or just favouritism, don't you think?" Deputy Pteran said. Tyrann didn't react, even when Pteran used a lower rank to refer to him, which I was sure he did on purpose. I let out a quiet growl.

"Just putting Nyx up to speed," Tyrann said.

"Oh yeah," Pteran let out a dry chuckle. "The agent who's so important he gets paid time off." He looked at me. "Just teasing, Agent Baryonyx. We are happy you are finally back at work."

The briefing began shortly after that. Allo gave some remarks about open investigations. Pteran kept saying assholy things—mostly boring stuff—until Tyrann took control, setting what the goals of the day's mission were. Tyrann gave Kylo the opportunity to explain her findings.

"From the data I cracked," Kylo said, "there's an exchange happening at—"

Pteran cut her off, raising his hand and avoiding looking at Kylo. "Tyrann, I am sure you are aware, but I am more than happy to remind you that you should verify the consultant's findings before we take them as fact."

Kylo rolled her eyes. "Yeah, Tyrann," she said, her voice fully sarcastic. "Because my completely accurate record isn't enough."

I leaned forward. "Well, if Kylo's the one who decrypted the messages," I said, "I'm fully confident it's correct."

Pteran's jaw tightened. "The rookie is telling us what to do," he said. "I thought we don't make decisions based on speculation, but who am I, right?"

"I don't speculate," Kylo shot back. "I can verify everything. You can have the tech team review them if you don't trust me. I'm sure the bad guys will wait until then."

I smirked. "I mean, if they take too long, we'll probably just miss the meeting. But I guess that's not our problem."

Chief Allo remained silent. Not sure if she was agreeing with Pteran or if she just wasn't in the mood for his usual smugness.

Tyrann cleared his throat. "If we're done arguing over whether we trust the expert hacker," he said, "we need to move. The confirmed meeting location is at The Last Drop. I'll be going on an observation mission, trying to see if we can find out who the dealer is."

Pteran was on his phone. After sending his email, text, or whatever, he leaned back against the desk, his gaze landing on me. "You know what? What if you go with him, Nyx? Might be time you actually do something after your little family vacation."

The way he said it set something off in me. My ears flicked, but I kept my expression neutral. "Oh Pteran, you know I'd be happy to be back in the action," I said smoothly.

Tyrann glanced at me. "You good with that?"

"Count me in," I said. "Just need to make a quick stop at my place to grab some fresh clothes. I've been crashing at my parents' place for the last few weeks, so I haven't been there much. I just hope Steg hasn't leased my room to someone else."

Tyrann nodded, and we dove into the details of the mission. Despite Pteran's apparent goal to kill my mood, I couldn't stop the wag of my tail for the excitement of being back in action.

I took the walk home from the office. Tyrann and I had agreed to meet at the club at 10:30, So I had plenty of time to rest before what promised to be a long, lacklustre night.

"Hello, stranger," Steg said with a grin as I walked into the apartment.

"Hey, bro!" I said back, my tail wagging. "Missed you at the office today. How was patrol?" All field agents were required to log 15 hours of patrol each month, so I assumed that's where Steg had been.

"Boring as fuck," he replied, leaning against the kitchen counter, tail wagging. "You know how it is. So... how's the fam?"

We chatted for a while, catching up on life. He told me about a few dates he'd been on, and I couldn't resist teasing him about finally settling down with a girl-friend. He denied it, insisting he wanted to keep his options open. After we made dinner together, I excused myself to change for the night.

I threw on one of my favourite hoodies—a thick, navy cotton one that cost more than any hoodie has a right to. "Screw it," I said. It was my first time hitting a nightclub in years; the least I could do was look decent, even if I was there for work.

I often get asked, *Why are you always wearing hoodies?* I usually brush it off with a dumb answer like, "It's what the cool VidTok kids wear," though the idea of doing one of those embarrassing dance videos makes my ears fold back.

But the real reason? It all started after the Emergence. A hoodie became my way of disappearing, an easy way to hide. Big and loose, it made it easy to blend into the background. I figured if people couldn't see the fox in me, they wouldn't ask questions. They wouldn't stare.

Now, though? They're just a part of me.

It sounds ridiculous, right? Like I'm attaching part of my personality to a piece of clothing. But it's true. Hoodies became my armour, my shield from the world. They've turned into a colourful security blanket I never leave behind.

Honestly, I'm still surprised the *GUIP Uniform, Equipment, and Appearance Standards* never came after me for it. I suspect Tyrann had something to do with that. He never said a word about it, but he had this way of watching out for me, like the big brother I never had. Always there—not in your face about it, but you know he takes care of you.

He's the one person who sees me for more than what I was. So yeah, I have this feeling he vouched for me, making sure I could keep my hoodies, even if it bends the rules a bit. But I'd never ask him—he'd just smirk and brush it off, anyway.

The Last Drop. It wasn't just any club; it was the spot to be on a Thursday night or whatever the cool day to go clubbing is. Housed in an old post office, it had been transformed into a maze of pulsating lights and thumping bass that could shake your insides.

As I approached, the bass thumped hard enough to rattle the walls, and the lights flickered like they were trying to hypnotize everyone into forgetting their troubles. aniforms and norforms alike moved to the beat, lost in their own worlds.

I just stood there, tail flicking nervously, feeling like an outsider looking in. It was a strange sensation—being in the middle of it all and still somehow alone.

I leaned against the bar, my eyes drifting over the crowd. Without really thinking, the words slipped out. "You know, I can't remember the last time I felt that relaxed," I said quietly, just loud enough for Tyrann to hear, my voice tinged with a wistfulness I wasn't even trying to hide.

Tyrann, scanning the room for our target, glanced at me with one of those knowing smirks. His ears twitched slightly. "When was the last time you went out?" he asked. "You know... just for fun?"

I straightened a bit, ears angling back. "It's been a while," I admitted softly. "I used to love going out, hitting clubs, dancing and whatever. But... I haven't really done much of that—or dated anyone—since the Emergence." My tail flicked again, betraying the unease I was trying to bury.

Tyrann studied me for a second. "Well," he said lightly, "consider yourself off duty tonight. Go on—take the night off. You said you loved dancing, right? Go have fun."

I blinked, caught off guard. "I dunno..." I scratched the back of my neck. "Doesn't seem very smart to take more time off after all the shit Pteran gave me."

"Well, I'm not going to tell him," he said with a conspiratorial grin. "Besides, your shift technically ended at five—this is just overtime."

Before I could come up with another excuse, Tyrann waved the bartender over, ordered a drink, and slid it into my paw. "Drink this. You've got five minutes before I push you onto that dance floor myself," he said. Despite the teasing, there was no mistaking the genuine warmth in his voice.

I opened my mouth to protest, but Tyrann was already unclipping my gear belt and badge. "You're off duty," he said, softer this time. "Just enjoy your-self." He placed my gear into his messenger bag with his usual calm efficiency.

I felt... *lighter*? It was weird, like the absence of that weight freed me from more than just my gear.

I made my way to the dance floor, feeling the unfamiliar tug of both nervous-ness and excitement. My tail twitched again, but this time, it wasn't from nerves.

I have to confess: I've never been good at picking up flirting signals. Usually, I'm completely oblivious when someone's showing interest in me.

But ever since I'd stepped into the club, I couldn't shake the feeling someone was watching me. Glancing around the crowded room, my gaze kept drifting towards a certain figure—a hyena who seemed to stare back more than casually.

As I tried to find my rhythm, the hyena appeared right beside me on the dance floor, felt like something out of a cheesy rom-com. Amber eyes, a mischievous grin, and perfectly groomed brown-and-grey fur.

"Hi there, handsome," the hyena said with a wink, slipping effortlessly into my stiff rhythm as if we'd been there all night.

He is cute, I thought, but that wasn't enough to silence the voice screaming in my head: *What am I doing? Why am I here?* My body refused to loosen up, every movement betrayed by my nerves.

I shot a glance back at Tyrann, still leaning against the bar with that infuriatingly knowing smirk. He raised an eyebrow and mouthed, "Relax. Just enjoy it."

"Right. Relax." I took a deep breath, closed my eyes for a second, and just... let go. Let the music take over. Somehow, the awkwardness melted away. My feet found the beat, my tail swayed to the rhythm, and for the first time in what felt like forever, I wasn't overthinking. I was just... there.

The hyena flashed me a grin, moving in sync with me. At that moment, I wasn't thinking about any of the other shit that weighed me down. It was just me, a beautiful stranger, the music, and the moment.

But, of course, Tyrann wasn't just there to have a drink and watch me loosen up; he was still on the job. As I caught a glimpse of him at the bar, I noticed his posture had shifted. His eyes narrowed, focused on something in the crowd.

That's when he spotted him—the dealer. The guy was inching toward the side exit, trying to blend in. Tyrann set his glass down and slipped into the crowd, disappearing into the shadows like he was born to do it.

Before he left, he paused and glanced back at me. I was still dancing, lost in the music, a smile tugging at my lips. He gave a small, proud smirk. I guess it's not every day you get to see the rookie unwind.

And then he was gone, following the dealer into the night.

The Next Day, the GUIP office buzzed with activity, as usual. Agents hustled around, the smell of coffee filling the air. You get the drill. I spotted Tyrann sitting in his office, talking with Kylo, who had her paws kicked up on Tyrann's desk, sipping her coffee.

As I walked in, my tail swayed with the confidence of someone on top of the world. I couldn't help it—I was still riding the high from last night. "Morning!" I said, grinning.

Kylo raised an eyebrow, lowering her cup. "Well, someone's in a good mood," she said, exchanging a curious glance with Tyrann. "What's up with you, Foxy boy? Is Pumpkin spice season already?"

Before I could even respond, Tyrann cut in, smirking. "He met someone last night."

Kylo's eyes lit up. "Oh? A hot date, eh?"

My ears flicked back, heat rising to my face as I tried to play it cool. "No, it wasn't a date—"

Tyrann chuckled. "Well, whatever it was, something happened. You're still wearing the same clothes from last night."

My fur bristled, and if I could blush, I would've. "I... well... I didn't... went home."

Kylo leaned forward, grinning. "So, you're telling me you're a fox who got done?"

My ears shot straight up, and I felt like I was on fire. "No! I mean... I did him—I mean! I didn't—ugh. I just didn't get home, okay?!"

The room erupted into laughter. Tyrann was shaking his head, chuckling. I crossed my arms, my tail flicking in frustration, but a small smile lurked on my face.

"Well," Tyrann said, still grinning, "whatever happened, it looks like it was exactly what you needed."

I glanced away, trying to hide my grin, but the truth was obvious. That night off had done me more good than I wanted to admit.

Still flustered, I cleared my throat, trying to steer the conversation away from me. "Alright, alright, enough about my night," I said. "What about you guys? Did anything happen after I, uh, clocked out?"

Tyrann's smirk faded, replaced by something more serious. "yeah. While you were busy on the dance floor, our friend made his move."

I straightened up, my earlier embarrassment evaporating. "The dealer? You saw him last night?"

Kylo, gave a mock gasp. "Oh, look at Nyx. Back to business already. But yeah, big guy here followed the suspect."

Tyrann nodded, his expression darkening. "I believe we have a probable location for the armoury. Intel is analyzing the data."

I felt my ears perk up. "Alright then, what's the plan?"

As Tyrann filled me in on the details I'd missed, I couldn't shake the thought of last night. It had seemed all too perfect, and I realized I would have to get used to not worrying about the things that weren't even happening.

The rest of the week went by uneventfully. I guess returning to work midweek has that effect. I even started listening to a book Steg recommended during my morning jogs. Oh yeah, I forgot to mention—I had begun to work out.

Anyway, it was a new week, and I was back in the office when my phone buzzed. I fumbled it out, expecting a text from Mom or maybe Steg sending me some weird meme. Instead, an unknown number flashed on the screen.

It's 2025—who even calls anymore? But I guess I was in a good mood.

"Hello?" I answered, my voice betraying my annoyance.

"Hey, It's Carlos from the other night," a voice replied cheerfully.

I frowned, trying to place a face with that name. "Uhh Carlos?"

"Yeah, the hyena? We met at The Last Drop last Thursday. I had a great time—hope it's cool I called."

"Oh yeah, Carlos! It's fine. I'm glad you called," I said, attempting to sound convincing. Trying to recall at what point I gave out my number. But again, I wasn't exactly counting drinks that night. Besides, the dancing, the night conversation, and the sex afterward hadn't been half bad, so I let it slide and kept the conversation going.

"Just wanted to see if you'd be interested in grabbing a coffee sometime. I know a great little spot by ByWard Market—great desserts too," Carlos added, his tone light and teased.

I hesitated, the familiar pang of doubt creeping in. *Did I really want to dive back into this?* It had been a while since I dated. *Was is it even a date?* A part of me wanted to cling to the distance, but the other part—the one that had enjoyed his company and felt a spark of excitement—was tempted.

"Uh, I'll have to think about it," I said, my heart racing at the thought of being vulnerable again.

"Come on, it'll be fun! I promise to spare you from seeing me dance again. Unless you liked it," he laughed, and I couldn't help but smile at the memory of how easily he had pulled me into the moment that night.

I took a deep breath, weighing my options. Sure, it felt risky to step into the unknown again, especially after everything that had happened. But maybe... maybe I was ready for a change.

"Alright, you know what? Let's do it," I said, surprising myself with my own enthusiasm. "When were you thinking?"

"How about tomorrow night?" Carlos said, his voice brightening. "We can catch up over coffee and see where the night takes us."

"Sounds good to me," I said, feeling a flutter of anticipation mixed with anxiety. It was a small step, but it felt significant. Maybe that time, I could allow myself to form a connection without overthinking it.

"Awesome! I'll text you the details," Carlos said, his excitement infectious.

"Looking forward to it." As we wrapped up the call, I couldn't help but reflect on the decision I'd just made. I was setting aside my hesitation to embrace the possibility of personal connections again. It was a step into the unknown, but it felt like the right one.

I returned to the office, the hum of activity around me a welcome distraction. Kylo was hunched over her desk, her focus laser sharp as she scrolled through reports. "Need help?" I asked, not wanting to disturb her concentration.

"Nah, thanks, but I'm good," she nodded, a faint grin appearing before fading. "Tyrann asked me to gather all the information we have about Chasing Tails, so it's not that complicated."

"Sounds like a headache," I said, leaning against the cubicle wall. "Are you sure you don't need my help?"

"Yeah, I got this," she said, though her tone was uncertain. I could see the tension in her posture as she glanced back at the screen, her brow furrowing.

I studied her for a moment. "You don't look so sure," I pressed gently. "Is something else going on?"

Kylo hesitated, biting her lip. "It's just... some of the dates in the reports don't match up," she said. "I thought it was just a glitch, or maybe it is?, but the more I look, the weirder it gets."

"Like how weird?" I asked, stepping closer, my curiosity piqued.

"Like... mission outcomes that don't align with what we've recorded. Or at least not how I remember them to be. I just can't figure out why."

The atmosphere shifted. "That doesn't sound good,"

"Tell me about it," she said, running a paw through her hair. "I'm trying not to jump to conclusions, but maybe there's something fishy going on."

I nodded,. "What do you think we should do?"

Kylo paused, glancing around the office to ensure no one was listening. "I think I need to dig deeper. But if I find something that confirms my suspicions... I might need your help to figure out what to do next."

"Count me in," I said. "Whatever's going on, we'll face it together."

"Thanks, Nyx," she said. "Now go away, so I can finish this."

I nodded with a grin and returned to my desk. I gave a quick glance towards Kylo, her fingers dance over the keyboard. I couldn't stop thinking *Who could we trust to help us?* No one seemed to have a hidden agenda.

Ugh... I'm being stupid here. It's called hidden for a reason.

Chapter 12

YOU PICKED THE WRONG BITCH

Wasn't it great? What more can I had asked for? It was 2:47 AM at GUIP headquarters, fuelled by curiosity, determination, and shitty coffee.

I saw my ears twitching in the reflection of my screen, picking up the hum of the air conditioning and the faint snores of the night security guard down the hall.

White-collar work wasn't something I ever thought I would do, but I have to say—it's kinda... *fucking boring.*

Or I thought it was. I even think I yelled, "What the fuck?", not caring if I disturbed the guard's deep sleep. But I was just trying to figure out what the hell was going on.

The dates didn't match the records, and the outcome... was completely different from what the guys had told me.

My heart raced as I pulled up file after file, uncovering a pattern of tampering that made my fur stand on end. Someone was altering mission data and erasing information.

"This can't be a coincidence," I growled. "Who the hell is doing this? And why?"

An email popped up just as I began to piece together the implications of what I had discovered. My first thought? "Who's up at 3 AM sending emails to me?"

The only ones who ever did it were Tyrann, Robert—my lovely parole officer—and that propagandist 'People and Culture' newsletter.

I clicked on the email, bracing myself for whatever nonsense awaited me. Check this steaming load of crap:

```
From: dangerous_dingo@anonemail.onion
To: ankylosaurus@ca.guip.int
Subject: Last warning


Message body:
```

```
Ankylosaurus.

You have no idea what you're messing with.

This is your first and last warning. Leave it

alone or it will be the last thing you ever

do.
```

"Dude. Are you fucking serious?" I said. The rational and annoying part of me screamed to slam the laptop shut and pretend I'd never seen any of that. But that's not who I am, you know? Kicking ass is how I clawed my way out of a life of crime and earned a conditional release from federal prison, so I wasn't about to back down.

"Nice try, asshole," I said, saving everything I'd found to an encrypted drive. "You picked the wrong bitch to threaten."

Once the backup was finished, I grabbed my coat, phone, and keys. I unplugged the charger for the annoying ankle monitor before heading outside.

Don't get me wrong; I'd take that stupid box of shame any day over spending time inside. Being conditionally released is a pain. For once, I'm not allowed to carry any weapons, which I've never really been into, but they seem handy for that kind of work. Still, I wasn't too bothered by it; I knew how to defend myself. But it probably wasn't a good idea to leave alone after that email. I needed to talk to someone, and the office wasn't the right place to do so.

GUIP HQ was in an old but renovated complex, sharing buildings with other federal government offices. On the basement level, there was an awful food court, a tunnel connecting to the Mapleview LRT system, and a public phone. A device that the phone company seemed to have forgotten about, but I appreciated it.

"Hey, Robert," I said to the man on the other side of the phone. "Sorry for the hour. I'm just reporting that I'm leaving work. But I won't be going home. I'll be at Nyx's place. Over Metcalfe Street."

"Reason for the change of routine?" the annoyed and half-asleep man asked.

"I had to catch up on work and forgot to check the time. I called Nyx; he's letting me crash on his couch since he's close to the office. Easier commute, you know?" Of course, I lied. But I knew Nyx would be okay with it.

Another annoying part of parole is that I need to notify my officer of any changes in my routine unless I want the MVPD biting my tail.

"Request granted," Robert said. "Please allow 15 to 20 minutes for the temporary exception to be added to your monitor, and... next time, call earlier, okay?"

"Yeah, yeah. I will," I replied, feeling a mix of annoyance and urgency as I hung up.

I set a timer on my phone. And went outside, lighting a cigarette and keeping a watchful eye out for anyone who might lurk around.

Twenty minutes and a cigarette later, I made my way to Nyx and Steg's place. Upon arriving at the building, I pressed the button for their apartment in the electronic directory. "Come on... hurry up," I muttered, my ears perked as I strained to listen for any approaching footsteps.

Nyx answered, "ugh... yes?" His voice came through the intercom, clearly annoyed. Nyx isn't exactly known to be a morning guy—especially not at 3:30 a.m. But this was important, and I needed someone I trusted.

"Nyx, it's Kylo. I need to talk to you. It's urgent," I said, keeping my tone serious.

"Oh, shit. Come on in." He buzzed me in right away.

I know this book is supposed to be Nyx's story, but if I can talk shit about him for a second, there's something about him I have always found annoying: he cares. *Fucking outrageous, right?* And it's not like he says it outright, but I've seen him stand up for Steg, other agents and whatever he went through to find his family says a lot about him. At that point, I've only known this fox for five or six months. It felt strange to say I trusted him. Well... to think about it. I'd be damned if I ever told him that.

Anyway, I got to his floor, and Nyx was waiting for me at the door. "Hey, Kylo," he greeted me. He looked worried. "Stupid question, but... everything okay?"

"Fuck no... or I don't know, maybe?" I replied, furrowing my brow.

"Want something to drink? Coffee? Tea?" he offered, probably just trying to chill me out.

"Beer. Or something stronger."

"All we've got is a peach-flavoured amber IPA. Is that okay?"

I smirked. "Fine, you guys and your hipster beers."

He handed me the beer, and we settled onto the couch. "Alright, what's going on?" he asked again.

"Do you remember I mentioned how some reports seemed off? At first, I thought it was a glitch or some sloppy data entry. But when I dug in, I found a ton of strange stuff," I said, trying to be as quiet as possible, still worrying someone might be listening.

Before I could go on, Steg walked out of his room, half-asleep in nothing but boxer briefs, his golden-ish fur all over the place. "Bruh, what's going on?" he said, rubbing his eyes.

I couldn't resist when I spotted him. "Someone's happy to see me, huh?" I said with a grin. "Or was it nice dreams?" His boxers weren't exactly hiding his...morning state.

"What are you talking about?" The clueless dog said, still trying to wake up.

But Nyx had to ruin the fun. "For fuck's sake, Steg, cover yourself!" he said, tossing him a cushion.

Steg finally caught on and held the cushion in front of his lap, trying to change the subject while he adjusted. "What are you two doing up so early?"

I refocused on Nyx. "I needed to talk to someone I trust."

Nyx met my gaze. "Alright, let's hear it."

I pulled my laptop from my bag and opened the files I'd found. "You know how Tyrann asked me to compile everything we have on Chasing Tails? Simple enough, right? Or so I thought. But as I went through, I noticed the records didn't match up. So, I went to check the logs to verify any changes."

"And?" Steg asked, tilting his head.

"They were deleted," I said, looking between them. "And it is not something anyone can do. You'd need top clearance for that—or at least to pull it off without a trace."

"Do you think is someone inside GUIP or someone hacked us?" Steg asked.

"I thought about hacking. But it'd have to be someone who knows the system. Both the changes logs and access logs were wiped. The existence of the access logs isn't common knowledge. Besides GUIP's encryption and firewall? Almost impossible to bypass, and believe me, I tried. How do you think I got this job?"

Steg's ears perked up. "Wait—is that how you got—?" He pointed to my ankle monitor.

"Nah. I was already locked up when I did it. One day, I was bored, and I used the prison library's computer to try to hack into it. I may or may not have been trying to see if I could change my sentence... anyhow, I was caught. I would probably get more years inside, but Tyrann saw potential or some fuckery like that, so here I am."

With his adorable curiosity, Nyx asked, "How did you manage that? Aren't those computers restricted?"

I swear I tried not to sound that snarky. "Bitch, please. Hacking those cheap-ass machines was easy," I said, smirking. "Outdated operating systems, shitty admin passwords, and guards who didn't care. Practically a walk in the park."

Steg chuckled, shaking his head. "Guess you were made for this, huh?"

"What can I say? I know my ways."

Steg settled onto the couch, his curiosity now fully awake. "So, back to the thing. Do you think is someone inside GUIP?"

"Definitely," I said, my voice steady. "And whoever it is has the clearance to do it. This doesn't feel like a simple error."

"It has to be the same person who let Seb in, right?" Nyx asked.

"Unless we have more than one traitor."

Nyx and Steg exchanged a worried glance. "What are we going to do about it? We might need to bring Tyrann in." Nyx said.

I hesitated. I liked Tyrann and wanted to believe he couldn't do that, but being skeptical is why I have survived this long. I opened with the boys. "I'm not sure we should involve him just yet."

Steg frowned, crossing his arms. "Come on, guys. It's Tyrann we're talking about. If anyone can help us with this, it's him."

I jumped in, asking whatever those cowards couldn't, "What if Tyrann's involved somehow?"

"I trust Ty. I don't think he could," Nyx said. "But before we drop this on him, we must dig up more. If someone's messing with our records, this could be bigger than we realize."

"Let's not jump to conclusions," Steg said, frustrated. "I just want to be careful."

"Alright," I said, trying to keep the peace. "Let's give it a day. I'll keep digging and see what else I find. Then we'll decide if we need to bring Tyrann in." We stayed in silence for a while, unsure of what to do. Nyx broke the silence with a yawn.

"Well... we should try to get some rest if we're supposed to be at work in four hours," Nyx said, frustrated with the upcoming sleep-deprived day.

Then he asked me, "You're crashing here, right?" I nodded.

Nyx stood up. "Let me grab you a blanket. There are extra cushions under the coffee table," said and headed to his room.

"Or, if you'd prefer, you can use this one," Steg offered, patting the cushion on his lap with a grin.

"Ew no, keep it. You might need it," I replied with a smirk, rolling my eyes.

Steg chuckled, getting off the couch, while Nyx tossed a blanket over me. "Let's try to get some sleep, guys,"

"Thanks... for, you know, letting me crash here," I said.

"Don't mention it; try to rest, okay?" Nyx said, trying to analyze my thoughts. "Is something else bothering you?"

Ugh... see? He cares, it's so annoying. I probably should have told him about the email, but that is something I wanted to figure out on my own.

"Nah, I'm just tired and frustrated. Go to sleep."

"Fine," he added, heading to his room. "If you need anything, let me know, okay?"

"Night guys,"

The apartment went quiet, just me and the soft hum of the old-ass fridge filling the space as I settled in.

I wrapped myself in the blanket, glancing at Nyx's and Steg's closed doors. Even though I was exhausted and totally in the dark about everything, I felt safe with them around.

Steg's morning energetic mood was borderline unsettling, especially compared to Nyx's, who looked about as alive as a corpse.

Naturally, we were late. We grabbed breakfast from the Tim Hortons down the block and made a run for the office.

I never quite felt like I fit in there, you know? And for the first time in a decade, it wasn't just because of my scrappy, *spoiled wolf* appearance.

Usually, I wouldn't care what people think—I'd just flip them off and mutter something rude about their mothers. But I was trying out the *Good Citizen* thing, so I kept it to myself.

It's not like everyone was openly hostile (some assholes were), but the looks said it all. Their eyes flicked to my ankle monitor before meeting mine, or they'd dismiss me outright because I'm "just a consultant."

I didn't know why, but I felt a real need to prove I wasn't just some screw up. Like it was my only chance to do something good, beyond all my *alleged* crypto scams or using dirty emails on some startup CEOs to fill my *not existent secret* bank account in some tax haven.

Now that I think about it, it was all Tyrann's fault. Childish to say, but he's the first person to see anything in me, to believe I had *potential*.

And how was I repaying him? By suspecting he was behind the inconsistencies in our system.

There's something I didn't tell Nyx about what I found: all the modified reports shared a key detail in the metadata. (For anyone with a social life, unlike me, metadata is a mix of useful and junk information attached to every file—creation date, file type, and, in this case, the identifiable details of the host computer that last edited it.) Every modified record traced back to Tyrann's machine.

Does that mean he did it? Not necessarily—anyone with his password or enough technical knowledge could have used his computer, or even spoofed the data. But more to the point, would he have even wanted to?

Here's a piece of trivia people forget about Tyrann—maybe because he never brings it up: *he's one of the founders of GUIP*. Roughly six years before all this mess, he was an ex-cop joining forces with other officers, soldiers, politicians, and intelligence agents to push for the *Interspecies Unity Treaty*, or whatever it's called. He could've taken any rank he wanted, but he chose fieldwork for some reason.

So, I couldn't make sense of why he'd want to tear GUIP down from the inside after fighting so hard to bring it into existence. Which leaves option two: someone's setting him up, counting on someone sharp enough to notice and implicate him.

Before I ended up being that someone who blames innocents, I needed to dig a little deeper.

After about a week, I started ignoring Nyx's daily "Did you find something else?" questions that he'd asked. Oh, I don't know, a dozen times per day. And, for the record, I had found more. But I wasn't ready to show it.

Each November, GUIP throws this gala thing. Supposedly, it's a chance to get together, mingle, and, you know, probably make some questionable choices with coworkers. Not really my scene. But that year, it seemed like the perfect opportunity to keep an eye out and maybe *chat* with some tipsy potential traitors. So, I had to fill the guys in.

"Are you sure?" Tyrann asked after I presented my findings to him, Steg, and Nyx. His tail was still, ears alert, focused, but doing a damn good job of not reacting. I'm sure he had trained hard for it.

"Yeah. I've been digging for weeks," I replied, showing him my screen. "I've been making copies of the latest reports using... well, let's call them unapproved methods, as soon as they're submitted, so I don't leave a trace. Then I compare them a few days later. And they don't match." I pulled up two versions of a report filed by Nyx.

"Look here," I pointed. "They're subtle, but the changes make it look like we—or Nyx, in this case—are incompetent." I tapped the screen.

Tyrann leaned in, eyes narrowing. "What's the objective of these changes?"

"I'm not sure yet, but it only happens when Chasing Tails is mentioned," I said. "Whoever's doing this seems to be trying to erase them from the official records."

The room went silent, everyone watching as Tyrann read through the documents. It was intense—until he finally broke the silence with a single, firm word. "Fuck."

That's right. *Profanity.* I don't think I'd ever heard Tyrann swear before that day.

"Does anyone else know about this?" he asked, voice low.

"Just us four," Steg replied.

"Well..." I began, lowering my ears, my tail curling under my legs. "There's one thing I didn't tell you. Back when this all started, I got an email—a really half-assed threat telling me to back off. I've been trying to find who sent it, but no luck so far."

Tyrann's eyes softened as he nodded, processing everything. "Alright. We need more answers before making any moves," he said, his voice steady.

"Good, because the gala's coming up," I replied with a smirk. "Perfect time to play detective. Ask a few innocent-sounding questions, maybe 'accidentally' find out what people know."

Tyrann looked hesitant, but Nyx jumped in. "Everyone's guard will be down. And with a free bar, someone's bound to let something slip."

"Alright," Tyrann agreed, though he still sounded reluctant. "But please. Be subtle."

The night of the gala was exactly what I'd expected: A room packed with agents dressed up and looking like they'd rather be anywhere else. My fur felt odd against the formal grey blazer and light blue blouse, paired with matching pants and stylishly uncomfortable heels—definitely not my usual look.

Mingling wasn't high on my list. But dressing the part made people more willing to talk.

We split up to cover more ground, keeping our eyes peeled and ears open. My first few conversations were with lower-level agents, a mix of rookies and those just coasting until retirement. I kept it casual, dropping hints about Chasing Tails to see if anyone reacted. It was a long shot, but I wasn't expecting much from the grunts.

Then I spotted her—Chief Allo, chatting with a few of the higher-ups, every bit the picture of confidence and authority. She had that kind of presence that filled a room without saying a word. But there was something off about her. I'd never been able to put my finger on it.

Memories started creeping in—maybe it was the drinks or the pants that barely let me breathe. She reminded me of my dad in a way. He had that same ability to make people feel small without lifting a finger. Growing up under that weight, I'd thought it was normal to feel like I was walking on eggshells every second. But there was a difference between him and Allo. She commanded respect because, well... she had actual power. My dad? He relied on fear. That's why I had to leave. But it hadn't been easy.

I was barely out of high school when I realized I couldn't take it anymore. I didn't want to end up like my mother, pushed into a life of conformity and addiction. That day, he was yelling about some stupid thing—can't remember what it was, but I'm sure it was dumb. By then, my mother was long gone, moved south of the border and left me with him. My memory's fucked, but I remember giving him the middle finger, a few things flying across the room, grabbing a bag, and taking off. Never looked back.

My survival options were pretty bleak. So, I dove into the one thing I was good at: cybercrime. It started small jobs to keep me afloat. But as I got better, the jobs got bigger, and soon enough, I was hacking into places I had no business touching. By the time I got caught, I was in way over my head, on the hook for half a dozen counts of federal-level hacking. Allegedly, of course. None of it was ever proven in court.

So, how did I get caught? Was it a daring hack on the Bank of Canada? Wiretapping? Maybe a data leak? Nah. I love making up different stories every time someone asks. The RCMP had been close, but they could never quite nail me—until they realized I hadn't paid taxes for twenty years. Yeah, I went to federal prison for tax evasion.

Then, yada yada yada, you know the rest. Me in federal (white-collar) prison, bored as hell, hacking GUIP on the prison library computers. Tyrann stepped in, saw something in me, and offered me a choice: stay locked up or use my skills for something that mattered.

That's how I ended up there. And maybe that's why I couldn't ignore my instincts now, especially when they screamed that Allo might be hiding something.

Taking a deep breath, I approached Allo, keeping my expression casual. "Chief, evening," I said, offering a polite nod.

Allo returned a slight smile, though her eyes stayed sharp. "Kylo," she replied smoothly. "Enjoying the gala?"

Across the room, I caught Tyrann's eye. He gave a slight nod, as if to say, be careful.

"Doing my best," I shrugged, keeping it light. "It's been a busy few weeks, though. Chasing Tails is keeping us on our toes. Seems like they're showing up in places we'd least expect."

Her smile faltered—just barely—and she recovered quickly. But I'd caught it. "Yes," she replied, choosing her words carefully. "We've got everything under control. That group is nothing more than a nuisance."

"So, you're not concerned?" I pressed, keeping my tone innocent.

She paused, fixing me with a sharp look. "What I'm saying," she replied, her voice carrying a quiet warning, "is that everything is exactly as it should be."

I started to push further, but the moment I opened my muzzle, she cut me off. Her gaze narrowed, though she kept a polite nod. "I'm stopping you right there. Rest assured, we're doing everything possible to remove the issue," she added, her tone leaving no room for argument.

To me Chief Allo was hiding something. Whether she was the traitor or just playing along with someone, I couldn't say. But I'd be damned if I backed down now.

I gave her a nonchalant smile. "Of course, Chief. Just playing agent here."

She gave me a dismissive nod, then turned back. I walked away.

As I moved through the crowd, I spotted Nyx and Steg, their eyes following her.

I made my way over to them. They were huddled near the bar, trying to look inconspicuous. Tyrann joined us moments later, his expression grim.

"Well, that was... interesting," I said, grabbing a glass of champagne from a passing waiter. "Anyone else getting major something's-not-right vibes from our esteemed chief?"

Nyx nodded, his ears twitching nervously. "Yeah, I tried chatting her up earlier. She shut me down."

"Same here," Steg said. "I mentioned double agents, and she looked like she wanted to bite my head off."

We started to head toward the exit. We'd mingle enough. It was time to go somewhere we actually wanted to be.

Tyrann's tail was up, a rare sign of agitation from our usually stoic leader. "This is... concerning. But we need to—."

He was cut off when the lights flickered, and every screen in the room—the giant displays on the walls—went dark. When they came back to life, they all showed the same image: my face, alongside details of my criminal record and my current status as a GUIP consultant.

*Alecia Green, 1566 Rue de la Fontaine, Rivière Fleurie. Tax Evasion and Unauthorized Computer **Access. Criminal. Untrustworthy**.*

"What the flying fuck?" I yelled, my fur bristling.

Before any of us could react, the doors burst open. A masked figure in tactical gear stormed in, weapon raised. Agents dove for cover, shouted orders, or scrambled desperately for their weapons.

The intruder moved with precision, zeroing in directly on us. In one swift motion, they grabbed Nyx, who was closest to the door, pressing a gun firmly against his head. "Nobody moves!" the masked figure shouted. "Or the fox gets it!"

"For fuck's sake! I have a name, you know?" Nyx shouted back, irritation cutting through his fear. The gun against his head was one thing, but apparently calling him "fox" crossed a line.

I met Nyx's eyes. And I sweat I can hear his annoying voice saying: *Don't do anything stupid, Kylo.*

But following rules has never been my strong suit.

I had a choice: do nothing or act. I knew whatever I did could send me straight back to prison, but right then, none of that mattered. My friend was in danger.

With a growl, I lunged for a nearby agent's sidearm. In one fluid motion, I aimed and fired, hitting the intruder's arm. They cried out in pain, and dropped their gun.

Nyx didn't waste a second—he drove his elbow into the captor's crutch, twisting free as they doubled over.

I stepped forward, gun straight at the intruder's head. "Who the fuck are you? And why are you after us?"

Before I could get any answers, a voice rang out, cold and commanding. "Alecia Green. Drop the weapon."

Confused, I hesitated. Had I heard that right?

"Consultant Kylo," Deputy Pteran repeated, his weapon pointed at me. That asshole prick—I never liked him. "You are under arrest for breaking the terms of your conditional release. Drop the weapon. NOW!"

"Are you shitting me?" I muttered, my eyes locking onto the masked figure slipping away. "Ignore me and go after that bastard!"

But Pteran's expression didn't budge; he continued, aiming at me. "Do it now."

With a sigh, I dropped the gun and look at Nyx's gaze. His expression was a mix gratitude and horror.

"I'm sorry," I murmured, feeling the cuffs snapped around my wrists.

Nyx stepped forward. "Leave her alone, you idiot!—she just saved my life!" He planted himself in front of me, blocking the agents surrounding us.

"Chief, you can't let them do this," he yelled.

Allo's face was cold. "Stand down, Agent Baryonyx. It's protocol."

Nyx didn't budge. "She doesn't deserve this. Hell with protocol!"

Tyrann stepped in, placing a firm hand on Nyx's shoulder, murmured something I couldn't quite hear. Allo gestured, and another agent pulled Nyx away, restraining him.

As they led me out in cuffs, I glanced back at the team one last time. I'd done what I had to do. I'd protected my friends, and whatever came next... I could handle it.

The doors closed behind me, locking me back into a life I thought I'd left behind. But even as they did, I knew this wasn't over. There were still too many unanswered questions, and I'd find my way back to them—no matter what it took.

Chapter 13:

UNTANGLING MESSES

I have never been a fancy kinda guy. For me, the perfect date is simple—good coffee, decent company, and a spot by the window where you can watch the world pass by.

On one of our dates, the aroma of freshly ground coffee swirled around us as I leaned back in my chair, feeling the warmth of the afternoon sun streaming through the cafe's front window. Outside, a white blanket covered the ground, a stark contrast suggesting winter's imminent arrival. Carlos sat across from me, his eyes twinkling with interest as he sipped his latte.

"So, stud," Carlos said, setting down his mug. "It must be pretty exciting stuff, right? I can only imagine the things you've seen."

I wouldn't have called myself athletic—I was more of an average build back then. Sure, I went to the gym every other day, but mostly for stamina. Carlos liked to call me *stud*, and I suspect he did it just to boost my confidence. It worked, though.

I chuckled, my tail swishing behind me. "Kinda... It has its moments. But most of the time? Not that crazy." I tried to play it cool. It wasn't often someone showed genuine interest in me or what I do.

Carlos was wearing a red winter jacket, which stood out against his hyena features and spotted fur. He leaned in, his voice dropping to a conspiratorial whisper. "Come on, SJ. You can't leave me hanging like that. What's the craziest thing you've encountered?"

I hesitated, drumming my fingers on the table. Protocol made it clear to disclose as little as possible with civilians, especially any ongoing cases. Normally, I'd deflect with a joke, but something about Carlos made me want to open.

Maybe it was his charming grin, the way his ears twitched when he listened, or that he was really listening—without judgment. Also, he paid for the coffee, so I felt like I owed him.

"Well," I began, leaning in, "there was this one time we had to step in during a heated debate about whether long-tailed Aniforms should pay extra for a movie ticket." I sipped my caramel macchiato. "Things got weird fast. We told the theatre owner that his 'policy' went against the Equal Interspecies Rights Act. But he didn't care. He wasn't against Aniforms, or at least he claimed, but his issue was that long-tailed ones shed too much, apparently, and he had to pay more for cleaning." I laughed as my own tail flicked, sending a tuft of fur into the air.

"To be fair, he had a bit of a point." Gesturing to my own fur. "Anyway, he called us biased since, we all have long fluffy tails. He got mad and tried to take a swing at Steg, and... yeah, he ended up in cuffs."

Carlos laughed. It felt good to share, to be seen as more than just the awkward fox-guy I was.

"Yeah, that was a weird day. But lately..." I continued, my tone shifted, my ears lowered, and my tail curled up against my legs, "things have been tense. We've been dealing with this group called Chasing Tails. They're... well, they're everything wrong with this world."

As soon as the words left my mouth, I caught a sudden shift in Carlos's expression. *Interest? Concern?* I couldn't quite place it. A small, nagging voice inside my head kept yelling that I should probably stop, but I pushed it aside. By that point, we had been on a few dates, and I had felt something I hadn't before. And although I'm no expert, I could swear Carlos felt the same.

"Chasing Tails?" he asked, his tone casual but his gaze intense. "Doesn't sound that bad."

I nodded. "Yeah, the name's... kinda lame. But they are not fans of Aniforms, to put it mildly." I fiddled with my cup.

Maybe I was saying too much. But the words kept coming, fuelled by my need to connect, to be understood. And Carlos, with his sympathetic nods and warm smiles, seemed like the perfect confidant.

"I'm so confused and angry about them. I feel like they're about to do something big."

"Do you know what?" he asked.

"Not yet. I'm not even sure if it's happening. Maybe they're just a fringe cult." I sighed, my ears flattening. I could've sworn Carlos' eye twitched slightly. "We were following some leads. It all seemed solid, but long story short, something went wrong, and it ended with the arrest of a friend—a colleague of mine."

Carlos leaned in, his expression serious. "Fuck. That's terrible, stud. What happened? Were they involved with that Tails group?"

I ran a paw through my fur. "No. She's the reason we even know about them. Kylo did nothing wrong—she's just... it's complicated. But she's one of us, you know? And now she's locked up, angry, probably scared out of her mind, and I can't do a damn thing about it."

Carlos nodded, his expression sombre, his gaze locked on mine. "It sounds like you really care about her."

"I do," I said. "We're a team—a family, really. And I can't help but feel so helpless right now."

As I spoke, my throat tightened. I hadn't realized how much it weighed on me until I said it out loud. Carlos reached over and gave my hand a reassuring squeeze, grounding me. I felt a rush of gratitude just for him being here with me.

I looked into his eyes. "Thanks, Yeen."

"For what?"

"You know... for listening," I said, managing a weak smile.

"Anytime, stud," he replied softly, grinning as he gently tapped the tip of my nose with his finger.

I hesitated for a beat before trying my luck. "Hey... um, want to come to my place? I could use the company." I even threw in a bit of a puppy-dog look, just to sell it.

Carlos smirked, clearly seeing through my attempt at manipulation. "Of course. Anything I can do to thank you for your service, stud."

He gave my hand another squeeze, warm and steady. We grabbed our things and headed to my apartment, where we spent the night watching cheesy movies and staying up way later than we should have.

The next day, the air of the office was filled with a sober atmosphere. The usually busy space was filled with an uneasy silence, broken only by hushed whispers and the occasional frustrated sigh. The kind of quiet that made you uncomfortable for no reason other than the sheer wrongness of it.

Steg and I stepped onto the 10th floor, my tail dragging behind me, ears twitching at every muted conversation we passed.

When we reached Tyrann's office, I hesitated at the door. He sat behind his desk, his expression neutral, but the tension in his shoulders told me everything. Steg stood behind me, silent but watchful.

"Morning, Ty," I said, poking my head in. "Any news?"

He didn't answer right away, just exhaled sharply before shaking his head. "Nothing yet. They've got Kylo under tight security. No visitors, no communication."

I slumped into a chair, running a hand over my face. "Isn't that a bit extreme? It's just... crazy."

Tyrann's expression remained unreadable. "It is" Tyrann said.

"And without Kylo, we're—"

"Screwed?" Steg finished for me, leaning back with a sigh.

Tyrann's jaw tightened. "The day seems to be a quiet one. Maybe try to focus on patrol or catch up on your filings today. I'm doing what I can to get Kylo back. I'll let you know if anything changes."

We nodded. "Thanks, Ty," I said, but the weight of everything made the room feel smaller, suffocating.

The three of us wore the same look—tension buried beneath anger. A quiet, collective fear no one wanted to say out loud.

This felt different. And it wasn't just because our friend was back in jail—though that was a big part of it. It was the uncertainty, the creeping sense that we were standing on the edge of something we couldn't quite see or understand.

I was about to sink deeper into my worries, drinking a cup of the bitterest coffee known to *humanity* and *animacy*, when Steg's tail started wagging, his ears perking up. "Wait a sec, foxy friend!" He said. "We're missing something obvious here!"

"What? The fact that this coffee sucks?" I said, though my curiosity was piqued.

Steg bounced on his feet, his enthusiasm contagious as always. "No, dummy! Well, yes... but I'm talking about Kylo's apartment! She wasn't trusting GUIP, right? So... if she found something big, she might've left it there. We gotta check it out!"

"Steg, that's... actually not a bad idea."

"Not bad? It's brilliant!" Steg said, tail wagging. "C'mon, partner! Adventure awaits!"

I couldn't help but chuckled as I followed him. "You know this isn't actually an adventure, right? We're just going to trespass and illegally snoop our friend's stuff."

Steg shrugged, flashing a grin over his shoulder. "Potato, po–tah–to," he said, unfazed. "Besides, it's for a good cause! And it's not like she'd mind if she knew we were helping her."

I raised an eyebrow. "Yeah, tell yourself that when we're explaining this to her—or to the police or, worse, the ethics committee."

Steg just laughed. "Come on, where's your sense of adventure?"

I shook my head, trying not to smile. "Fine. Let's hope we don't end up needing bail for ourselves."

The drive to Rivière Fleurie was quick, but my mind screamed at me the whole way. *What if we found nothing? What if we found something that made things worse?* I pushed the doubts aside as we pulled up to Kylo's building.

Steg bounded out of the car. I hesitated, my hand on the door handle. "Hey, Cooper?" I called softly. "What if... we don't like what we find?"

He paused, his usual exuberance fading. "Then we deal with it, Spence. That's what friends do, right?"

I nodded, feeling a surge of gratitude for my overeager partner. We made our way up to Kylo's floor, the hallway eerily quiet. We opened the door using the spare key she had given us for emergencies.

The apartment was a mess. Not trashed *per se*, but far from its usual order. Papers scattered around, drawers slightly open. My fur rose as we moved through the space.

Kylo knew how to access anything digital, even when she wasn't supposed to, so it was no surprise she preferred using physical media for things she wanted to keep private.

"Looks like someone beat us here," I said, carefully picking up a fallen picture frame.

Steg nodded, his nose twitching as he sniffed the air. "Recently, too. Within the last day, I'd guess."

We began our search, methodically going through Kylo's belongings. Although with each passing minute, it felt incredibly pointless. Whatever Kylo had been onto, it seemed like someone else had gotten to it first.

She always said the best way to hide something was to leave it in plain sight. I wasn't sure how true that was, but as I rifled through a stack of seemingly mundane reports, Steg's sudden, excited yelp made me jump.

"Nyx! Over here!"

He was crouched by Kylo's desk, his tail wagging furiously. "Look at this!"

I hurried over, heart racing. Steg had pulled out a box labelled secrets. Inside was a collection of sentimental mementos—a letter from an ex, tickets from her first concert, little things that didn't seem important to anyone but her.

Steg ran his finger along the underside of the box, and with a soft click, a hidden compartment popped open.

"Damn it, Alecia," I muttered, a grin spreading across my muzzle. "Our Kylo's got some tricks up her sleeve."

Inside the false bottom was a sleek flash drive, nestled beside a business card from a local brewery Steg and I liked. It felt out of place, almost like she'd left it there for us—a hint, a message, something.

My fingers trembled slightly as I pulled the drive out.

"Think you can crack Kylo's encryption?" Steg asked, practically vibrating with excitement.

"I hope so." I plugged the drive in, along with a second flash drive loaded with hacking tools Kylo had given me "just in case" into a brand-new computer we'd picked up on the way there.

Now, you might ask—*why all the extra trouble?* Simple. This was the safest way to do it: a completely new device, never connected to the internet, with zero personal information. If anyone was tracking us, they'd be left in the dark about what we were up to.

"Give me a few minutes."

As I waited, my eyes drifted back to the business card. It featured a colourful print of a duck—the brewery's logo—along with stylized, random characters woven into the design. At first glance, it looked like a regular modern brand design. But the odd text, the weird phone number and address and other subtle inconsistencies hinted at a hidden pattern.

I tried to recall some of the cryptographic tricks Kylo had drilled into me. Then it hit me.

"Salted hash!" I blurted out, causing Steg to whip his head around like I'd finally lost it.

"Uh... what?"

"Look at these random characters." I pointed at the card.

Steg nodded slowly, clearly humouring me but intrigued.

"That's hashed data—basically a scrambled version of the original info. To decode it, we need the encryption algorithm and the salt—a key used to generate the hash. And look here." I tapped the address. "*PBK DF2* doesn't follow real postal code formatting. I think it's a reference to the algorithm, and these odd letters mixed into the address and email? I'm betting that's our salt."

I pulled up a tool Kylo had shown me once. "We'll run a brute-force program to test different passwords until we find a match." I set it up, watching the screen flood with scrolling lines of text.

Steg let out a low whistle. "For someone so private, Kylo sure loves leaving breadcrumbs."

I chuckled. "Yeah, well, maybe she knew we'd need to find this someday."

The computer beeped. I grabbed the decryption key and entered it into the drive.

As the files loaded, my ears perked up, my tail following suit. Then my excitement turned into immediate exasperation.

"Really? You've got to be kidding me! I don't believe it."

Steg tensed. "What? What is it?"

I started clicking furiously, perhaps a bit too hard. "Fuck off. No, I don't want to use OneDrive. Fuck, Microsoft,"

After that little battle, the files finally began populating the screen. My frustration melted into shock as I scrolled through them.

"Holy shit," I breathed. "Steg, look at this. Financial records, surveillance footage, encrypted communications. Kylo's been busy."

As we dug deeper, things started falling into place. The evidence pointed to a GUIP agent tangled up in a conspiracy that went way beyond simple corruption.

Steg whistled softly beside me, shooting me a sideways glance. "Why didn't she tell us about any of this?"

I shrugged, still trying to process everything. "Not sure, Coop. Maybe she wasn't ready yet."

I grabbed my phone and called Tyrann. It rang four times before he picked up. "Agent Tyrann," he said, all business, as usual.

"Hey, Ty. Sorry to bother you, but Steg and I were, uh... helping a friend who just moved out of their place, and... well, we kinda need a hand with something. Think you could swing by?"

I'm not exactly known for my lying skills, and moments like that made me wish I'd taken some improv classes. But who knew if anyone was listening? I had to be subtle—well, subtle for me.

Naturally, Tyrann, completely clueless about our little "mission," wasn't impressed. His tone turned sharp. "Nyx, you know I'm accessible, but I expect you to handle personal matters off duty."

For a split second, I almost lost it. *Holy fuck, Tyrann, it's about Kylo! Just get your ass over here!* I bit back the impulse, taking a deep breath instead. "Yes, sir, I know. But this is... important. About a friend in a, uh, temporary situation. Just... meet us at the same place where we had those homemade fajitas on Steg's birthday, alright?"

Tyrann paused on the other end, clearly processing my awkward phrasing. "Nyx... what are you—?" Then it clicked. "Oh. Do you need any additional help or supplies?"

"Nope, all good," I replied, struggling not to sound exasperated. "Just meet us there as soon as you can."

"Fine. I'm on my way," he said, sounding equal parts annoyed and intrigued.

I hung up and looked over at Steg, who was barely containing his laughter. Tail wagging. "Nice code work there, Agent Subtlety."

I rolled my eyes. "Shut up. I got the point across, didn't I?"

Steg smirked. "Sure, sure. Just don't expect anyone to nominate you for 'Undercover Agent of the Year.'"

I punched his arm lightly. "Hey!"

We shared a tense laugh.

"You know, Spence, we should order a pizza," Steg said.

"Steg, this isn't a party,"

"Yeah, I know, but everything's better with food,"

I nodded. "You're right. Order whatever you want—just no pineapple, okay?"

Steg grinned. "Fine, but one day, you're gonna realize pineapple on pizza is life changing."

"Ugh. Keep talking like that, and we're gonna have to rethink this friendship."

He smirked, leaning back with an exaggerated air of confidence. "Nah. I make your life way too interesting for you to ditch me."

I rolled my eyes, unable to hold back a smile. "Sure, keep telling yourself that, bud."

And with that, he placed the order and waited.

Forty-five minutes, a pizza, Tyrann's arrival, and a heated debate over whether pineapple belonged on pizza later, we finally got back to business.

"Do we have any clue who this guy could be?" Tyrann asked.

"Nope," I replied. "I think that's what Kylo was trying to figure out. There's a list of names and aliases—Victor, Adam, Maddison, Mansi, Sarah, Taylor and so on—but none of them ring a bell. All communications mention someone called 'Hargrove' as the one pulling the strings." I said. My ears lowering, "If only we could ask Kylo about it."

Tyrann's ears flattened slightly. "I tried to visit her, but she's under restricted access."

"Don't you basically run the place?" Steg asked, half-joking, half-annoyed. "Can't you just, I don't know, ignore that it and go see her?"

"No," Tyrann said, voice sharp. "I just vouched for GUIP's creation. Beyond that, I'm no different from any other agent."

"So... what are our options?" I asked, trying to mask my irritation with a grin. "Petition the prime minister? Try a dramatic prison break? Carrier pigeons?"

"Close," Tyrann said, with a slight smirk. "Allosaurus or Pteranodon could get us access—they have the clearance, or at least enough clout to allow a phone call."

I nodded, but a doubt crept in. "But Ty... what if Allo's involved too? Kylo had a hunch about her at the gala, remember? And right after talking to her, she was arrested. Allo didn't exactly step in to stop it."

Tyrann hesitated, then sighed. "I know how it looks, Nyx, but I've worked with Allo for years. I'm sure there's an explanation. You trust me, don't you?"

"You? Yes... Allo? I'm not so sure," I said, trying to keep my tail from twitching.

"We can't just sit on this," Tyrann said firmly. "We're running out of options. Let's head back to HQ, and I'll talk to her. I'll approach it carefully, see if anything feels off, okay?"

I wanted to say no, but he was right. *Annoyingly right.* If we were going to get anywhere, we needed someone with clearance and inside knowledge of GUIP.

"What about Pteran?" I suggested. "I mean, the guy's an—and I say this with all due respect—a self-centred douche. But he's always going on about our 'mission' and the 'importance of balance.' He might actually be interested in sniffing out a traitor."

Tyrann tried to hide a grin, but I caught it. Clearly, he thought similarly about Pteran. "Let's try Allo first," he said. "If anything seems wrong, then we'll go to Pteran."

"Fine," I muttered, crossing my arms. "Let me back up this drive first, then we'll head over."

After backing up the files, we packed up the evidence and got ready to leave. My mind was racing. How deep did this conspiracy go? And more importantly, how were we going to stop it?

I drummed my fingers on the conference table, stealing glances at Tyrann's stoic expression. Allo stormed into the room, and we straightened instinctively at her commanding presence. It was automatic—something we all did without thinking.

"So, boys," Allo said, her voice edged with annoyance. "What's so urgent that it couldn't wait until tomorrow, forcing this lovely gathering at 5 p.m.? And make it quick. I have theatre tickets."

Tyrann gestured for her to sit and began easing her into the findings. Allo's face remained expressionless, occasionally breaking to ask pointed questions. "Is that verifiable? Has anyone else seen this?"

When Tyrann finished, the room fell into silence as she flipped through the documents, then through the mission reports—both the modified and the originals. "Who obtained this information?" She didn't wait for an answer. "Was Consultant Ankylosaurus? Wasn't it?"

"It was," I said quickly. Silence again.

Allo's gaze shifted to Tyrann, her tone colder. "Agent Tyrannosaurus, why weren't these inconsistencies reported sooner?"

"Kylo was working on it—right before the attack at the gala," Tyrann said. "We believe the attack was an attempt to silence her. After she started uncovering the discrepancies, she received an anonymous email warning her to stop. Whoever was behind this must've seen you speaking to her and panicked."

Allo's face softened as the realization dawned. "So that's why she was asking all those questions at the gala... I suspected we'd been infiltrated, but I was beginning to think she might be involved. I feel like an idiot now."

"Is that why she's under restricted access?" I asked. Allo didn't look at me; her eyes were fixed on the papers in front of her.

"It was part of—" Chief Allo froze, her face shifting from irritation to shock. "No... it can't be..." she muttered, frantically flipping back through the documents. Her voice dropped to a whisper, almost as if she couldn't believe what she was seeing. "Victor Hargrove..."

She looked up at us; her face was grim. "That bastard made me think you were chasing ghosts."

I appreciated the unintentional pun, but it didn't feel like the right moment to point it out.

Tyrann's tail twitched irritably. "Victor? Who exactly are you talking about?"

"Deputy Pteranodon. His real name is Victor Hargrove."

"Do you know his name?" Steg asked, tilting his head.

"I know everyone's name, Cooper," Allo said in a firm voice.

Steg jumped in. "Wait, Chief Allo, did I just hear you say my name? Isn't that a serious violation of the rules?" He flashed a grin, clearly mocking the time he'd almost been fired for saying his.

Allo gave him a withering look. "Would you like to revisit your case, Agent?" Her tone made it clear she wasn't nearly as amused.

"Nope thanks, I'm good." Steg replied, backing down quickly.

"Hold on," I interjected, my ears perking. "Our esteemed second-in-command, the guy who's never shuts up about the 'importance of our mission,' has been working with Chasing Tails—the group that wants us wiped out?"

Allo nodded, swallowing hard. "Kylo's evidence looks rock solid. Financial trails, encrypted messages... all of it, plus."

Her voice grew darker. "He's been trying to convince me that the traitor was someone on your team, Tyrann. Feeding me a false narrative, painting Nyx, and Kylo as the ones we couldn't trust."

The room erupted into a cacophony of disbelief and anger. I caught snippets of "impossible" and "how did we not see this?" My own thoughts were a chaotic mess. *How long had this been happening, right under our noses?*

Tyrann raised a paw, silencing the room. "Chief. How should we proceed? Kylo's data is solid, but probably not enough for an arrest," he said, his voice low and menacing. "If Victor's compromised, who knows how far is his reach, or how many are involved,"

The seriousness of the situation was sinking in, and it was terrifying. One of our own, from an organization whose prime responsibility was to protect ani-forms—*and technically all sentient species*—had been infiltrated by those who wanted us gone.

"Whatever we do," I said, surprised by the determination in my voice, "we need to act fast. If Victor realizes we're onto him, who knows what he might do next?"

The room fell silent.

I hesitated, before speaking up, unable to keep the worry from my voice. "And what about Alicia? I mean... Kylo."

Allo shot me a glare, clearly not thrilled with me using Kylo's name so casually. "Agent Baryonyx," she said, her tone firm. After a pause, her expression softened slightly. "Let me see what I can do. I can't order her release without raising suspicions, but I'll do everything in my power to get her out of there."

I nodded, grateful but still tense. This wasn't over—not by a long shot. But at least now, we had a plan. And for Kylo's sake, I hoped it was enough.

Each of us sat there, processing how deep this conspiracy went. Tyrann's tail twitched with barely restrained anger, his eyes fixed on some point in the distance, no doubt picturing exactly what he'd do to Victor if he got the chance.

Allo gathered her things, her expression hardening as she pulled herself back into the role of our commanding officer. "We'll reconvene tomorrow morning. I'll put in a request to speak with Kylo. It's a risk, but if she has more information, we need it now."

"What should we do in the meantime?" Steg asked, glancing around as if the answer might magically appear in the room.

"Go home, rest, and keep a low profile. We don't know who else might be involved, so no unnecessary chatter, no slips. And definitely no sarcastic remarks." She said and shot me a look—which kinda felt personal.

We nodded.

"Good," she replied, giving each of us a final, hard look. "Thank you, agents."

With that, she turned and left the room, leaving the three of us in silence.

"Well, Tyrann," I said, glancing over at him. His eyes widened slightly as he looked up at me. "Gotta give it to you. When you offered me this job, you said I wouldn't be bored. Mission accomplished, sir."

Tyrann let out a tired laugh, leaning back in his chair. "Honestly, I was thinking more of the usual grind. Nothing like this. I need a beer—care to join?"

"You read my mind," I replied. "Steg, you in?"

Steg grinned, leaning in with a glint in his eye. "Yeah. Your treat, by the way. You know, as an apology for the noise from your date last night."

"Oh... yeah. Sorry again about that."

Tyrann raised an eyebrow, smirking. "Wait... are you still seeing that hyena guy? Spill—I need details."

I rolled my eyes, unable to hide a grin. "Maybe, maybe not. But you'll have to buy me a drink first."

Steg chuckled, nudging me as we gathered our things. "Your 'late-night wrestling routine' kinda gave it away."

My ears went hot. "Okay, okay—just don't make it weird."

The three of us walked out, the crisp night air hitting us as we left the building behind. Despite everything we'd uncovered, there was a strange comfort in these small, familiar moments.

"First rounds on me," Tyrann announced as we headed toward the bar.

"Deal," I replied. And as we stepped into the warm glow of the pub, I was unable to shake the feeling that maybe, just maybe, we'd find a way to get through this together.

For now, we had each other—and a night to pretend that everything wasn't falling apart.

One of the things I never thought I would do is to be tucked in the back of a truck heading to Mapleview Federal Prison, disguised in a prison guard uniform. But there was the only way to keep a low profile.

Once inside, I shuffled into the private room usually reserved for high-profile cases, my tail twitching nervously. The harsh fluorescent lights flickered overhead, casting a stark, almost clinical glow on the place. I slid into the cold metal chair, my heart pounding as Kylo entered the room. Her usually pristine silver-grey fur was ruffled, her eyes shadowed but sharp.

"You look like hell," I said, hoping to break the ice.

Kylo's lips curled into a wry smile. "Thanks. I see you're charming as ever, Spence."

By that point, we had abandoned GUIP's stupid rule about using codenames, at least between Steg, Kylo, and me. Yes, we intentionally broke the rules, and we were okay with it. And as much as I hate to admit it, Seb was part of the reason. Using codenames instead of our actual names felt like a way to strip away our identity, and none of us were okay with that.

"So, what's up? Finally remembered I exist?" she said, her tone sharp with anger but undercut by something else—a hint of hurt, like she thought we'd forgotten her.

"Are you serious—" I started to snap back, frustrated after everything we'd done to get this visit approved. I took a breath, holding back, trying to see things from her perspective. "We've been trying to come since day one, Alicia, but you were under restricted access. They wouldn't let us near you," I said, softer now.

She let out a sigh, her shoulders slumping. "So, what changed? Did they finally realize me being here is stupid?"

I leaned in, lowering my voice. "Kinda. We went to your apartment."

Kylo's ears perked up, her posture straightening. "What the hell were you doing in my apart—wait, did you find the drive?"

"We did. And after analyzing it, we finally found the traitor." I watched her eyes widen as she processed the news.

She exhaled sharply, her claws tapping against the counter. "Let me guess— your good friend Chief Allo, right?"

"Actually, Chief Allo arranged this visit off the books. She's been helping us investigate."

Kylo's expression darkened at Allo's name. "Nyx, be careful. Allo might be deeper in this than you think."

"Trust me, she's not," I said, my tail bristling. "She's been supportive. She was just misled, thinking one of us was the traitor."

Kylo stared at me, her suspicion fading slightly. "Okay, so if it's not her, who is it?"

"Victor Hargrove," I whispered. "Our own Deputy Pteranodon."

"What?" she blurted out, so loudly the guard outside the door peeked in through the window to check if everything was okay.

"That self-centred bastard," she muttered, glancing down in disgust. "He's been acting all high and mighty this whole time... I can't believe he's the one pulling the strings."

"We haven't been able to prove it, but we believe Victor was the one who helped Seb. Which, I'm happy to report, he's still in the detention centre. Guess Seb stopped being useful to Pteran."

Kylo let out a small chuckle. "I didn't know if I was going to see any of you again. But... I hoped I would, so I kept myself busy."

"What do you mean?" I asked, narrowing my eyes.

Kylo lowered her voice to a near whisper, glancing around as though the walls themselves might have ears. "I've been hearing things. Rumours about a coordinated attack on aniforms over the holidays. Something big."

"Any details?"

She shook her head, frustration flickering in her eyes. "Nothing solid yet. But whatever it is, it's bad."

"We'll figure this out, Kylo," I promised, trying to keep my voice steady. "We're doing everything we can to clear your name and stop whatever's coming."

As our time ran out, I pressed my paw against hers, her fierce and determined eyes meeting mine.

"Be careful, Nyx," she murmured. "And whatever you do, don't let your guard down. Not for anyone."

I nodded, my throat tight, watching as she was led away. Time was running out, and the stakes had never been higher.

Back at HQ, I gathered the team around the conference table. "We've got a problem," I said, my voice grave. "Kylo's heard rumours of a planned mass attack on Aniforms during the holidays."

Steg leaned forward, his brow furrowed. "What kind of attack?"

I shook my head. "Not sure yet. Details are scarce, but if it's true, we need to act fast."

Steg chimed in, his voice tense. "We're already stretched thin trying to clear Kylo's name and expose Victor's conspiracy. How are we supposed to prevent an attack we know nothing about?"

I paced the room. He was right. We were up against the clock and fighting an uphill battle.

"What if we go public with what we know about Victor?" Steg said, his tail twitching nervously. "If we expose the conspiracy, maybe it'll force them to call off the attack."

We all fell silent, considering the idea. It was a bold move, one that could change everything. "It's a gamble," I said. "But if we can get the truth out there, it could turn the tide in our favour."

Tyrann spoke up, his voice steady but firm. "It could also backfire. If Victor's backed into a corner, he might escalate things. Retaliation could come faster than we expect. First, let's assess the threat before going public. We need something concrete."

"Then, Let's get to work. We've got an attack to stop, a conspiracy to expose, and a friend to let out of jail."

I glanced at Kylo's empty desk, a bittersweet reminder of what we were up against. "Hang in there, Ky," I whispered. "We're going to make this right. I promise."

Returning to my computer, I took a deep breath, ready to dive headfirst into the fray. The fight against Victor and his minions had only just begun, but one thing was certain: we wouldn't back down until they were stopped.

The next morning, I took a steadying breath, the weight of the mission settling on my shoulders. Tyrann usually led these briefings, but that day, I didn't hold back. "Listen up, everyone," I began, my voice stronger than I expected. "We've got a job to do, and failure is not an option. Aniforms across the city are counting on us, and we're going to deliver."

Tyrann raised an eyebrow but didn't interrupt. He leaned back, arms crossed, letting me take the lead.

"Steg, you've got a knack for finding the strangest shit on VidTok, so you're on intel gathering. Track Victor and his minion's movements and monitor any chatter about the attacks."

Steg grinned, already tapping at his keyboard. "On it, Boss Jr."

I smirked, shaking my head. "It's Mr. Boss Jr., thank you."

Steg gave a mock salute. "Yes, sir."

Turning to Tyrann, I met his serious gaze. "We need to identify potential targets—places where aniforms are likely to gather during the holidays. Events, meetups, anything popular. Can you pull that together?"

For a moment, he didn't respond, just held my gaze with that unreadable look of his.

"Please?" I muttered, lowering my ears and tail slightly.

A faint smirk broke through his stoic expression. "You got it, Boss."

Feeling the tension ease, I continued. "As for me, I'll shadow Victor. It's risky, but I know how to stay invisible. If he so much as breathes near a potential target, I'll be there. Got it?"

The room went silent. Allo and Steg exchanged a glance before turning to Tyrann.

Tyrann nodded, his approval clear. "You heard Mr. Boss Jr. Let's move."

"Alright, briefing dismissed," Allo said, her voice firm. "Let's get this done."

As the team began to disperse, Chief Allo approached me. "Agent, I want you to know I'm doing everything I can to secure Kylo's release. I'll keep Victor off your tail as best I can, but you need to act quickly. We're running out of time."

I met her gaze and nodded. "Thank you, Chief. We won't let you down."

As I stood there, watching the team spring into action, the enormity of what we were up against hit me. A conspiracy embedded deep within GUIP. A traitor who had once stood beside us. And now, a looming threat that could shatter everything.

But even as the weight of it pressed down on me, one thing became clear: we weren't backing down. Not now. Not ever.

Somewhere out there, aniforms were living their lives, blissfully unaware of the coming storm. They were counting on us—even if they didn't know it.

To protect the innocent. To fight for a world where aniforms and Norforms could coexist in peace.

I glanced around the room, catching glimpses of Steg's focus, Tyrann's determination, and Allo's quiet intensity. Together, we were stronger than any conspiracy, hate group, or threat that dared to cross our path.

The challenges ahead were daunting, but so was our resolve. And with that, we were ready to face whatever lay ahead—together.

Chapter 14

RANT OF THE DAY

Okay, so things are getting pretty intense, right? Kylo's in prison. Our second-highest boss turns out to be a rat (not literally—just a regular, shitty human), and we're up against a group that wants us gone and is about to attack. You know, casual stuff.

So, as the great writer I am not, what better moment to take a breather and share the not-so-glamorous side of being half-fox? Sure, being all *animalized* has its perks, but it also comes with a fair share of really irritating quirks. Let's talk about them.

Fur, Fur, and More Fur!!

I shed. Constantly. My clothes, my bed, the shower, and yes, sometimes even my food—fur is everywhere. A robot vacuum becomes your best friend, as long as you remember to empty it almost daily. And don't even get me started on lint rollers. They're useless.

Doors: Your Tail's Worst Enemy.

Ever tried getting through a door without smashing your tail at least once? Yeah, me neither. It's a daily struggle. Cars, light rail doors, elevators—anything that closes are a tail accident waiting to happen.

Doctor or Vet? Yes.

People love to debate where we should go when we're sick: Doctor? Veterinarian?

Here's the secret—it's kind of both. We see A.I.M.D. Physicians—*An Intellectus Animalis Medicinae Doctor*. Fancy talk for a doctor with a mix of human and zoological knowledge.

Aniforms like us are still pretty new in the world, and while our bodies mostly work like regular humans, we've got our own quirks, which vary depending on our species.

Fun fact (I guess.): canid Aniforms, like me, can eat chocolate.

No Sweating Here.

Speaking of quirks, here's a fun one: I don't sweat anymore. Sounds like a win, right? Saving a fortune in deodorant! And it mostly is... until July rolls around, and I'm roasting in a permanent winter coat.

So, how does our body regulate heat? Well, depends on the species, of course. For canids like dogs and foxes, our thing is panting. It's something about air passing over the moist surfaces in our mouth, cooling the blood vessels there—or something like that.

Wet Dog Smell.

I stink when I get wet. Rainy days, baths—basically, anytime I get even slightly soaked. It's annoying, and that's about all there is to say.

But why? Because life's a bitch sometimes. Apparently, it's something to do with the natural oils on our skin and the friendly neighbourhood bacteria they bring along for the ride. And before you judge us, remember human skin is also full of bacteria.

And sure, I might save on deodorant, but I end up spending a fortune on shampoo.

Technology Hates You.

Screens, keyboards, touchpads, face unlock, smartwatches—you name it. None of it's designed for people with claws, fur, or ears in all the wrong spots. Autocorrect is now my sworn enemy.

Oh, and speaking of technology, let me tell you about IDs, passports, and anything else that depends on a photo. After the Emergence, all of ours became completely useless. You'd think it'd be an easy fix, right? Just pop down to the nearest service office, take a new picture, and done!

Wrong. Government IT offices suddenly had to figure out how to add species information and claw-friendly biometrics to their systems.

And don't tell Tyrann, but I may have skipped renewing my driver's license before getting my GUIP-issued one. Since we're not allowed to reveal our real identities outside GUIP, they issue us everything we need: health cards, licenses, passports; you name it. At least that part's convenient.

How Does a Fox Wear Pants?

Under the tail? Through a special hole? Or just stick it through shorts? It's more complicated than you'd think. Bottomless might be a choice, but only if you're not worried about spending a night in jail.

Personally, I go for pants with a flap in the back for my tail. But every tail's different, which means finding a decent pair of jeans that actually fit is an ongoing battle.

Weird Food Cravings.

I don't know what it is—maybe instinct or something—but try ignoring a sudden craving for raw meat or wild berries. Or resisting the urge to chase things. And, by the way, every smell is now annoyingly strong.

Dude, really? That's Your Question.

"Can you talk to animals? Do you howl at the moon? Can you see colours? Do you eat dog food?" Ugh! It's outrageous! And don't get me started on the inappropriate questions. "So... how's your... you know," while pointing down. My go to answer? "Try Googling it, with safe search off."

Pet, Pat... Put Your Hands Away from Me.

I get it. We're soft, we look cute, and people are curious. But seriously, I'm not a petting zoo. And no, I don't want my ears scratched. Well... maybe I do, but that's beside the point. Personal space, people!

And yeah, there's the social prejudice, rejection, and constant criticism—those definitely suck. But, hey, it's not all bad.

There are some perks, like the sharper senses. I can hear things across a room, pick up on subtle scents, and my night vision? Way better than it used to be. Then there's the stamina—I can run longer and climb faster, and my reflexes are off the charts, which is a solid advantage for my line of work. Plus, I've been told I make an excellent cuddle companion, and I've got a tail now; that alone is pretty awesome when it's not getting rammed in a door.

Alright, that's my rant for the day. Hope you took this breather to grab a tea or something. Now, let's get back to business... things are about to get heavy.

Chapter 15

PUNCHING BAG

The holiday season was never something I got overly eager about. Don't get me wrong—I get the appeal. The time off from work and school was always welcome. And it's not like I didn't enjoy spending time with my family. I did. We did a lot together. It's just... those dates never seemed particularly special. At least, that's how it was—until that year.

Carlos and I wandered through the holiday market. The crisp, cold air carried the scent of cinnamon, pine, and something sweet I couldn't quite place.

Around us, laughter and cheerful voices filled the air, blending with the soft crunch of boots on the snow-dusted ground. For once, the season didn't feel so ordinary.

I tried to lose myself in the festive atmosphere, letting my brain rest and enjoy the time off. But no matter how hard I tried, those nagging thoughts lingered— muted whispers of danger threatening to ruin this tiny slice of normalcy I'd carved out.

"Hey, check out those hand-carved ornaments!" Carlos said, grinning, grabbing my arm and pulling me toward a stall dripping with glittering baubles. "Aren't these cute?"

I couldn't help but smile at Carlos' excitement. Something about him just made it easier to lower my guard. "Yeah, they are, dude."

We kept wandering from stall to stall, oohing and aahing over the random stuff people were selling. Carlos kept pulling genuine laughs out of me I hadn't felt in weeks.

But as we paused near a band playing carols—familiar tunes with a bit of a twist—I caught myself scanning the crowd again, searching for... I don't know what. Trouble? A threat? Ever since visiting Kylo in prison, I couldn't stop doing it. I was always on edge.

"Hey, stud?" Carlos waved a hand before my face, snapping me out of it. "You still with me? You've been kinda zoned out."

I blinked, scrambling for an excuse. "Yeah, sorry. Just, uh... thinking about what to get my brother for Christmas."

Carlos squinted at me, clearly not buying it, but he let it slide. "Umm. But how about this: we grab a bottle of frozen grape wine, maybe one of those pies from back there, head back to your place, and I'll make dinner. You can tell me what's really on your mind."

We had the apartment to ourselves for the next few days, since Steg was with his parents. The way Carlos said it, so warm and genuine, made me want to just unload all the crap swirling in my head. But I couldn't drag him into my messy world, let alone tell him anything classified.

I gave him my best reassuring grin. "I appreciate it, dude. But I'm good, I promise. Definitely not saying no to dinner, though."

Carlos slung an arm around my shoulders as we headed toward the wine stand. His voice flowed easily, jumping between random topics. I let myself relax in his warmth.

For one night, I wasn't Agent Baryonyx of GUIP. I was just Spencer. The real me, a regular guy wandering through a holiday market with someone who cares about me as much as I care about him.

And that was enough.

But, of course, the warm, fuzzy feeling didn't last. A buzz from my phone shattered the moment. I planned to dismiss it, but my frown deepened as Chief Allo's name was displayed on the screen. With an apologetic glance at Carlos, I stepped away to answer.

"Baryonyx. What's up, Chief?" I said through the phone.

"I apologize for interrupting your evening, but we have a situation, and we urgently need you at HQ." Allo's voice was sharp.

Carefree night, nice dinner, and cheesy movies? Poof. Gone. "Understood. I'm on my way." I said to her.

As I hung up, Carlos caught a glimpse of my face, and his ears drooped.

"Something came up, didn't it?" The resignation in his tone was unmistakable.

I nodded. "The chief needs me. I'm sorry, Carlos. I know we had plans, but... this seems urgent."

He waved off my apology with a small, understanding smile. "Hey, no worries. Go save the world, stud."

I looked at him, every fibre of my being resisting the pull of responsibility. "Thanks for understanding. I'll make it up to you."

Carlos pulled me into a tight hug, his fur tickling my cheek. "Just be careful out there, okay? And call me later, so I know you're safe."

"Will do." I squeezed him back, reluctant to let go.

I knew I shouldn't have told him. But when Carlos looked at me like he trusted me to make it back, it was hard not to imagine... falling for him. I needed him to be safe.

I pulled back slightly, holding his shoulders. "Listen, I need you to go home right now, and stay in tonight. There's a chance Chasing Tails is planning something. I'm not sure what yet, but I believe it's what we are about to try to stop. I swear I'll explain everything later." I hugged him again, tighter this time, trying to say everything I couldn't. "And Carlos, I lo—" I hesitated, chickening out. "I'll call you soon."

I navigated through the crowd, dodging giggling children and tipsy adults. I caught a final glimpse of Carlos. He raised a hand in farewell, tail wagging slowly, his smile tinged with worry.

The laughter and music of the holiday market faded behind me. As I headed toward HQ, bracing myself for the what awaited, I couldn't shake the image of Carlos' worried smile, a reminder of what I was fighting.

I strode through the HQ doors, rushing to the elevator and repeatedly jabbing the button for the 10th floor. Agents huddled in small groups, hushed conversations punctuated by keyboards clacking.

Then I saw her. Standing by a desk, arms crossed, that familiar grin tugging at her lips. "Holy fuck Ky. You're here!" I said.

"Hey, stranger," Kylo muttered, her smile breaking through.

"Good to see you back where you belong,"

Kylo's grin widened, though it didn't quite reach her eyes. "Feels good to be out of that cell. Even if I'm still on a leash." She jangled her ankle for emphasis, the blinking green light of the monitor casting an faith glow.

I clasped her shoulder, feeling the tension thrumming beneath her fur. "You know me—relentlessly annoying. I'll bug them until they take it off."

She chuckled. "Sure thing, foxy. By the way, where's your little brother?"

"Who... Steg?" I asked. Although, of course, was him. Unless she and Andy had somehow started to hang out. "He's driving back from South Algonquin," I said. "His parents have a cottage up there. I called him an hour ago—he should be here in an hour if the roads aren't too bad."

"Can't wait to see that furball." Her eyes darted around the room, her tail flicking with nervous energy. "Any idea what's going on? Allo sounded urgent."

"No clue, But it can't be good if she calls us on a holiday."

Kylo snorted. "When is it ever good news around here?"

I couldn't argue with that. And as if on cue, Allo strode into the room, her expression as grim as ever, with Tyrann following close behind. The chatter died instantly, all eyes turning to her.

"Thank you all for coming on such short notice," she said, her voice tight. "I'm afraid we've got a situation on our hands."

Tyrann stepped forward. "We have reason to believe Chasing Tails are planning to strike tonight. Intel suggests three potential zones."

Carlos's warm smile started to feel like a distant memory.

I forced myself to focus, locking on Tyrann. There would be time to panic later.

As Tyrann outlined the potential targets, Government buildings, public spaces, holiday events—nowhere seemed safe.

"They're trying to stir up fear," Allo said. "We can't let that happen."

The meeting got interrupted when the door banged open, and Steg stormed in, his tail accidentally knocking over a metal trash can. The loud crash made everyone jump.

"Sorry!" he muttered, hastily picking up the trash before grabbing a seat.

Kylo leaned forward, her ears flattened. "So, what's the plan, boss? We can't exactly be in three places at once."

"We'll have to split up. Cover as much ground as possible. Coordinate with local law enforcement, shore up defences where we can."

Splitting up meant dividing an already thin team. But what choice did we have? We still had no clue who we could trust. We had to be smart.

My phone buzzed. A text from Carlos lit up the screen.

Stud. I hope you are okay.

Six simple words, enough to make my chest feel a little lighter.

Yeah, @ office rn

I replied, typing as discreetly as possible during the briefing. My fingers moved quickly, not wanting to draw Tyrann's glare.

His reply came almost instantly.

That's good.

I'm happy you're not somewhere dangerous.

Will you head out tonight?

I glanced at the group, my ears twitching as Tyrann outlined the plan. My thumb hovered over the screen for a second before I replied.

me stay ty and allo going to the market.

146

I winced at the sloppy typo and the overall lack of grammar. It's hard to text when your boss is staring you down, especially when everything feels like it's on the verge of blowing up. I just hoped Carlos could decode my rushed message.

My attention went back to Tyrann's commanding voice. "To recap: Team Whistler—" That was the one Steg, and I were on. And yes, they reused the code-names from our trainee days—apparently, it's cheaper than printing new uniform patches.— "you're heading to ByWard and Lowertown. Team Blackcomb will cover the Glebe and Lansdowne Park."

Tyrann assigned tasks to the remaining agents before turning to Kylo. "You're our eyes and ears from here. The tactical team is prepped and will deploy once we confirm the target. Clear?"

A unified "Yes, sir!" rippled through the room.

"Good," Tyrann said. "This is going to be a long night. Keep your comms open. Watch each other's backs. And stay safe."

As the team began prepping for their assignments, Tyrann moved closer to me. "Be careful out there, Nyx."

I cracked a smile. "Of course I will. Who else is going to keep you in check?"

He let out a low chuckle.

Steg and I stepped out into the cold night air. I took the driver's seat of a cruiser, but before starting the engine, I glanced at Steg, who was already buckling in.

"Mind if I call my parents real quick?" I asked, my hand hovering over my phone.

"Not at all," Steg said, leaning back in his seat. "I should probably call mine too."

I smirked at that. My fingers tapped the call button. The phone rang twice before my dad picked up, his warm, familiar voice filling my ears.

"Spencer! *Mijo, ¿Listo para Navidad?*" His enthusiasm immediately made me smile.

"*Hola, pa,*" I replied, though my tone didn't match his cheer.

"By the way," he added, his voice teasing, "your mom says you've been dating someone for a bit. If he's not busy, we'd love to have him over. Andrew's bringing his girlfriend."

I chuckled softly, leaning my head against the headrest. "That's nice, Pa... but—"

"What's up, kiddo? Is everything okay? Did you break up? Because if you did, we can say mean things about him if you'd like." His tone was light, but I could hear the underlying concern.

"No, he and I are still together. Listen..." I took a deep breath. We'd already spent so much time apart this year, and I hated disappointing him. "I... I might have to miss Christmas this year, Dad,"

There was a pause, long enough to make me feel even guiltier. Gently, he asked, "Are you okay? Please tell me you're safe, SJ."

"I'm fine," I assured him quickly. "It's work, Pa. I can't talk about it. But I'll call you as soon as I can, okay? Rain check on that dinner with Carlos—my boyfriend. And please hug mom and Andy. *Los amo, y espero verlos pronto.*" My Spanish wasn't perfect, but I knew he appreciated the effort.

He never said it outright or insisted we speak it, but there was always a light in his eyes when Andy and I tried, especially when we'd use it to mess with each other.

"¡*Eres un pendejo*!" Andy would yell at me, and from the other room, Dad would chuckle every single time.

"Kids, stop fighting," he'd say in that playful tone. "You both are."

We never knew what "*pendejo*" meant, but it always made us laugh and stopped the fight.

"We'll miss you, son," Dad said, his voice steady. "Just... be safe, okay?"

"I will, Dad," I said, my throat tightening.

"We love you too, SJ."

As we hung up, I stared at the blank screen. I didn't want to admit it, but I hated the toll the job took on me and the people I cared about.

Steg finished his call before me. "You good?" He asked softly, his gaze flicking toward me.

I nodded, tucking my phone back into my pocket. "Not really. But let's go."

I pulled out of the lot, headed toward the unknown.

The ByWard Market was filled with life. Strings of colourful lights stretched overhead, casting a festive glow over the streets as banners flapped gently in the breeze.

I stopped the patrol car under a *No Parking sign*. The red and blue lights pulsed against the nearby storefront windows. *Just leave them on*, I thought. *Not like a city bylaw officer was going to ticket a GUIP vehicle,* or at least, I hoped not.

The team split into smaller groups, spreading out to cover as much ground as possible.

Steg and I stuck together, weaving through clusters of laughing shoppers and families sipping hot drinks. The air smelled of roasted chestnuts and burning firewood. My gaze swept over faces, scanning for anything that seemed out of place.

Steg broke the silence. "So... what exactly are we looking for?" His tail flicked restlessly, ears swiveling at every sudden noise.

"Something suspicious?" I said, eyes darting toward a dimly lit alley. "Honestly, I don't know. Maybe just us being here is enough to spook them into backing off. Or maybe..." I trailed off, spotting someone cutting through the crowd a little too quickly. *It was probably just a guy in a rush. Right?*

Steg sighed, shoulders slumping. "So... our strategy is being paranoid?"

"Pretty much," I said, offering him a half-smirk.

"T. Whistler, head over to York St.," Kylo's voice crackled through my earpiece. "We intercepted CT text hinting at activity near Mapleview's city sign. You're the closest. Proceed to canvas the area." Of course, the actual message was in the usual coded jargon—but I've translated it for you.

"Copy, T. Whistler," I replied, "heading to York St."

Our little team regrouped and made our way toward the open market sprawled across the intersection.

People drifted between stalls selling everything from hand-knit scarves to fresh pastries. At a glance, it looked normal. But something wasn't quite right.

Vendors stood too still behind their booths. Their smiles felt hollow. Conversations quieted as we passed—eyes lingered on us just a little too long. My tail twitched.

"Steg?" I murmured. "Is it me, or does it feel—"

"Like everyone's staring at us?" he finished, glancing around.

"Yeah... I don't like this."

His gaze snagged on something. "What is that?" He gestured to a cylindrical container, conspicuous enough to stand out but ordinary enough to pass as vendor equipment.

"Should we call it in?" Steg asked.

"Not yet," I said. "The last thing we need is to cause a panic if it's nothing. Let's check it out."

We pressed on, nerves tight, trying to keep our focus and remember our training. As we got closer, the bustling crowd began to thin. Moments ago, people had been browsing—now they slipped downside streets, leaving behind only a few bystanders, oblivious to the tension in the air.

We reached the container. The lid was loose, barely covering whatever was inside. I pulled a pair of gloves from my belt and cautiously lifted the lid.

It was empty. It looked brand-new—no markings, no signs of use.

"It's clear," I called out, a collective breath releasing from the team.

Relief that was short-lived. A note taped to the underside of the lid:

The Reversionists are the future. Embrace purity. The fall of the false protectors will arrive soon.

"Why the fuck would Chasing Tails be this obvious?" I said, staring at the message. And glancing around. My ears flicked forward, tail going stiff. It made little sense.

Then it hit me.

"Oh, fuck. Fuck. Fuck," I barked, my gaze darting across the market. Grabbing Steg's arm, I shoved him away from the container and turned toward the rest of the team. "Guys—"

Kylo's alert voice came on our earpiece. "T. Whistler, evacuate the area! Now!! It's a—"

Kylo's message was interrupted by a deafening roar that tore through the night, louder than anything I'd ever heard. The windows of the nearby store shattered, shards of glass raining down. The force of the explosion hit us, throwing us to the ground.

I slammed into the pavement, the impact knocking the air from my lungs. The world blurred into an inferno—blaring noise, searing heat, and frantic shouts. My ears rang so violently it drowned out the screaming around me.

I pushed myself onto my hands and knees, coughing as the acrid stench of burning plastic and wood clawed at my throat. Flames devoured the buildings, thick black smoke curling into the cold night sky.

Civilians screamed and scattered, their terror blending with the wail of distant sirens.

"Spencer! You okay?" Steg's voice cut through the ringing in my ears.

I nodded, wincing as I brushed the debris off my fur. "Yeah, I'm good. You?"

Steg gave a quick nod. "What the fuck was that?" he said.

"Nothing good," I muttered, scanning the chaos. Two agents were down—one unconscious, the other clutching their side. Agent Velociraptor staggered to her feet, coughing but alert.

"Velo, are you good?" I called out.

She wiped the blood from her fur and nodded. "Yeah."

"Good—can you check on those two?" I pointed toward the injured agents. "Steg and I have the civilians."

"Got it!" Velo said, rushing toward them as Steg and I pushed deeper into the destroyed street, pulling people out of harm's way.

My radio was gone—probably blown by the blast—so I took out my phone, coughing through the smoke as I dialled.

"Nyx!" Kylo's voice crackled in my ear. "You need to get out of there—"

"Kylo," I cut her off, scanning the wreckage. "There was an explosion. No idea where my radio is. Call Tyrann—send rescue and medical to York Street and Sussex Drive. Civilians and agents are down."

"Got it," she said quickly. "What about you and Steg—?"

"We're fine," I snapped. "Just send them fast." I shoved the phone back into my pocket. I let adrenaline take over and sprinted into the smoke filled street.

A cluster of terrified Aniforms huddled near a collapsing building. "This way! Stay low!" I barked, guiding them toward safety as Steg struggled to free a young girl pinned beneath the debris.

Steg's muscles strained as he lifted the rubble, his voice calm. I couldn't catch every word, but it was something around, "It's okay; you're safe now," as he handed the crying girl to her mother.

We moved in sync, our actions focused even as everything crumbled around us.

We spent the rest of the night tending to the injured, doing what we could—rushing from one to the next. No matter how hard we worked, how many we helped, it felt endless.

It must have been around 6 a.m., though I couldn't be sure—my iPhone had died hours prior. Tyrann approached me, his expression a careful mix of authority and empathy.

"Nyx," he said, his voice soft but firm, "we've done everything we can here. It's time to head back to HQ. Let the first responders take over."

I stared at him; the words forming in my throat but refusing to come out. Instead, I clenched my fists, claws pressing into the pads of my hands until it hurt.

Tyrann didn't need me to say anything; he could see the turmoil across my face.

"I know how you feel," he added gently. "But if we want to ensure this doesn't happen again, we must keep moving. We have to go back and keep working."

"Fine," I muttered, swallowing the rage and sadness that threatened to spill over. I couldn't argue with him. As much as I hated to leave, he was right.

The scent of smoke clung to our fur as we trudged into HQ hours later, a grim reminder of what we'd failed to stop. The air inside felt heavy, replaced by a sombre stillness.

I caught sight of Kylo, hunched over her computer, her eyes dulled by exhaustion and guilt. "Kylo," I called.

She rose and ran towards me. She gave me a hug and, sobbing, said, "I'm sorry."

"It's not your fault." I returned the hug.

She glanced up, her ears flattening. She leaned back and started roaming the room like a caged wolf, claws clicking against the tile. "I should have seen it coming," she muttered. "The messages, the patterns... It was all there, If I had realized sooner."

I placed a hand on her shoulder. "Alecia, stop. We all missed it. It's not your fault." I reassure her.

She shrugged off his touch. "But Spence. It's my job to catch these things. If I had just been faster, maybe we could have—"

Steg burst into the room, his tail swishing wildly. "Guys, you have to come over," he blurted out, interrupting us. "Quick. Conference Room 4." He rushed back.

Kylo and I exchanged a look before following him.

When we stepped into the room, Allo and Tyrann were already there, their gazes locked on the large screen on the wall. The local news was playing.

"What's going—" I started, but Allo raised a hand, silencing me.

Victor's face was on the screen. His voice carried the same self-righteous tone I'd grown to hate. "Today, you witnessed the incompetence of those sworn to protect you." Victor said.

My fists clenched. The audacity of this guy to gloat after everything he'd done.

He continued, "This isn't the first time they've failed you, is it? GUIP has always been a lie—a crutch for the weak, a shield for the unnatural. They cannot protect this world because it was never theirs to protect. The real guardians of this country—of this world—are rising. A new era is coming. One where the true order of things will be restored. Where nature reclaims its balance, and mistakes are undone. No one can stop us. We'll see you soon."

The broadcast cut off, and we stayed silent for a moment, although our faces said it all.

"Fuck him!" Tyrann growled, breaking the silence. And hitting the table with his fists.

Allo turned to us, her face grim but composed. "I know we're all tired and devastated, but our priority is stopping whatever he's planning. We can't let him gain any more ground. Expect possible attention from the media; no one talk with them until an official statement is released, understood?"

We nodded, forming a huddle to strategize, but I couldn't focus.

Then I remembered to charge my phone—it had been dead for hours.

As soon as the screen powered back on, a flurry of notifications lit up the screen: hundreds of texts from my mom, dad, and Andy, along with several missed calls and voicemails. Each one seemed more panicked than the last.

"Oh Shit," I muttered. All eyes turned to me.

"What's wrong?" Allo asked.

"My phone died last night. I forgot to call my parents," I said, getting up. "They're probably worried sick. I have to call them."

Without waiting for permission, I bolted out of the room and dialled the first contact on my list.

"Hey, Andy," I said, trying to sound casual. "I saw your call... so... uh... what's up?" My voice carried a fake cheer I didn't feel.

"What's up?!" Andy snapped, his voice practically vibrating with anger. "What's the fuck up!? How about the fact that we had *zero idea* if you were alive or dead?! And all you can fucking say is 'what's up'?!"

My ears flattened, my tail curling between my legs. "I'm sorry," I said. "Stupid question. I'm fine, Andy. Something came up last night, and we focused on helping people, and then my phone died. I... I just forgot to check in."

Andy's voice softened, but the edge was still there. "Spencer, you can't just *forget*. Mom's been a wreck, Dad's been pacing the house, and I've been... I've been..." He trailed off, but the hurt in his voice was clear. "Not important right now. I'm pissed at you, man. We thought we'd lost you."

I leaned against the wall as I took in his words. "I know," I said quietly. "I screwed up. Are Mom and Dad with you? I want to tell them I'm okay and apologize. I didn't mean to scare you guys."

I heard Andy call out in the background, summoning our parents. He returned to the line. "Bro, don't be sorry. Be better," Andy said, his voice a mix of frustration and relief. "Spence, I need my big brother... don't do that again."

"I won't, I promise." I said, my voice full of guilt and sincerity. "I love you too."

"I didn't say I loved you," he shot back immediately.

"Yes, you did," I replied, channelling my usual big brother mocking tone.

"Shut up, dork," Andy muttered, but there was a little laugh in his voice.

Relieved, I spoke with my parents next. I explained what little I could without breaking any rules, reassured them that things would be okay, and told them I loved them.

Dad asked about Carlos, and that was when I realized I hadn't heard from him all morning. The thought sent a ripple of worry through me. After apologizing again to my family, I ended the call.

I tried calling Carlos, but it went straight to voicemail. "Oh, great," I muttered. As I started typing out a message, a text came through.

Hi Stud.

Can't talk right now.

Talk later, okay?

I paused, deleting the draft of my own text, and replied simply.

Hey,

No problem.

Just reporting that I'm okay.

The little "delivered" tick popped up, but no reply came.

I stared at the screen for a moment, my tail twitching anxiously. Something felt... wrong, but I couldn't grasp it. Shaking my head, I tucked the phone away. There was no time to dwell on it.

With a deep sigh, I pushed off the glass door and returned to the conference room.

We resumed our meeting, but only a few minutes later, a commotion outside interrupted us. We rushed to the windows. A crowd had gathered outside, their angry voices carrying through the thick glass.

"GUIP has failed us!"

"Where were you when we needed you?"

"How can we trust you?"

The shouts blended into a cacophony of anger and fear. News vans were pulling up and reporters were setting up their cameras.

"This is bad," Kylo muttered beside me, her ears drooping.

I nodded. "It's about to get worse," I said, pointing to the display where a live broadcast was playing. The ticker at the bottom of the screen read *BREAKING: Traitor Within GUIP Revealed.*

Tyrann let out a heavy sigh. "We knew this might happen. Public relations will have to handle the civilian reaction."

I just nodded numbly. Steg said something, but I wasn't paying attention. My focus was on the angry crowd outside. All I knew was that we were in deep trouble, and the people we'd sworn to protect were turning against us.

Allo's phone rang before we could fully process what was unfolding. She answered and stepped out of the room. I saw her face tighten through the window.

When she re-entered, her expression was unreadable. "The Prime Minister wants to see us. Now," she said, her tone clipped. "Nyx, Tyrann, and Steg—

you're coming with me." And Velo? Well, she didn't feel well, so she was in the emergency room.

"Me?" Steg muttered, his tail flicking nervously. "Why me... uh.. us? Are we getting fired?"

"The Prime Minister doesn't have the authority to fire you directly. I need you there because you were at the scene." Allo said.

Then her eyes landed on me. "And you. Go to uniforms on the fifth floor and ask for something more formal."

I glanced down at my hoodie—a light grey one with the logo of the local hockey team—and my ears flattened. "Oh, yeah. Sorry. I wasn't exactly planning to meet the head of government yesterday when all I wanted was to buy hand-crafted ornaments, and high caloric treats," I grumbled, unable to keep the annoyance from my voice.

Her gaze narrowed, and I quickly corrected myself. "On it, chief. Sorry, Long night." I headed for the elevator, the weight of the moment pressing down on me harder with every step.

The short drive to Parliament Hill felt like an eternity. My reflection in the tinted windows didn't do me any favours—dishevelled fur, tired eyes, and the look of someone who had barely held it together. What a mess.

"Anyone want to bet this is a friendly chat about our stellar performance?" I said, forcing a grin to break the tension.

Steg snorted. "Oh, for sure. They're probably announcing us as the new faces of the toonie."

Even Tyrann cracked a faint smile, but the humour didn't last long.

We parked behind Parliament's West Block and passed through security. A polar bear aniform, manned the checkpoint, his eyes cold. "Phones and gear in the locker," he said gruffly, motioning us to an array of small lockers.

The wait outside the committee room dragged on. My claws tapped idly against my thigh as I tried to keep still. Steg ran his fingers along the worn armrest of a nearby bench, and even Tyrann's tail twitched softly.

The doors opened. "Agents, the Prime Minister is ready for you," the clerk announced.

We stepped inside, and there she was—The Honourable Prime Minister Savage, seated behind an imposing desk. Her sharp eyes on us, taking in every detail.

"Chief Allosaurus," she began, her tone icy. "I hope you understand the gravity of the situation you and your team are in."

Allo straightened her shoulders, her voice calm. "Madam Prime Minister, I assure you we are doing everything—"

The PM's hand shot up, cutting her off. "Let me stop you right there. It's clearly not enough. Effective immediately, GUIP will suspend any active operations. The RCMP will take over."

Tyrann stepped forward, his voice firm. "With all due respect, Madam Prime Minister, that would violate the *Interspecies Protection Treaty*. GUIP was established for threats like this."

She met his gaze without flinching. "I am enacting emergency measures to protect the public. GUIP is not going anywhere... yet."

My mouth opened before my brain caught up. "Wow. That's a very stupid idea."

The prime minister's eyebrows shot up. "Excuse me?" All eyes in the room turned to me.

I ignored Tyrann's and Allo's silent warning glance. "We've been tracking Victor and his minions for months. We know their methods. The RCMP doesn't have the experience or intel to handle this."

"Agent Baryonyx is right," Steg added, stepping beside me. "We're not perfect, but we're the best chance you've got."

The Prime Minister's tone got even tighter. "If GUIP is so capable, explain to me why last night's tragedy happened under your watch. Why am I fielding calls from every level of government demanding accountability? Why are people and aniforms dead?"

The anger inside me rose, and I couldn't stop myself. "Because we're the only ones who give a fuck! The only reason this is even on your radar is because regular forms got hurt. If it were just Aniforms, you'd ignore it like always." I blurted out.

My fist closed, and my tone was slightly elevated; I could see from the corner of my eye that the parliament police were ready to put me down. Fortunately, Tyrann stepped in, his voice calm.

"What Agent Baryonyx meant," he said, shooting me a look that screamed *shut the fuck up*, "is that the situation's urgency outweighs any political considerations. Lives are at stake. And we are the best option to protect both sides."

"Don't lecture me about urgency, Agent Tyrannosaurus. I'm well aware of what's at stake. But people have lost faith in GUIP, and I have a responsibility to act. Until Parliament reconvenes and we can discuss GUIP's future, your involvement in any matter is officially over."

Allo's face was unreadable, and her professionalism was an unbreakable wall. "Yes, Madam Prime Minister," she said, her voice steady. "We will comply and facilitate the transition."

We filed out of the parliament like ghosts. As we stepped into the biting cold air, I muttered, "Not voting for her party next election."

Steg chuckled. "Assuming we're still around to vote."

I shot him a faint grin. "Thanks for the optimism, bud."

"Just calling it like I see it," he replied, his smirk fading as quickly as it had appeared.

The walk back to the car was painfully quiet. We'd been sidelined—shut out—at the worst possible time. And though I hated to admit it, a small voice in the back of my mind whispered that maybe we deserved it.

At HQ, Allo's voice cut through the silence. "Steg, call Kylo and have her meet us in conference room five. We need to gather everything we have to transfer it." She turned to Tyrann next. "And Tyrann, please talk with your agent." Her gaze briefly flicked to me, her frustration clear.

"On it, Chief," Tyrann replied, his voice steady. He gestured for me to follow him. As we strolled into his office, he closed the door behind us and lowered the blinds with a sharp tug. The room felt smaller, the tension suffocating.

"Listen," he began.

"Yeah, yeah. I know," I interrupted, my voice rising before I could stop myself. "I could've handled that better, right?" My tail lashed behind me. "But before you fire, suspend, or yell at me for speaking my mind, answer me this—do you think any of this is fair?"

Tyrann didn't respond immediately, his steady gaze watching as I paced the room.

"Don't you believe in GUIP and what it's supposed to stand for? Because since I joined, what have we done? Nothing! Isn't it our mission to protect everyone, no matter what they are? Now we have a chance to actually *do* something, and you want me to just sit back and let them sideline us? You expect me to stand down while Victor and Chasing Tails try to destroy everything?"

My voice cracked, the anger bubbling up. "And excuse me, buy I'm not going to just sit with my tail under my legs while our kind is at risk."

"You're right," he said simply, surprising me. "None of this is fair. But losing our temper in front of the Prime Minister doesn't help. We're already on thin ice;

now, she sees us as emotional and unstable. You didn't do us any favours today, Nyx."

My ears flattened, and I looked away. "Don't you think I know that? And this might be selfish, but..." I hesitated, my voice breaking slightly. "I've finally started to make peace with what I am. And... I don't know what to do to keep it," I muttered, the fight draining.

Tyrann pushed off the desk and touched my shoulder, his voice softening. "We *are* supposed to protect everyone. And if we're going to do that, we can't waste time feeling sorry for ourselves. For now, our best option—"

I cut him off, my voice rising again. "Oh c'mon, cut the crap, Ty. Leave the bureaucrat bullshit. Tell me the guy who fought to make *this*,"—I gestured broadly with my hands— "is just going to sit down and do nothing."

Tyrann's expression was hard to read. I was too mentally exhausted to keep arguing, so I plopped into the chair and stared at the floor. My tail and ears drooped, the weight of the past 48 hours crushing me.

"Fuck it," Tyrann muttered, breaking the stillness. "You're right. I can't sit and do nothing."

I looked up, my ears perking slightly. "What are you saying?"

"I have to do something," Tyrann said, leaning forward, his tone resolute.

"What exactly do you have in mind?"

"It's better if you don't know. I need you to go back and act like everything is going as normal."

I studied him for a long moment, my tail swishing thoughtfully. I stood up. "If you're going to do this, I'm going with you. No way am I letting you take this on alone."

Tyrann sighed. "I can't ask you to do that. We could lose everything—our jobs, freedom, and lives."

"And if we do nothing, innocent people will lose theirs," I countered. "You're not asking—I'm just letting you know I'm coming."

"Nyx," Tyrann said, his voice low. "Do you know this means the possibility of becoming criminals ourselves?. No matter what happens, there's no turning back."

"Well, we all knew it was just a matter of time before I ended up in prison. Might as well do it with style," I said, trying for humour, as I tried to keep my voice from cracking.

We sat down and devised a plan, listing what we might need. Stealing weapons and equipment seemed like the least troublesome thing we were about to do. We agreed not to tell Kylo or Steg. It wasn't a matter of trust—it was about keeping them out of what would become an outright act of rebellion.

Before leaving the room, I picked up my badge, thumbing over the embossed GUIP logo. With a deep breath, I set the badge down on Tyrann's desk. "Here. If they ask, I went on my own. You were just trying to stop me, okay?"

Beside me, Tyrann did the same, the soft clunk of his badge on the wood sounding deafeningly final. "Nah," he said, his lips curling into a faint smile. "I want some of the credit, too."

We waited until most agents had gone home for the night. Tyrann used his clearance to access the weapons locker. We grabbed what we needed.

As we walked out of the building, I realized it might be the last time I would be in it.

The doors closed behind us, and we stepped into the cold night air, a shared, silent understanding passing between us.

This wasn't about glory or rebellion.

This was about doing what was right. No matter the cost.

Chapter 16:
THE ONE I USED TO KNOW

I like to think I'm good at adapting to change. Maybe I've always been like that. And yet—here's the thing about change. I *fucking* hate it.

All my life, I did everything I could to hold on. Keep things familiar. Keep things safe. But that time? Well, I don't think I regret letting go.

Sure, I was walking away from the security of a job. Deliberately breaking the law by going rogue. Probably running headfirst toward a short, messy, and painful death. But, damn it. It felt like the right thing to do.

Hero calling or pure stupidity? Yes.

The cool air hit my face as Tyrann and I slipped out of the GUIP building. My fur bristled—whether from the snowy chill or the gut-clenching uncertainty, I wasn't sure.

Behind us, the sleek glass structure loomed, its towering windows mostly dark. A handful of late-night offices still glowed, silhouettes moving behind the glass.

I tried not to think about how, just hours ago, I'd been one of them. To avoid awkward conversations with Steg, we agreed for me to stay with Tyrann at his place.

Tyrann's tail swished nervously as we crossed the empty parking lot. "Are you taking your car, Nyx?" he asked, breaking the tense silence.

I winced, my ears flattening. "Ah, about that... I haven't gotten a new one," I said

Tyrann's ears twitched, his brow furrowing. "Really? It's been almost a year since yours... uh... went up in flames. At least you got the cheque from the GUIP victims' fund, right?"

GUIP has a fund for personal property lost in active operations. Makes sense when you're an organization prone to blowing up cars, homes, and sometimes entire streets. And since I was just a food delivery guy when my car got obliterated, I got a cheque.

"I have," I admitted. "Haven't cashed it, though. It's sitting next to the one from my insurance."

"Why the hell not?"

I shrugged, shoving my hands into my hoodie pockets. "Been busy. I'll get to it eventually… assuming we don't end up in prison, or dead, or I dunno, something in between."

Tyrann rolled his eyes, but I caught the hint of a smile. "Fair point. Come on, we'll take my truck."

I followed him, kicking at a patch of slushy snow as I tried to shake off the doubts creeping into my mind.

I had known Tyrann for about nine months by then—not a long time— but it felt like we'd been through enough to make us more than just coworkers. He was like the big brother I'd never had, and I was the younger, sometimes annoying one. Still, sitting in his truck, I realized how much I didn't actually know about him.

"I didn't peg you as a truck guy," I said, glancing around the cabin of his black F150 lightning. "For some reason, I thought you'd have a Mercedes or something fancy like that."

Tyrann chuckled as he started to back out. "It's handy."

"Handy? Do you haul stuff often? Secret lumberjack side hustle we don't know about?"

"It's handy for Costco and IKEA trips," he said, his tone so matter of fact it caught me off guard.

"Makes sense." I leaned back in the seat, glancing out the window at HQ one last time. The building stood silent and imposing, a reminder of everything we were leaving behind.

The truck engine hummed softly as we glided through the quiet streets. Tyrann's hands stayed steady on the wheel, but the way his jaw clenched gave him away. He was just as wound up as I was.

"You okay?" His gruff voice broke the silence.

"Yeah. I guess. Forty-eight-plus hours awake is finally catching up to me." I hesitated, staring out at the empty streets illuminated by faint streetlights. "Ty, what if… what if we're making a huge mistake?"

He didn't answer immediately, the hum of the engine filling the space between us. "Sometimes doing the right thing means bending the rules, Nyx. And we both know GUIP's hands are tied on this one."

I nodded, even though his words didn't quite ease the worry.

We pulled into the parking lot of Tyrann's apartment complex. The building caught me off guard. It was one of those modern, minimalist places, all clean lines, and neutral colours.

Inside, his apartment was spotless—immaculate, really. Everything looked like it had been placed by a professional organizer with a grudge against clutter. Not a single speck of dust in sight.

"Wow," I whistled low, glancing around. "You could perform surgery in here, T."

Tyrann grunted as he hung his jacket with a kind of precision that suggested it was a ritual. "Just because I'm part animal doesn't mean I have to live like one."

I left my boots at the door and wandered farther in, my tail swishing as I took in the sparse decor.

Few personal photos. Not many knick-knacks. No signs of hobbies or personality—just furniture, some books, and appliances that looked like they'd barely been used.

"So, uh, nice place you got here," I said, trying to fill the silence. "Very... you."

Tyrann raised an eyebrow. "What's that supposed to mean?"

"Oh, you know. Neat. Organized. Functional and probably equipped with something that'll take me down if I open the wrong drawer."

"It's cozy," he replied, letting out a chuckle. "plus, I don't spend much time here, anyway."

"Yeah, I can see that," I muttered, eyeing the perfectly aligned books on a shelf.

"Make yourself at home," Tyrann said, though the place itself seemed to disagree with the concept. "Get some rest, Nyx. We've got a long day ahead of us tomorrow."

"Will do," I mumbled.

"And here," he added, handing me a pillow and blanket. "Please let me know if you need anything, okay?"

I hesitated for a moment, the lingering scent of smoke on my fur making me self-conscious. "Actually, uh... would it be okay if I showered first? I don't want your place reeking of smoky fox."

Tyrann smirked lightly, nodding toward the bathroom. "Good idea. Towels are in the cabinet. Take your time."

I headed to the bathroom and let myself enjoy the warm water for a while. It felt like the grime and tension of the day were finally washed away, replaced by a fleeting sense of relief. As I was rinsing off, Tyrann's voice called through the door. "Hey, Nyx," he said. "I left you something on the couch. Figured you'd appreciate it."

"Thanks," I yelled back, curious.

I stepped out of the shower wrapped in a towel, feeling worlds better. As I walked into the living room, something on the couch caught my eye.

A neatly folded pile: GUIP training T-shirts, standard-issue underwear (not the comfiest, but they'd do), some sweatpants, and—best of all—a pair of clean hoodies. I ran my fingers over the soft fabric.

"Are these yours?" I called, smirking as Tyrann reappeared from his room.

"Not quite," he said, casually leaning against the doorframe. "Picked them up from the uniform storage earlier. Figured you'd rather have those than one of my shirts."

He wasn't wrong. I pulled one of the hoodies over my head, even though my fur was still slightly damp. The familiar weight of it was grounding. "Thanks, Ty. This is... really thoughtful."

"Don't get used to it," he teased, though there was something genuine behind his low voice. "Now, get some rest, okay?"

"I'll try. Night, Ty."

"Night, Nyx."

The door to his room clicked shut, leaving me alone with my thoughts—and the unexpected comfort of a clean hoodie. I quickly finished dressing since the idea of being unclothed in his apartment felt wrong.

I plopped onto the couch. Which, like the rest of the apartment, felt too pristine to truly relax in. I stared at the ceiling, clutching the blanket as if it might hold off the storm in my mind.

It didn't.

Tyrann's absence left too much room for doubt to creep in. The silence wasn't comforting—it was intrusive, amplifying every worry.

As I lay there, trying to find sleep, one thought refused to let go. I wasn't sure who I trusted less right now—Victor, GUIP, or myself.

I woke up with a groan, my back protesting every movement. Tyrann's couch had all the comfiness of a rock wrapped in regret. The smell of bacon and coffee wafted through the air, though, so at least there was that.

"Good morning!" Tyrann's gruff voice called from the kitchen. His tail wagged as he worked at the stove. "Breakfast is almost ready."

"Ugh, morning. Thanks," I muttered, dragging myself upright. My tail swished irritably as I stretched, trying to work out the knots in my back.

"Oh yeah," Tyrann said, glancing over his shoulder. "Forgot you're not a morning guy. Coffee's ready if that helps."

I padded into the kitchen, my nose twitching at the smell of fresh coffee.

"Sleep well?" he asked, a hint of amusement playing on his face.

I rolled my shoulders with a grimace. "Yeah, well... kinda. Since you're making breakfast, I won't talk bad about your couch."

"Should've warned you," he replied, his ears twitching slightly. "5 minutes and breakfast is ready."

I ducked into the bathroom to splash some cold water on my face. When I came back, Tyrann was already plating bacon and eggs, his movements quick and efficient.

"Need a hand?" I offered, more out of politeness than anything else.

"All done. Mugs are in that cabinet," he said, nodding toward the kitchen. I grabbed two mugs and started pouring coffee when something on the counter caught my eye—a sleek wooden photo frame. Inside was a picture of Tyrann with an attractive woman. His arm rested around her waist, her hand was on his shoulder, and they both wore the kind of unguarded smiles that hinted of a good story.

"Who's this?" I asked, unable to contain my curiosity.

Tyrann appeared behind me. He hesitated before finally answering. "That's... Amelia," he said softly. "She's my fiancée."

My ears perked up. "Fiancée? Didn't know you weren't single." I stopped, realizing I might've crossed a line. "Sorry for being noisy. I'm just surprised."

He waved off my apology, his tail swishing slowly. "Well, you never asked. And I don't exactly broadcast my personal life. Though, if anyone's worth bragging about, it's her. She's... impressive."

"She looks it. How long have you been together?"

"Six years. We have been engaged for two."

I let out a low whistle. "Wow. That's been a long time. How come I've never met her?"

"She's in the U.S. military," he said, his tone a mix of admiration and resignation. "Deployed more often than not."

The stark simplicity of his apartment made more sense. It wasn't just discipline—it was a placeholder, a space waiting for someone to come home to.

"That must be tough," I said softly, feeling a pang of sympathy for my usually composed partner.

Tyrann's eyes met mine. "It is," he admitted quietly. "But we knew what we were signing up for. We make it work. We understand each other's service."

I nodded, unsure how to respond. "Sorry, I didn't mean to pry," I added quickly, though I didn't regret asking.

"Nothing to apologize for," he said, his gaze lingering on the photo for a moment longer before turning away. "We all have our reasons for what we do this job."

"Guess so," I murmured, my mind racing as I pieced together fragments of who Tyrann really was. I knew some of the battles he'd fought—both external and internal—the struggles he endured to become who he is today.

But now, the reason he fights so hard felt clearer. The risks, the sacrifices... the stakes we were both willing to gamble in a game where the odds never seemed to stop climbing.

I settled at the table, setting down the mugs. "Well, if she's anything like you, I'm betting she's pretty damn good at her job."

Tyrann turned, a faint, almost wistful smile pulling at his lips. "She's better," he said simply. "Way better."

Before I could respond, he chuckled and slid a plate of eggs and bacon in front of me. "Eat up. We've got a long day ahead."

I dug in, surprised at how good Tyrann's cooking was. Between bites, I asked, "So, what's the plan?"

Tyrann sighed as he sat across from me, his fork spinning aimlessly in his hand. "Honestly? I have no idea. We're in uncharted territory now."

I pushed the eggs around the plate, my brain racing in a thousand directions. "What about Seb?"

"What about him?"

"Not sure," I said, shrugging. "But maybe he knows something. He used to be Victor's right hand."

Tyrann's ears flattened slightly. "Nyx, I don't know. We can't trust him and let's be real—he's not exactly your biggest fan."

"Yeah," I said, poking at a piece of bacon. "But think about it. He was so sure Victor was going to let him out, and... well, he didn't. Something tells me Seb's the resentful type. Maybe I can use that. Plus," I added with a smirk, "I'm not an agent anymore, right? So maybe that'll soften his hatred just a bit."

Tyrann didn't look convinced, but I could tell he was mulling it over. "You think you can get him to talk?"

I shrugged. "Only one way to find out. And it's not like we have GUIP resources to fall back on anymore." Then it hit me. "Fuck. Right. How are we even supposed to get in to talk to him?"

Tyrann leaned back, his tail swishing lazily. "Well, technically, we didn't give a formal notice of resignation. So I think we're still in the system, or at least I am. And... the correctional director owes me a favour. I'm sure I can get us in."

I grinned, leaning forward. "See? That's why you keep me around—I'm great at improvising."

Tyrann's face softened, hinting at a smile. "And that's exactly what worries me," he muttered, standing to clear the plates.

"Hey, look at us. Two rogue agents with no backup, no resources, and no idea what we're doing. What could possibly go wrong?"

He shot me a look over his shoulder. "I'd say don't jinx it, but it's probably already too late."

I laughed, but the weight of what we were about to do settled heavily between us. For all our banter, we were stepping into the unknown—two agents against a storm far bigger than either of us could see.

The *GUIP Detention Facility* had that sterile, suffocating vibe that always made me uneasy. Tyrann and I were led through the halls by a bored-looking guard who barely spared us a glance.

"This better be worth it," Tyrann muttered as we approached the holding cells.

"It will be," I said, though I wasn't sure if I was convincing him or myself.

Seb was lounging on the bench inside his cell, looking far too comfortable for someone locked up. When he spotted us, a smug grin spread across his face, his wolf eyes gleaming with amusement.

"Well, well, if it isn't my favourite fox and his oversized guard dog," Seb drawled, leaning back like he owned the place. His gaze locked on Tyrann. "Or whatever you are supposed to be. A cat?"

Tyrann growled, but I held up a paw to stop him. "Hello, Sebastian," I said flatly. "We need to talk."

"Really, Jean? After all this time?" He tilted his head, feigning curiosity. "I guess things are really going to shit if you're here to beg for my help. Oh, how the mighty have fallen."

"I don't have time for your crap," I snapped, stepping closer to the bars. "Victor left you here to rot, didn't he? You're not part of his plan anymore, which means you've got nothing to lose by talking to us."

Seb's grin faltered for just a moment, but he quickly recovered, leaning forward with mock interest. "Nice jab. But why would I help you? You know what I think about you and other 'agents', like big guy over there."

"Look," I said, forcing my voice to stay calm. "You don't owe me anything. You don't even have to like me. But you've got to see what's happening here. Victor's actions just got aniforms killed. And for all the hateful shit you say about us, I don't think you're a sociopath who's okay with that. Am I wrong?"

Seb's smirk twitched. I could see the wheels turning in his head. Tyrann stayed silent behind me, his arms crossed and his presence looming. I hoped it was as unsettling to Seb as it was comforting to me.

"Victor promised you freedom, didn't he?" I pressed. "And yet, here you are. Tell me—how's that working out for you? Has he even given you a call? Because, from where I'm standing, it looks like he disposed of you the moment you stopped being useful to him."

Seb chuckled dryly, his tone sharper now. "I'll give you this, Jean—you've got a hell of a smart mouth. Gotta say, you almost believe your own bullshit. GUIP's manipulation skills are rubbing off on you."

"I'm not an agent anymore," I said, my voice cutting through his sarcasm.

Seb's ears perked up, and he leaned closer to the bars, his curiosity momentarily overriding his usual smugness. "Really? What? Do they finally got tired of your fake moral high ground act?"

I crossed my arms, meeting his gaze. "Big guy and I decided we weren't fans of their methods."

Seb chuckled, leaning back again with a skeptical look. "Oh, I see what's happening. Now that you're out of the game, you're here to play the renegade card. Let me guess—you're doing this for justice, for the poor aniforms, for the 'greater good,' or whatever other crap GUIP preaches?"

Tyrann growled softly behind me, but I ignored him, keeping my focus on Seb. "Believe whatever you want, but here's the reality: you're in here because Victor doesn't need you anymore. And I'd bet good money he'll throw you under the bus again if it benefits him."

Seb's smug grin faltered, his jaw tightening ever so slightly. "And what makes you think I care what Victor does anymore?"

"Because you're not stupid, Seb," I shot back. "You may hate me, but you hate being played even more. And that's exactly what Victor's done to you. He used you, just like he's using everyone else in his little game. But unlike the others, you're in a position to do something about it."

Seb stared at me for a long moment. He leaned forward again, his voice low. "Alright, Jean. What's in it for me?"

I glanced at Tyrann, who gave a slight nod before adding, "I'll make sure the assault and trespassing charges vanish. Call it a clean slate."

Seb let out a dry laugh. "Now we're talking. See? Could've saved ourselves half an hour if you had started with that. Fine, Jean, you've got my attention. What do you want to know?"

Relief flickered through me, but I didn't let it show. "We know the attack at the market was just the beginning. Victor's planning something bigger—

something that could kill a lot of people. Where, when, and/or how. Anything you've got."

Seb's smirk widened, his expression infuriatingly confident. "I got something from big dog over there. But if you want my secrets, I'm going to need one of yours. Tell me your name. Your real name."

I hesitated. "All my friends call me SJ." I said.

"SJ, eh?" Seb tilted his head, his grin curling wider. "Keeping it cryptic. Fine, I'll talk—because I like a mystery and I also kinda like chatting with you."

He leaned back lazily, his tone casual. "Chaudière Island," he said. "Last I heard, phase two involves the old hydro plant. What exactly?, no idea. But you can start there."

"How do we know this isn't another one of your games?" Tyrann asked.

Seb shrugged, his grin sharp and infuriating. "You don't. But hey, what choice do you have? Believe me or don't. Either way, I'll be here, nice and cozy."

As much of a manipulative bastard as he was, Seb never struck me as a liar—at least not for the things that mattered to him, anyway. I could see the desire to take revenge on Victor. "Alright," I said finally. "Thanks for the tip."

Seb leaned back against the wall. "Don't thank me yet. If I'm right, you're walking into hell."

As Tyrann and I turned to leave, Seb called after us one last time. "Oh, and SJ? Try not to get yourself killed. I'd miss our little chats."

I didn't dignify him with a response. Tyrann and I exited the facility in tense silence, our footsteps echoing in the halls.

We had a lead. We had a chance. But every step forward felt like we were only getting closer to a cliff's edge. Or some poetic shit like that.

The drive to Chaudière Island was tense. Every second felt like an eternity.

"Think they'll let us share a cell?" I asked, trying to break the silence. "You know, if we don't die."

Tyrann snorted; his eyes fixed on the road. "Yeah, I don't think they're that accommodating. Maybe for me. But you? Probably solitary."

"Funny," I muttered, forcing a grin.

We approached the hydroelectric facility. Its weathered façade loomed against the darkening sky, the aged structure a stark reminder of how much history the place held.

"Charming, do you think they do tours?" I said.

Tyrann's only response was a low growl as we pulled up and parked.

The Chaudière Island facility was a relic, one of the country's first hydro plants. Though some power was still produced here, it was mostly a historical site, a testament to old technology trying to remain useful. But its critical role in controlling the river's flow meant it couldn't just be abandoned.

Tyrann made quick work of the lock, the security woefully outdated. We slipped inside, greeted by dim, empty corridors. Our footsteps echoed ominously in the silence.

"I don't like this," I murmured, my fur prickling. "It's too quiet."

"Stay alert," Tyrann whispered back, his ears swivelling to catch any [sound.

I was about to fire off a retort when a distant clang made us both freeze. We pressed against the wall, straining to listen.

Footsteps echoed closer, and three figures emerged from a nearby room. They were dressed in plain, nondescript clothing, that made clear—they weren't hydro workers.

As they passed, I caught snippets of their hushed conversation.

"...timer set... showtime in forty-five..."

The moment they disappeared down the hallway, we crept toward the door they'd come from.

It led into one of the plant's decommissioned turbine rooms. Normally, I'd be geeking out over the sheer size of the machinery—massive metal constructs, once responsible for powering half the city. But my eyes locked onto something far more pressing.

A device sat in the centre of the chamber, wires sprawling out from its metallic casing, snaking into the walls and floor. And at its heart, glowing ominously, was a familiar blue-lit box. A Zenitharian energy core.

"Nyx," Tyrann said, his voice grave. "That's a bomb."

"Fuck, The good news is that at least Seb wasn't bullshitting us."

We approached cautiously. Tyrann crouched beside the contraction, his eyes scanning the setup. His ears flicked as he traced the wiring, his fingers hovering near the core but not daring to touch it.

"It's a complex setup," he muttered. "Those are plasma emitters. If this goes off, it won't just take down the building—it'll incinerate everything in a two-kilometre radius. They seem to be using the old chamber to amplify the effect."

"Well," I exhaled, forcing down the rising panic. "Guess we're on the clock. So... can you disarm it?"

"Not in time," Tyrann said, pointing to the pressure mounts beneath the device. "Look here. It's rigged. Any tampering triggers an immediate detonation."

"Shit," I said, attempting to keep my tail still—no sudden movements, no accidental nudging of anything in this death trap. "Okay, so what do we do now?"

Tyrann's eyes darted around the room, scanning every corner. He pointed toward the far end. "The turbine gates. Zenitharian tech and water don't mix well. If we flood this room, the water might dampen the power of the explosion and absorb enough of the blast to prevent catastrophic failure."

"Flood the room?" I echoed. "Crazy plan, but sure, let's do it—so we can get the fuck out of here."

Tyrann shook his head. "It's not that simple." His tail flicked as he gestured toward the rusted machinery. "This turbine was decommissioned decades ago. The gates have to be opened manually."

"So.. does that mean—"

Tyrann met my gaze. "Someone has to open the intake valve in the catwalk in here and ensure the water flows into the turbine chamber. And the other has to handle the controls for the main gate, which can only be accessed from outside."

"Should we call for backup?—Allo can pull a team together. We don't have to do this alone."

Tyrann's voice sharpened. "We don't have time for backup. Even if they scrambled a team right now, they wouldn't make it here before the timer runs out. You know that."

"Okay... so let's do it together!" I said. "You handle one gate, I'll handle the other, and we'll both get out of here!"

"It doesn't work like that," Tyrann replied, his tone soft but resolute. "The second the intake valve opens; this room will start flooding. The pressure will trigger the bomb if it's not controlled properly. Whoever stays won't have time to escape."

My ears flattened, my mind raced for alternatives. "Then let me stay!" I said, my voice cracking. "You go handle the outside gate. I'll take care of the intake valve."

Tyrann said nothing, his expression unreadable.

"Tyrann, this is insane!" I pulled out my phone, desperate to call for help, only to see a "No Service," icon. "Fuck. At least can we just go outside and try calling Allo from there? Maybe we can find another way."

Tyrann's mouth twitched, almost like he wanted to smile. "I guess we can try that. But let's Hurry."

We turned toward the exit. My tail swished anxiously behind me as I tried to come up with an alternative plan. My thoughts were interrupted by a loud clang. I whipped around to see Tyrann slamming the door shut, the sound of metal scraping as he locked it from the inside.

"What the fuck?" I shouted, running back to the door and pounding on it. "Tyrann! Open this fucking door right now!"

"I can't," came his muffled reply, steady but firm.

"Bullshit!" I barked, slamming my fists against the cold metal. "Let me in!"

"I can't do that, Nyx," Tyrann said, his voice softening. "We both know you'd try to stop me. And I can't let you throw your life away. Besides, someone needs to be out there to call for help, to make sure this doesn't get worse."

I pressed my forehead against the door, my ears flattening against my head. "And I'm supposed to just leave you here?" My voice cracked as desperation clawed at me. "Come on, T, there has to be another way. I'm begging you—don't do this! Please Tyrann."

"It's Riley." He said. His voice was softer.

My ears stood up. "Riley?, Wait. Why are you telling me this?" I asked, my voice cracking.

"Because I trust you," he replied.

My throat tightened, tears pricking at the corners of my eyes. "Man, think about it," I tried to convince myself as much as him. "Think about Amelia."

"Promise me whatever it happens you'll tell her I love her. And that I'm sorry."

"Don't talk like that. You're going to make it out of this. You don't get to pull this hero shit and leave me here to clean up the mess afterwards. Ty—uh, Riley, don't do this. Please, I need you."

A sudden shout broke the moment.

"Hey you, fox! What the fuck are you doing here?"

I spun around to see a broad-shouldered guy with a no-nonsense scowl, already reaching for the gun tucked at his back. Adrenaline shot through me, and I dove for cover behind a stack of rusted pipes.

My mind torn between the immediate danger and the friend I might be losing.

"Hydro maintenance, sir!" I yelled back. "Just here to check the turbines!"

"Nice try, asshole." He growled, drawing his weapon.

He opened fire. The sharp crack of gunfire rang through the facility, deafening in the enclosed space. My fur bristled as I pressed myself flat against the pipes.

I fumbled for my sidearm, the cool grip grounding me. Taking a steadying breath, I peeked out, just as another bullet pinged off the metal near my head.

"Shit! Focus, SJ, focus!" I muttered, tail curling tight.

He had a good spot, shifting between cover near the far end of the room, keeping me pinned. I popped out and fired off a shot—the bullet ricocheted harmlessly off a pipe near him.

"Damn it!" I hissed, ducking as another round tore through the air above me.

"You think you can stop this?" the guy taunted, his voice echoing through the space. "You're out of your depth, fox!"

"Maybe. So it's really gonna suck when I beat you."

I returned fire. This time, my shot grazed past his shoulder—close enough to leave a nasty cut, but not close enough to go through. He stumbled with a grunt of pain, clutching his arm.

Taking advantage of the opening, I sprinted toward the intake valve ladder. My boots clanged against the metal.

More bullets whizzed past—one grazed the side of the ladder, a searing sting cutting across my arm.

"Fuck!" I cried, shoving the pain aside and climbing faster. My focus locked on the valve handle above. Below, the sharp clack of his weapon as he reloaded.

Reaching the top, I crouched low and grabbed the valve. It resisted at first, rusted from years of disuse, but I gritted my teeth and forced it to turn. The faint rush of water told me it was working.

"Gotcha!" the man said.

I barely had time to duck before a bullet whizzed past my head. He was already climbing after me, his steps slamming against the metal rungs.

"Oh no, you don't!" I kicked out, my boot smashing into his hand. His gun clattered to the floor below. He yelped but didn't stop, his massive frame still hauling itself upward.

Then he reached for his hip.

I saw the movement before I saw the weapon—his fingers curling around something, yanking it free. A sidearm. Smaller than the first.

I pulled my own gun, heart pounding. "Don't," I warned, my voice sharp. "Just stay down."

He didn't listen. He lifted the weapon, aiming straight at me.

Training kicked in before my mind could catch up. I fired.

The shot was deafening at close range. He choked out a strangled sound, his body going limp as he slid down the ladder, hitting the ground with a sickening thud.

I stayed frozen, gun still raised, breath coming fast and shallow. Shocked at what I had done.

However, I didn't have time to fully process it. I couldn't. I turned back to the valve, forcing it another wrench. The roar of rushing water filled the chamber, drowning out the ringing in my ears.

I tell myself there was no other way. That it was him or thousands more besides me. I just did what I was trained to do.

I scrambled down the ladder. My legs pumped as I sprinted toward the turbine room. The sound of water rushing through the intake mixed with the faint whine of machinery struggling to contain the pressure.

"Riley!" I shouted as I neared the sealed door. My heart clenched as I slammed into it, pounding with both fists. "Riley, I did it! The valve's open! Let's go!"

There was no response. Panic clawed at my throat. "Riley!?" I screamed again, my voice cracking.

The ground beneath me bucked violently, and I was thrown off my feet. A deafening explosion rocked the facility. Smoke filled the air, a blinding flash searing my vision. My body hit the ground, the impact knocking the wind out of me, *the second time that week.*

For a moment, everything was silent—except for the dull ringing in my ears. Disoriented, struggling to make sense of what had just happened, I forced my gaze toward the turbine room door. Warped. Charred. Barely hanging onto its frame.

My breath hitched. "Fuck... Riley..." My voice cracked. Tears blurred my vision as I forced myself upright, every muscle in my body protesting the effort.

Stumbling outside, I fumbled for my phone, my hands trembling as I searched for a signal.

When Chief Allo's voice finally came through, her words felt distant—like static inside my head.

I pressed the phone tightly against my ear. "Chief..." I barely held it together. I could hear the anger in her tone, but I cut her off, my throat too tight to speak properly.

"We... I need medical," I stammered, my words broken and uneven. "And rescue units. There's been... a situation—" My breath hitched again.

Silence stretched between us, except for the sound of Allo's steady breathing. Then, cool and clipped, she said, "Agent Baryonyx, may I remind you that no operations are permitted at the moment? Return to HQ immediately."

I clenched my jaw, my grip tightening around the phone. My eyes flicked back to the ruined facility, smoke pouring into the frigid air. "Chaudière Island," I forced out. My voice wavered. "Agent Tyrann... He's... down."

The sharp intake of breath on the other end told me everything. For the first time, Allo's professional mask cracked. "Shit, What?" she snapped. "Stay where you are. I'm sending units now. Tell me what happened."

The words wouldn't come. The truth was too heavy. Too raw.

"Agent. Are you there? What happened?" Allo's voice pressed through the haze, but I couldn't answer.

The phone slipped from my fingers, landing in the snow with a dull thud. I sat there, staring at the wreckage, my chest rising and falling in uneven breaths. No tears came—just a hollow, all-consuming ache.

I dragged in a shaky breath, my gaze drifting back to the turbine room. The broken shell of it loomed in the distance.

I didn't think. I just moved.

One step. Then another.

I turned, pushing forward, heading back inside. Just hoping for something... Anything.

Chapter 17:
NEVER GONNA NOT FIGHT AGAIN

I've always been a rule-breaker—not the reckless kind, not the one who does it for the thrill, but someone who breaks the rules because, well, they were wrong. Rules must be bent, twisted and shattered if they mean standing up for what's right.

Now, staring at the unknown ahead of me, I wonder if this will be the last time I break the rules. I don't regret it—not even for a second.

I wasn't always this confident, though. Growing up, I was a rebellious teenager—well, that's how the world labelled me back then. "She's just strong-opinionated," my mother used to say. "I'm sure Wylie will grow out of it." But even then, something about that never felt like it belonged to me. I felt out of place in my skin, like I was forced to perform a role that didn't quite fit.

Still, I had one thing going for me: I couldn't stand by when someone needed help. I was the first to intervene if someone was bullied or mistreated. Even if it meant detention—or worse—I acted. Decisive, yes. Naïve? Perhaps. But it set the foundation for who I'd become.

When I was 19, I thought I'd finally found my place. I joined the police academy, determined to channel that streak of rebellion into something meaningful. To my surprise—and everyone else's—I excelled at the top of my class. The instructors didn't quite know what to make of me: a fiery, determined, kick ass recruit who outshot, outran, and out-thought most of her peers.

Getting a spot on the force was easy. Understanding who I was? That was the real challenge.

As my career took off, a nagging feeling that something wasn't right remained. It was like I was living someone else's life, walking in someone else's shoes. The signs had always been there—small, persistent reminders I buried because confronting them felt impossible. But at 25, I couldn't keep pretending. I took the leap. I embraced who I was.

It wasn't easy becoming the man I knew I was. It felt freeing, sure, but the journey was anything but smooth. Policing wasn't exactly known for welcoming change. At first, the pushback was subtle—a lingering glance, an ill-intentioned comment. Then, it wasn't subtle at all. My every move was scrutinized. My career nearly fell apart.

Nearly.

But if there's one thing I've always been, it's stubborn. I wouldn't let anyone take away what I'd worked so hard for.

By my mid-30s, I'd finally found some stability. Twelve years into the force, I was on track for a higher rank. Things were steady. Predictable, even. And then came the Emergence.

I remember that day in May as if it had just happened. One minute, I was on patrol, laughing at some rookie dumb joke, and the next, everything changed. My reflection in a store window caught my eye, and there they were—feline ears and a tail where there had been none before.

Disorienting doesn't even begin to cover it. But I've always been good at adapting. Once the shock wore off, I accepted the changes. They became part of who I was, and I embraced them.

However, society didn't feel the same way.

The fear and prejudice that swept through the population after the Emergence were unlike anything I'd seen. People like me—Aniforms—became scapegoats. Despite my good record and years of service, I wasn't spared. They dismissed me from the force. Officially, it was "due to restructuring." But we all knew the truth.

It was devastating, like losing a part of myself. My years of hard work, gone. But giving up? That's never been my style.

If I couldn't fight from within the system, I'd fight from the outside. I joined an underground group dedicated to promote the rights aniforms. It was dangerous, gruelling, thankless work, but it gave me purpose again.

We started small—anonymous actions, protests, and spreading awareness online. Slowly, our movement gained traction. People began to listen. Against all odds, we made our voices heard.

Then came our most significant victory: the formation of the *Global Unity for Interspecies Protection*. I was there when the *Interspecies Protection Treaty* was signed. I watched GUIP take shape from the efforts of many who refused to give up.

Not long after, I was offered a high-ranking position. A cushy desk job overseeing operations. But that's not who I am. I turned it down. The real work isn't done behind a desk. It's done in the field, where people need you most.

Looking back, I don't regret that decision. It's what brought me here, to this moment, standing alongside people like Spencer—or Agent Baryonyx, as he's officially known.

I remember the day I met him—a witty fox delivering food who jumped into a dangerous situation because it was the right thing to do. At first, I thought he was crazy. Someone caught in the adrenaline rush. But as I spent more time with him, I realized there was something more.

Nyx reminded me of a younger me: messy, reckless, relentless. But with a heart that couldn't ignore someone in need.

That fox has potential. I see it in him, even if he doesn't see it in himself yet. And maybe that's why I trust him.

Because at the end of the day, this fight isn't about me. It's about the people out there and those who will carry it forward when I'm gone.

I look back on my life, from the Wylie I was, to the Riley I became. From the rebellious teenager the world saw to the man standing here today. I see the struggle, the pain, the growth. And although I am unsure what the future holds or how long I'll be here, one thing is for sure:

I am so proud of the man I came to be.

— Riley Brian Moore

GUIP Sr. Tactical Operations

Agent Tyrannosaurus.

Extracted from Tyrann's Daily Log, December 26, 2025

Chapter 18:

RISE FOR THE FALLEN

Loss. You never get used to it. You just learn to live with it, to channel it so it doesn't consume you. There are plenty of reasons new agents don't last long, but losing someone you care about? That's the one that breaks the most.

After ending Allo's call, I couldn't move. The possibility of Tyrann being gone had me frozen. But if there was even the slightest chance he was alive, I had to take it—I couldn't live with myself if I didn't.

I went back in—back into the wreckage, back into the danger—because there was no other option.

I climbed over chunks of concrete like they were nothing more than scattered papers, my hands scraped raw, my lungs burning. Every breath tasted like dust and smoke, but I kept going.

"Tyrann!" My voice echoed through the ruins, bouncing off twisted metal and shattered pipes. My heart pounded against my ribs, the silence stretching too long, too heavy.

"Come on, Ty, where are you?" My paws scrabbled against a cold slab of what had once been a wall. My voice cracked. "Answer me, damn it!"

Panic filled my chest with every passing second. I tried calling again, my voice shaking. "Riley, please!"

The desperation cut deeper as I hurdled over a splintered beam. He wasn't just a mentor—he was the person who, for some reason, had believed in me when even I hadn't. The one who taught me to channel my mess of emotions into something useful.

Without him, I was just a fox playing hero. A kid with delusions of grandeur.

The facility's guts were a maze of destruction. Jagged metal jutted from the walls, water trickled ominously, and the air was thick with smoke and the smell of scorched wiring.

"Please be okay, please be okay," I kept repeating. My eyes darted over every twisted piece of rubble, every shadowy corner.

Tyrann couldn't be gone. The team needed him. I needed him. His fiancée needed him.

Tyrann was a fighter. The guy who never gave up. A little dust and debris couldn't be the end of him.

Could it?

"TYRANN!" My voice echoed, a lonely sound swallowed by the vast wreckage. My throat burned from shouting.

I could hear his voice in my head, clear as day.

"Remember, Nyx, hesitation is a luxury we can't afford."

His tail had twitched with that familiar impatience as he lectured me, back during my first training days.

The taste of iron lingered on my tongue as my breaths came faster. There was no room for hesitation.

"TYRANN!" I screamed again, louder, rawer.

I pushed forward, clawing away chunks of wall with my bare paws. My claws scraped against concrete, my pads raw and stinging.

I could still see his grin in my mind—all encouragement, no pity.

"You'll get there," he'd told me once, after I'd fumbled my first rooftop jump in training. He'd laughed it off, confident I'd figure it out someday.

"You can't do this to me, man," I muttered. "Not today. Not when we've come this far."

I caught my breath, the dull roar of water filling the surrounding silence. My paws trembled as I leaned against a broken beam.

The thought of losing him felt like losing a piece of myself—of everything I'd worked so hard to believe in.

"Hang on, Riley," I whispered, forcing my legs to move again. "I'm coming."

I pushed forward, clawing my way deeper into the damaged facility.

My eyes locked on a brown, slick tail poking out from beneath a slab of wall. With that distinctive pattern that marks him unique.

"Oh no... Tyrann!" My voice cracked as I stumbled forward, collapsing beside the rubble that buried him.

His body lay still. *Too still.*

"Come on, Tyrann," I pleaded, unsure what I could do—but I had to do something. I grabbed his hand, trying—and failing—to check his pulse. I was vibrating too much to feel anything. "Don't do this to me. Please."

My Mentor, Friend. My big brother in all but blood.

He couldn't be gone.

Not like this.

"Riley," I whispered, the name catching in my throat. Dust hung thick in the air, choking every breath.

"Damn it, Riley, wake up!" My shout echoed through the remains of the turbine room, raw and desperate. My hands were slick with grime and blood—his, mine? I didn't even know anymore.

My strength gave out as tears spilled down my face. My breath hitched, and the sobs I'd been holding back finally broke free.

I slumped over him, my forehead resting against his shoulder.

"I need you, Riley," I choked out between broken gasps. "Please. I can't do this without you."

The silence was unbearable. Heavy. Unforgiving.

Barely broken by a faint, gravelly murmur beneath me. "Seven lives left."

I froze. My ears shot up.

A loud, high-pitched, half-hysterical laugh broke out of me before I could stop it, raw and uncontrollable.

"You scared the absolute shit out of me!" I choked, brushing dirt from his face as his eyes fluttered open.

Tears blurred my vision as I shook my head. "I'm planning to take another one off," I teased, my voice breaking.

Tyrann managed a weak, bloodied smirk.

I let out a shuddering breath. "Don't ever do that again, you asshole."

"Will see," he muttered.

I bit back another laugh, still lightheaded from the sheer insanity of relief. He was alive. Bruised, battered, and bleeding—but alive. And for that moment, it was enough.

"So..." I exhaled, my hands still shaking as I checked him for injuries. "Still in the habit of making me save your ass, eh?"

Tyrann let out a chuckle mixed with a groan as he shifted, trying—and failing—to push himself up.

"Don't move," I whispered, pressing him back down. "Help is on the way."

"Did you call Allo?"

"I did." I said with a half-smile. "By the way, she's not exactly thrilled about our little adventure. I might need to borrow one of your lives, friend."

"Deal." His smirk cut through the exhaustion.

In the distance, the faint wail of sirens grew louder.

I let out a slow, shaky breath, leaning back on my heels beside him. My tail swished slowly as the weight of everything finally started to settle.

After a couple of bandages and a generous dose of painkillers, I was cleared to go back to work. But I wasn't exactly eager to face Steg's inevitable rant, so I made a detour to the downtown mall to pick up some new, less-burned clothes instead of going home.

Without my badge, my only way to enter GUIP was to go through Kingston, doing my best to keep my tail from curling between my legs.

He glanced up from the front desk. "Agent Nyx! Welcome back," he said. His tone was surprisingly friendly—or maybe it just felt that way after what we'd survived in the last few hours.

"Hey, K." My voice came out rough. "If I'm not fired yet... think you can let me in?"

"Oh, Agent. I wish I could," he said, grinning in a way that made me more nervous than it should have. "But I've got something better for you."

"What?"

He opened a drawer and pulled out two vanilla envelopes—one labelled *A. Baryonyx,* the other *A. Tyrannosaurus.* He took out the contents of mine, revealing my badge and keycard.

My ears perked up, tail giving a small swish. I extended a paw. "Oh—thanks, K."

He frowned, holding the badge just out of reach. "Don't thank me yet... I was told to give this to you after letting you know the Chief wants to see you ASAP. Like, now-now."

"She's not happy, is she?"

"Nope. So... hurry your fluffy butt up there. Or, you know, be smart and leave the country."

I sighed and snatched the badge from his hand. "Comforting as always. Thanks, K."

He chuckled.

I left the reception area and made my way to Allo's office. After a gentle knock, she called me in.

"Please, have a seat," she said.

The Chief sat behind her desk, the sharp lines of her suit as precise as her expression—clean, composed, and unforgiving. Her office always felt sterile, like a place where warmth dared not tread.

"Field Agent Baryonyx," she began, her tone slicing through any pretense of a cordial meeting. Hearing my official title made me flinch—it always felt too formal for a guy whose wardrobe was 80% hoodies.

"Chief," I said, ears lowered. "Let me explain—"

"Silence," she snapped, slamming a stack of papers onto the desk with a force that made me jump.

"What exactly were Tyrann and you thinking? Acting on your own against direct orders? I can expect this kind of reckless behaviour from a rookie like yourself, but a senior agent?"

She shook her head, pacing now. "It was stupid, idiotic and out of line. Now, thanks to your little stunt, I'm buried under a mountain of political and bureaucratic fallout."

"Screw the Politics," I murmured, though loud enough for her to hear. "We reduced the impact of the attack, didn't we?"

"Politics aren't optional, Agent," she said, her voice cutting through the air. "They're part of the job. You can't just charge in tail-first without considering the consequences."

"Look, I know we messed up—" I started, but her raised hand silenced me.

"Your actions have political implications that reach far beyond your little act," she said, her eyes drilling into mine. "The *Interspecies Protection Treaty* is hanging by a thread, and your escapade might've just frayed it even further."

"We saved lives, didn't we?" I shot back, planting my feet as I met her gaze.

That gave her pause. Her shoulders relaxed, just slightly, and the fire in her eyes dimmed. "Yes," she admitted reluctantly. "The mission was... successful in that regard. Despite your unorthodox methods."

"Unorthodox is my middle name," I quipped, attempting to lighten the mood. It landed awkwardly, but I caught the faintest twitch of her lips.

Chief Allo sighed, leaning back in her chair, her gaze hard and calculating. "Be that as it may, this isn't over," she said, her tone sharp and measured. "We're already walking on eggshells with the feds. Your actions didn't just jeopardize yourself—they put this entire organization at risk."

I hesitated, unsure of how to respond. Then, an idea sparked.

"Let's use this," I said, stepping forward, my tail swishing nervously. "Show them that GUIP isn't the waste they think we are. Show them that we can protect everyone—our own, and theirs."

Her brow furrowed, and for a moment, I thought she might laugh outright. But instead, her expression shifted, softening just enough to suggest that my words might've hit their mark.

"Your optimism is... refreshing," she said finally, her voice quieter but no less firm. "But don't mistake this for leniency. Try anything like this again, and I won't just take your badge—I'll personally ensure you spend the rest of your days in a cell. Are we clear?"

"Yes, Chief," I said, swallowing hard.

"Good." She straightened in her seat, her composure returning. "For now, go home. Take the rest of the week off. Spend time with your family. We'll discuss this after the New Year."

"Understood, Chief," I replied, nodding.

"Dismissed," she said, her focus already shifting back to the stack of papers on her desk.

I turned to leave, my shoulders sagging slightly under the weight of exhaustion. But just as I reached the door, her voice cut through the silence.

"And James..." she said, her tone softer than before. "Good job."

I froze for a moment, caught off guard. Turning back, I caught a glimpse of her face—hard as ever, but with something just beneath the surface. Not pride, exactly, but something close. Softer, more cautious.

"Thanks, Chief," I said quietly.

I stood in front of the elevator, staring at the polished metal doors. It should have been simple—walk in, head to the 10th floor, tell the team what happened.

But somehow, running towards bullets or explosions felt easier than facing this. They deserved to know, though.

I took a deep breath and stepped inside the lift, the hum of it changing floors doing nothing to quiet my nerves. My reflection stared back at me in the mirrored doors—still dishevelled, bruised, and looking like I'd been through hell. Which, I suppose, wasn't far from the truth.

When the doors opened, I stepped out into the familiar workspace. The scent of stale coffee and the sound of Kylo clicking away at a keyboard filled the air. She looked about as thrilled as someone stuck watching paint dry.

Meanwhile, Steg was enthusiastically flicking a paper football across the desk to himself, completely engrossed in his one-man championship.

"Hi, guys," I said awkwardly, breaking the relative silence.

Both heads snapped up immediately. Steg was on his feet in seconds, closing the distance between us with a speed that made me remember how big he was. "SJ!" he shouted, pulling me into a crushing hug before I could react.

"Hey, bud," I croaked, patting his back weakly as he squeezed the air out of me.

When he finally let go, he stepped back, his sharp eyes scanning me like he was checking for damage. "What the fuck happened? We thought you and Tyrann quit or something! Allo hasn't said a word!" His voice hovered somewhere between relieved and accusing.

Before I could answer, he punched my unharmed arm—hard enough to sting but not enough to bruise. "Ouch!" I yelped, rubbing the spot. "What was that for?"

"For not calling!" Steg barked, his frustration spilling over. "Tyrann and you disappear. Allo goes into lockdown mode, and we're just supposed to sit here and guess what's going on? We thought you were dead, taken by aliens or something, man!"

I winced, rubbing my arm again. "Sorry," I mumbled. "That's on me. I should've let you guys know."

Kylo swiveled her chair around, her sharp eyes narrowing as she crossed her arms. "And Tyrann?" she asked, her voice calm but filled with concern.

"He's okay.," I said finally, exhaling deeply. "With a couple of bruises and a dislocated shoulder, but nothing serious. He'll be okay."

Kylo's face softened slightly, though her concern lingered. Steg looked like he was debating whether to punch me again.

"Look," I started, running a hand through my fur, "I can't get into everything right now. Allo's handling it, and it's kind of a long story. But I promise I'll explain soon. Just... know we stopped something big. Tyrann and I—we did what we had to."

Steg let out a long breath, his shoulders relaxing as he clapped a heavy hand on my shoulder. "You're an idiot," he said, his tone balancing exasperation and affection. "But you're our idiot."

Kylo gave a small nod, leaning back in her chair. "Good to have you back, Fox. Just don't make it a habit to ghost us like that again."

I chuckled weakly. "Noted."

For a moment, the room felt lighter, the tension dissolving into something that felt like normalcy. The three of us stood there, in our little corner.

"Alright," I said, stepping back and glancing at the clock on the wall. "I'm heading to the hospital to check on Tyrann. Wanna tag along?"

"I'm busy," Steg said, flicking his paper football with exaggerated precision. "Let me finish this. Goal!" he shouted, raising his arms triumphantly. Then he grinned. "Okay, let's go."

"Dork," Kylo said with a shake of her head, though her grin matched his.

The day had been long and brutal, but I wasn't alone in this fight. There were still questions to answer, consequences to face, and battles to fight—but for now, I had my team, my friends. And that was enough.

The warmth of home was almost disorienting after the week I'd had. The smell of my dad's famous holiday roast filled the air, mingling with the faint scent of pine from the slightly lopsided Christmas tree in the corner. My mom fussed over the dining table, straightening napkins that were already perfectly aligned, while Andy and Dad argued over hockey.

It felt like everything might be okay.

They didn't ask about what had happened last week. Maybe they were waiting for me to bring it up, or maybe they preferred not knowing, trusting that whatever I was involved in, I'd done my best. Either way, the silence on the subject was both comforting and unnerving.

Dad's voice broke my thoughts. "So, how's Carlos? We still want to meet him. Maybe he can come tomorrow if he's not busy."

My ears twitched. Carlos. I hadn't spoken to him much since December 23rd. A couple of texts, mostly just a few words, exchanged. Between the attacks, the mission, and everything in between, we'd drifted. *Could he be mad that I'd ditched him that night? Could that be it?*

"He's okay," I said to my dad. "We haven't seen this week. I've been busy. I can ask him if he wants to come tomorrow."

I pulled out my phone, typing out a quick message.

Hi Yeen! Happy almost-New Year!!

I miss you. Just wanted to check in and see how you're doing.

Dad's asking about you again.
He invited you over tomorrow if you're free.

His reply came quickly, but the words felt distant.

Hey.

All good.

Busy with family stuff.
Happy New Year too.

I stared at the screen, rereading his message. It wasn't like Carlos to be cold— at least, not with me. I thought about pressing, but I didn't have the energy for it. Not when it felt like the start of a breakup.

However, I wasn't going to hold back telling him how I felt, not after that week. I wanted to say it in person, but I needed him to know.

Love you,

Hope we can see each other soon.

A reply didn't come right away. I shoved my phone into my pocket, deciding to let it go for the night. This was family time, and I wasn't going to let my doubts overshadow it.

The hours slipped by in a mix of laughter and food. Andy dragged me into a heated debate about the best sci-fi movie of the year while Mom rolled her eyes, and Dad cracked open the good champagne a little early.

The countdown was about to begin. Ten seconds to midnight, and I tried to let the moment carry me. *Finally, this shitty year would be over.*

For what comes next, I don't know exactly what happened. I wasn't there. But if I had to imagine, it went something like this:

Carlos sat alone in his childhood bedroom, staring at his phone. My last message glowed on the screen.

Love you,

Hope we can see each other soon.

His thumb hovered over the keyboard. He could lie again—tell me he loved me too, and keep playing with me.

But he couldn't. Not anymore. The weight of everything was crushing him.

He typed and retyped his reply, each draft feeling more hollow than the last. The words blurred together as the enormity of his actions bore down on him.

He took a deep breath, and before he could stop himself, the truth slipped out:

Spencer. I need to be honest with you.

His text came while I was halfway through a sip of champagne. I picked my phone up, ready to take a midnight picture, but the words on the screen weren't what I'd expected.

I am a member of Chasing Tails, and

I've been working with Victor for a while.

The room seemed to tilt. My fingers tightened around the phone as I set the glass down. My heart hammered against my ribs, and the air felt thick, suffocating. I forced myself to keep reading, each word sharper than the last.

At first, it was just about getting close to you.

To trick you into giving me information GUIP had about us.

But... things changed.

I got to know you, and I fell for you.

Victor told me no one would get hurt, and I believed him.

The attack on the market. I gave them the location. I misunderstood your message, thinking you were going to stay at GUIP.

I didn't want any of this to happen.

I'm sorry.

The message trailed off, but I couldn't bring myself to read it. Around me, my family cheered as the countdown echoed through the house.

Ten. Nine. Eight...

The words blurred on the screen, but I couldn't look away. Carlos. The one I'd let into my life—into my heart. And he'd been the one to betray me.

Seven. Six. Five...

Tears pricked at the corners of my eyes, but I refused to let them fall. The cheers around me felt like mockery, a cruel reminder that the world kept spinning while mine had stopped.

Four. Three. Two...

I clenched the phone in my hand, the glass of champagne forgotten on the table. My mind was a storm of emotions—anger, heartbreak, sadness. But beneath it all, a single, burning thought took hold: *This isn't over.*

One.

Fireworks lit up the night, their bursts of colour painting the sky outside. The surrounding cheers grew louder, but all I could hear was the pounding of my own heart.

I stared at the message one last time before locking the screen. The phone felt heavy in my grip, as if it carried the weight of every decision Carlos had made.

He had made his choice. Now I had to make mine.

Chapter 19

LOST CONTROL

Anger is a powerful tool. It pushes you forward. Makes you do things you never thought you were capable of.

But anger is also dangerous. It clouds your judgment, blinds you to reason, and makes you forget about yourself and about the people around you.

And when you mix anger and heartbreak?

Shit goes downhill. Fast.

The months after Carlos' confession, I was a walking shit show. Doing everything I could to take down the bastards who send him my way.

With Tyrann still out of commission, I took the lead against Chasing Tails. Looking back, I shouldn't have. I went over my head—I was reckless, stupid, and a liability to anyone.

And honestly, Alicia? Cooper? How the fuck did you two let me? I mean, don't get me wrong—I'm grateful you stuck by my side even when I didn't deserve it. But still, what the fuck guys?

I wasn't thinking. I wasn't planning. I was just moving, one target after another, hoping to fill the void inside me with a victory that never felt close enough.

So, here's how it went down:

The warehouse door blasted inward with a sharp crack, splinters flying. My pulse surged as we stormed inside.

It was the third raid that month. I should've been running thin, but adrenaline and anger kept me moving. Every hideout we hit was another step closer to Victor. Another step closer to payback.

"Clear the area!" I barked, sweeping every corner.

Steg fell into position next to me, his golden floppy ears pinned back.

"Nyx," he muttered, his voice mixing with the crunch of our boots against the dusty floor. "Maybe we should slow down."

I didn't even look at him. "We can't afford to slow down," I said, snapping at him, tail lashing. "Every second we waste, these bastards get stronger."

Steg frowned but didn't argue. He knew better by then.

Kylo had tagged along, despite not being cleared (or allowed, really) for field-work. I hadn't cared. My trust was stretched thin, and I only brought people I knew wouldn't fuck it up.

"Yeah, because sleep is for the weak, right?" Kylo said dryly, ducking under a rusted beam. Her ears twitched. "Who needs rest when we can just grind our-selves into the dirt?"

I ignored her, already rifling through a desk piled high with scattered papers. My hands trembled—not from fear, but from too much caffeine and not enough of anything else.

I couldn't stop. Not when we were that close.

The constant flashing of Carlos' face on my mind—his lies, the pain he helped cause. And the memory of Tyrann, bloodied and unconscious, barely clinging to life. My vision blurred with anger every time. It had to end, and I had to be the one ending it.

"I found something!" Kylo's voice snapped me back. She held up a crumpled paper stack, a sharp grin showcasing her excitement. "Looks like shipping routes. Contracts and stuff like that. Could be useful."

I snatched it from her, scanning the words.

"Good work Kylo," I muttered, my voice rough. "Lets go back to HQ so we can analyze it."

By the time we got back, I was filled with exhaustion, but I refused to give in. One by one, the others headed out for the night, leaving only the hum of the computers, the distant murmur of late-night agents in the halls—and Steg's snores after he collapsed, dead tired at his desk.

I went over documents and cross-referencing locations. My head was killing me, my eyes burned, but I had to keep going.

A chair scraped behind me. I turned and spotted Kylo, arms crossed, fur ruf-fled from exhaustion, her tail flicking in irritation. "SJ, please go home."

"I'm fine," I said, my voice annoyed as I shook my head.

Kylo didn't move. "Bullshit Spencer. You haven't slept properly in weeks."

"I don't need sleep, Alecia," I shot back, sharper than I intended. "I need re-sults."

"I make you a deal." She said, although her expression didn't change. "I'd show you what I found, but only if you promise to head home after. Deal?"

I let out what what it sounded like a dry angry growl. "Ugh. Fine."

She pulled out a USB drive and held it up. "Good. Because you're gonna love this."

I frowned as she plugged the drive into the terminal. The screen came to life, revealing images of a fortified warehouse on the outskirts of town—satellite images, blueprints, shipping manifest, stuff like that.

The exhaustion disappeared. My ears perked, tail going still. "Shit. Is that...?"

Kylo's grin was sharp, triumphant. "Chasing Tails' primary base of operations. Spence, we finally found it."

"Holy fuck, Kylo!" I shouted.

Steg jolted awake at my outburst, ears twitching as he blinked rapidly. He scrubbed a paw over his face, squinting at the screen.

"What?" he blurted, his grin spreading as he leaned in. Then his expression hardened. "Wait—is that...?"

I clenched my fists, anger spilling out. "It is, Coop! And I just hope Victor's ready to get fucked."

"Hell yeah, dude!" Steg echoed, followed by a loud yawn.

"Let's go home," I said, my voice softer now. "We need to plan how we're taking them down."

That was it—our best shot at shutting them down for good. And making Victor pay.

We were ready, and this time, Chasing Tails wouldn't know what hit them.

The following weeks were a blur of planning—gathering intel, studying every inch of the base, and vetting every agent we could. There was no room for error.

We stood outside the looming warehouse. (Yes, another warehouse. Apparently, it's the number one real estate choice for illicit activities.)

The hulking structure cast long shadows under the dim moonlight, its metal siding groaning against the winter wind. My fur bristled as we approached, every nerve humming with anticipation.

Steg moved in sync beside me, his presence a steadying force against the storm in my head.

"Alright," I whispered, barely audible over the distant hum of traffic. "You know the drill. Breach team, prepare to enter hot. Stick to the plan, and keep comms open. If you need support, use your radio—Kylo's on standby."

Steg's warm paw landed on my shoulder. "Be careful in there, bud. Don't do anything I wouldn't do."

I snorted. "That leaves a lot of stupid options open, doesn't it?"

"Hey!" Steg's offended tone was lighthearted, but guilt crept in as soon as I heard him. I exhaled. "Sorry, I'm not in the best mood."

Kylo's voice crackled in our earpieces, cutting through the moment. "Cut the chatter, boys. Outer sensors are down. You're clear to move."

We slipped into the shadows, each agent splitting off to secure different parts of the unit. My breath was steady, but my heart was quite the opposite.

Inside, the warehouse was a maze of towering crates and rusted industrial equipment.

Moving cautiously, I picked up snippets of hushed conversations between Chasing Tails operatives, their voices had a hint of excitement.

"...biggest hit yet..."

"...show those freaks what real humans can do..."

My claws flexed involuntarily. It took everything I had to not act, not to tear through them right then and there. But Victor was the target. Everything else was just noise.

I pressed my back against a stack of crates as they strode past.

"...Hargrove said the bombs will be ready by dawn..."

A low growl started in my throat before I swallowed it back. *Focus, Spencer. Stick to the target.*

I moved deeper, each step measured, each creak of the floorboards making my muscles tense. The dim lighting and eerie silence made the space feel alive—like the shadows were watching me.

At the end of a long corridor, I found him. Victor.

He stood in a dimly lit office, back turned, sifting through neatly stacked documents on his desk. Everything about the space reeked of arrogance—sleek furniture, polished metal accents, expensive liquors crap like that, it was the kind of place designed to remind everyone that he was in control.

I pressed my fingers to my earpiece. "Got visual on the target. North upper side," I murmured.

Slipping inside, I shut the door with an audible click.

Victor turned slowly, his smirk already in place.

"Well, well, well," he said, spreading his arms theatrically. "It was about time for GUIP's favourite little pet to arrive."

He leaned back against his desk, studying me like I was exactly where he wanted me.

"Pseudo-agent Nyx. The petite Spencer James," he drawled, shaking his head in mock disappointment. "You're becoming terribly predictable."

My fur bristled, every nerve on edge. "Game's over, Victor. We know about your plans. They end tonight."

He chuckled, the sound grating and self-satisfied. "Oh, Bary. Can I call you Bary? Bary it is," he said, as though the decision was his to make.

"It's *Agent Baryonyx*," I snapped, refusing to let him see how much he was getting under my skin.

Victor's grin widened, his eyes glinting with amusement. "Oh, I don't think so. Bary suits you better—short, simple, and insignificant, like you." His tone was casual, but every word was calculated to dig deep. "You really think it's that simple?" He continued. "That you can just waltz in here and stop it all? You're nothing but a pawn in a game you are too stupid to even begin to comprehend."

"Save it," I barked, raising my weapon. "You're coming with me."

Victor's eyes flickered with predatory amusement, his smug confidence unshaken. "Tell me something, Bary," he said, his tone sharp. "Did you really think Carlos cared about you? That anyone does?"

The words hit me. My grip faltered, memories of Carlos flooding my mind—his smile, his touch, the sting of his betrayal.

"Shut the fuck up," I hissed, my voice trembling with rage. "And again, it's *Agent Baryonyx* to you."

Victor tilted his head, his smile widening as he leaned into my hesitation. "Face it, little Bary. You're a freak. A mistake. Even your own kind can't stand you."

My weapon rose, my left hand trembling as I aimed at him. His words burrowed deep, unearthing doubts I thought I'd buried long ago. Just as I tightened my grip, Kylo's voice crackled in my earpiece, cutting through the fog of my thoughts.

"Nyx, status update. What's going on in there?"

Her voice grounded me, snapping me out of the spiral. I adjusted my grip, forcing my hand to steady. "All good," I murmured into the comm. "Target is restrained. Requesting backup for arrest."

Victor's smirk faltered, if only slightly, as I stepped closer. *It's over*, I told myself. *His game ends here.*

He yawned theatrically, feigning boredom. "You're so naïve. You've never done anything right in your life, so why pretend now?"

Red blurred the edges of my vision, his words triggering every insecurity I'd fought to bury. My finger twitched on the trigger.

"You don't know anything about me," I snarled, but a small voice in the back of my mind whispered: *What if he's right?*

Victor leaned forward, his tone dropping to a low, venomous whisper. "Don't I? Carlos did. And well, he told me you're alone, Bary. I know you're scared. And I know, deep down, you're just like us—angry at the world for what you are. Desperate to be normal."

I wanted to pull the trigger—every fibre of my being screamed for it. A simple motion, a single act to silence him forever. But something held me back. Morality? Fear? Or was it the gnawing thought that Victor might be right?

"You're wrong," I said, but my voice lacked the conviction I wanted. "I'm nothing like you."

Victor's smile widened. "Aren't you? You want to pull that trigger, don't you? Come on, little pet. Show me what kind of monster you really are."

"Shut up! Shut the fuck up!" I snarled, the pressure in my chest building, my finger tightening on the trigger. I stepped closer, extending the weapon closer to Victor.

Just as I felt myself teetering on the edge, a familiar voice broke through the storm in my mind. "You're not like him, Nyx," Steg said, steady and urgent. "You're better. Don't let him pull you down to his level."

I blinked, the red haze clearing as Steg's golden fur came into focus. His eyes filled with concern—and something I hadn't realized I needed: unwavering faith.

"Pests need to be exterminated," I muttered, hovering over the trigger, my voice cracking under the weight of my emotions. "He needs to be stopped."

"I know," Steg said gently, but firmly. "But this isn't the way. This isn't you."

Victor's grin faltered for a split second before he sneered, recovering quickly. "How cliché," he drawled. "The freak show sticks together."

Before I could retort, a loud *crack* shattered the tension. A bullet collapsed with a nearby shelf, sending shards of glass flying as an expensive wine bottle exploded.

Followed a piercing alarm blared, and red lights began flashing throughout the warehouse.

"Shit," I muttered, my instincts kicking in as the sound of footsteps filled the air. Chasing Tails operatives poured in from every entrance, their weapons trained on us.

"We've got company!" Steg said.

Gunfire erupted, sharp and relentless. I yanked Victor forward, snapping handcuffs onto him before dragging him behind a stack of crates. My heart hammered in my chest, but the chaos faded into a sharp, focused calm. *This,* I thought grimly, *I can handle.*

"So much for a quiet arrest," I said, crouching beside Steg. He returned fire.

"Any bright ideas?" he asked, ducking as more bullets tore through the air.

"Yeah," I replied. "Walk out of here alive."

We sprang into action. I pushed Victor forward, forcing him to stumble ahead of me, my tail swishing behind as I darted between crates. My ears twitched, catching the click of a rifle being raised.

"On your left!" I shouted, spotting a cheetah aniform taking aim at Steg.

Steg pivoted, but not fast enough. The crack of a shot was followed by his pained yelp. I panicked as I saw blood seeping through his sleeve.

"Shit!" he barked, gritting his teeth.

"Steg!" I said, rushing to his side.

He waved me off, his voice rough but steady. "I'm fine. It's just a scratch," he growled, raising his gun with his good arm. "I'm not out of this fight yet."

"Alright, tough guy. Let's finish this."

Steg's resilience ignited something in me. As we pressed forward, the adrenaline pushed aside my doubts.

"Can you just give up already?" Victor said, his tone maddeningly calm, like he wasn't standing in the middle of a war zone. "Don't get me wrong, I've enjoyed watching you take out some of those idiots—useful, sure, but entirely expendable. Face it: you're not walking out of here alive. And I've got dinner reservations."

"Shut up!" Steg and I barked in unison.

I tapped my earpiece. "Kylo, we need backup! Shots fired. Now."

"On it," she replied, her voice clipped but reassuring.

Steg smirked through his pain, aiming at another operative. "Let's show these assholes what real tails can do."

"Save that line for when they turn this into a movie." I said.

Victor groaned dramatically. "Ugh. Neither of you are funny."

"Shut up!" Steg and I barked in unison again.

One step at a time, we'd bring these bastards down. And no matter what Victor thought, we were getting out of this alive.

Smoke filled the air, mingling with the scent of gunpowder. My ears twitched, catching snippets of panicked shouts from Chasing Tails members as the thundering sound of GUIP reinforcements storming the warehouse. The tide had turned, and they knew it.

"They're falling back!" I yelled, my tail swishing with adrenaline. "Time to wrap this up!"

More agents poured in, corralling the scattering remnants of Chasing Tails into submission. The once-menacing operatives now looked like rats abandoning a sinking ship, their faces pale as agents secured the building. Steg gave me a bloodied thumbs-up as he leaned against a crate.

Things began to quiet down. I scanned the room, checking if it was safe to leave cover. That's when I caught a door swinging shut—behind a familiar silhouette.

"Fuck. Steg, Victor!" I growled, my fur bristling.

I bolted for the exit. My footsteps echoed against the concrete as I burst through the door, the noise inside fading to nothing. But when I hit the alley, he was already gone. The narrow street stretched out empty, save for a couple of toppled trash cans and the distant hum of the night city beyond.

"Dammit!" I snarled, slamming my fist against the wall. My claws scratched against the cold stone.

"Kylo," I said into the comm, "please tell me we've got air support. Victor's heading west side of the building!"

"Chopper's three minutes out," she replied, her voice strained but steady. "We've locked down the perimeter. If he's still in range, we'll find him."

Three minutes felt like an eternity. Victor was slippery, and I knew better than to underestimate him. My fists clenched as I forced myself to breathe, scanning the empty alley for any sign of him. But the only movement came from the wind stirring discarded trash.

Behind me. GUIP agents moved with precision, hauling operatives into armoured vehicles, confiscating weapons and Zenitharian artifacts. Chasing Tails' infrastructure was crumbling before my eyes. I knew I should've had to be happy, but the absence of their mastermind made it feel hollow—unfinished.

Steg appeared at my side, his face tight with pain he tried to mask. "We'll get him, SJ," he said, his voice firm but gentle. "We will."

I nodded. "We sure will," I muttered, mostly to myself. For a moment, we just stood there, panting, the adrenaline crash hitting both of us. I glanced at him, noticing him shifting his arm awkwardly, his sleeve darkening with blood.

"How's the arm?" I asked, raising an eyebrow.

He blinked, glancing down at the injury as if noticing it for the first time. "Oh, right!" he yelped, flashing a sheepish grin. "Guess I should hit medical before this gets worse."

I shook my head with a small smile and clapped him on the back. "Yeah, you think?"

Together, we trudged back inside. The sight of the dismantling Chasing Tails' operation brought a flicker of satisfaction to my chest. Weapons were being secured, computers confiscated, and data drives extracted for analysis. Kylo, having left her monitoring van, stood over a laptop at a makeshift station, her fingers flying as she decrypted files in real time.

"Got a list of their safe houses," she announced, her wolfish grin spreading as she glanced up. "And a lot of dirt on their supporters. This is going to take them years to recover from."

It was a win. A big one. But as I stared at the wreckage, my mind kept drifting to Victor's mocking smile, his taunts ringing in my ears.

"You good, Nyx?" Steg's voice cut through my thoughts, softer this time. He was studying me carefully.

I didn't answer right away. My fists clenched at my sides as I took one last look at the shattered remnants of Chasing Tails. Then I muttered "yeah."

Steg placed a hand on my shoulder, his grip solid and reassuring. "Don't worry bud. We'll find him."

I met his gaze and nodded, "Yeah," I said, my voice steady now. "We fucking will."

As I stepped back into the ruined warehouse, I made a silent vow. This wasn't over. Victor could run, but he wouldn't get far. I'd find him—no matter what it took.

Hours later, I stood outside Tyrann's apartment, the city's quiet hum a stark contrast to the tension clawing at my chest. I hesitated before knocking.

The door opened before I could second-guess myself, and there he was—Tyrann, his feline features etched with weariness. His sharp eyes softened when they landed on me, a small smile breaking through his usual stoic demeanour.

"Nyx," he said simply, stepping aside. "Come in!"

The words spilled out as soon as I crossed the threshold. "We did it. Ty. Chasing Tails is finished." My tail wagged briefly, a flicker of triumph quickly snuffed out. My ears dropped, and my tail followed. "But Victor... he escaped. I couldn't stop him."

Tyrann's tail twitched, but his voice remained steady. "Sit down. Want some tea?"

I nodded, sinking onto the couch as he disappeared into the kitchen. The adrenaline had long worn off, leaving behind only the raw ache I'd been holding back. The silence in his absence pressed on, amplifying my doubts.

When he returned, he handed me a mug and took the armchair across from me. His sharp gaze met mine, unwavering. "You can't blame yourself, Nyx. Victor's been at this game a long time."

"But I let him escape," I snapped, my tail lashing against the couch. "How many more people is he going to hurt because of me? I let everyone down."

Tyrann studied me for a moment before speaking, his tone firm. "You didn't let anyone down, Nyx. You took down an entire organization today. That's a huge win."

"It doesn't feel like a win," I muttered, gripping the mug tightly. "I was so close, Ty. I could have ended him. "

His ears flicked, his expression hardening—not with anger, but worry. "To end him?" he asked, his voice low and pointed.

I avoided his gaze, staring into my tea. "I had him, Ty. I could've k—. But I didn't. I couldn't pull the trigger."

We remanded silent for a while. I stared at my mug. Tyrann's tail stilled. Finally, he exhaled. "Do you know what would've happened if you had?"

"I don't know!" I snapped, my voice cracking. "But maybe I wouldn't feel like this—like I failed."

Tyrann leaned forward, locking eyes on mine. "You think it would've fixed everything? That all your anger would've disappeared? Let me tell you something—it doesn't. I've been there. It really doesn't."

I opened my mouth to argue, but nothing came out. He was right, and I *fucking* hated it.

"You didn't fail," he continued, his voice softer now. "You made a choice—a hard one. And that's what makes you better than Victor."

I stared into my tea, my ears drooping. "It doesn't feel like it. It feels like I let everyone down."

"You didn't," Tyrann said, his tone resolute. "Actually, you did the opposite. This job breaks people, Nyx. It twists them up and leaves them hollow. But you? You held on. That's not failure. That's strength."

I let out a shaky breath. "I just... I feel so lost, Ty. I don't even know who I am anymore. How am I supposed to pretend everything's okay when it's not? I finally let someone in and I hate that I still love that *fucker* after everything he did to me—to us."

Tyrann's expression softened, his sharp gaze laced with understanding. "It's not wrong to feel hurt, Nyx. You have every right to be angry. But don't let it control you. Anger can drive you forward or destroy you. The choice is yours."

I nodded faintly, his words slowly sinking in. "Ugh. I guess I have a decision to make.."

He stood, setting his mug aside and ruffling my ears like a big brother might. "Yeah. Now drink your tea, rookie. And cut yourself some slack—you did good today."

I smirked faintly. The heaviness in my chest eased just a little. "Now that you've petted me, how about a treat?"

He chuckled softly, shaking his head.

And for the first time that night, I felt a flicker of something I hadn't in a while—hope. Tyrann's quiet faith in me was grounding in a way I hadn't expected. It didn't fix everything, but it was a start.

"Fuck. I should probably apologize to Kylo and Steg." I said, my ears lowering.

He chuckled. "Probably. I'm sure they understand what you've been through. They're tougher than they look, but an apology wouldn't hurt."

I nodded, letting out a small sigh. "Yeah, you're right. I've been kind of an asshole to them lately."

"They'll get over it," Tyrann said with a reassuring smile. "Just don't keep them waiting too long."

"I won't," I said softly, looking at him. "Thanks for being there for me, Ty."

"Anytime, Spence," he replied with a grin.

"Hey! You said my name! Does this mean I can call you Riley? Or maybe Ry? Or Riles?" I asked with a smirk. Then Victor's mocking voice echoed in my head, and I grimaced. "Ugh. I sound like him. Victor tried to call me Bary. Nothing wrong with the name, but definitely not for me, you know?"

Tyrann chuckled, "I can get used to Bary," he teased.

I snorted, leaning back. "Please don't."

He laughed, his tail swishing. "Riley is fine. Just not at work. We don't need to give Allo more reasons to chase our tails."

I burst out laughing. "That was the perfect pun."

Tyrann leaned back in his chair. "You know," he said, a smile tugging at the corners of his mouth, "I've got some news that might interest you."

My ears perked up. "Oh yeah?"

"Doc's clearing me for field duty. I'll be back in action in a few weeks."

I blinked, surprised by the rush of emotions that washed over me—relief, excitement, and maybe a little anxiety. "Seriously? That's... that's great Riley!"

He nodded, "yeah I'm ready to get back out there. Someone's got to keep you kids in line, after all."

"Hey, I resent that. I'm at least a full-grown fox by now."

"Keep telling yourself that, rookie," Tyrann shot back. The warmth in his voice was undeniable.

The banter felt easy. We chatted a bit more, mostly about mundane things, which were something I really needed. As I stood to leave, I felt... lighter somehow. Tyrann's resilience, his unwavering commitment to the cause despite everything he'd been through—it was infectious.

"Thanks again, Riley," I said softly. "For everything."

He simply nodded, but in his eyes, I could see it—the same determination and faith he'd shown me since the beginning. No words were needed. We'd both been through hell, but we'd kept going together.

As I stepped back out into the city, the hum of the streets felt less oppressive. I could help but smile at the calmness of it.

The next day, back at the office. Tyrann's words from last night replayed in my mind as I made my way to the medical bay. The door was marked with a handwritten sign: *"Dogtor's Office"*—a friendly touch from the bear Aniform who ran the place. It brought a faint smile to my face.

Inside, Steg was perched on one of the examination tables, his arm wrapped in a crisp white bandage. His golden fur was slightly ruffled, but his trademark grin was firmly in place.

"Well, if it isn't the agent of the hour," I drawled, leaning against the doorframe. "How's the wing, bird dog?"

Steg barked out a laugh, flexing his arm dramatically. "This? Pfft. Just a scratch. You should see the other guy."

I rolled my eyes, but the smile tugging at my lips betrayed me. "I did. They were dragging him out in a bag. So yeah, you're definitely better."

The doctor, a sturdy-looking bear aniform, finished checking Steg's bandage and gave him a firm pat on the shoulder. "You got lucky. No surgery needed, but you need rest—four to six weeks, minimum. No fieldwork until then, got it?"

Steg winced slightly as he moved, though he tried to play it off. "Got it, Doc. No problem."

"Careful there, bud," I teased, stepping forward. "Need a hand?"

Steg smirked, hopping down from the table with exaggerated bravado. "Seriously, I'm fine. A little sore, but worth it. Besides, the ladies love scars, you know?"

I raised an eyebrow. "What the ladies like is way out of my area of expertise," I said, deadpan.

Steg chuckled, throwing an arm around my shoulder. "Fair enough. Either way, I'm cashing in on some serious sympathy points for tonight's date."

I snorted. "Of course you are."

"Damn right," he said with a wink.

As we slipped back into our usual banter, the tension of the past few weeks began to melt away. Victor was still out there, and the fight wasn't over, but for now, I let myself enjoy the small win.

I took a deep breath, steeling myself for what I needed to do next. "Alright, Cooper. Let's grab Kylo. There's something I need to say."

"Uh-oh. Sounds serious." He said.

"Kinda," I admitted, my tail swishing nervously behind me.

A few minutes later, we were in the briefing room. Kylo perched in a chair, her ears twitching as she watched me. Steg leaned against the wall, trying to look nonchalant despite his bandaged arm.

I took a deep breath. "Look, guys," I began, my ears flattening slightly. "I've been a huge asshole these past few months. I let my anger get the best of me, and I put you both in danger because of it."

I paused, swallowing hard. "I'm sorry. You deserve better. Hell, I need you guys more than I can say. Who knows where I'd be without you?"

Kylo's sharp expression softened, and she leaned forward. "Hey, Spence. Don't beat yourself up. You've been through a lot."

"Yeah, but that's no excuse," I said, shaking my head. "You've had my back, and I've probably owed you my life—and definitely my sanity."

Steg smirked, pushing off the wall with a wince. "Well, I wouldn't go that far. Your sanity's always been questionable at best."

I chuckled. "Thanks, bud. But seriously, I'm lucky to have you both as friends. I'll do better. I promise."

The mood in the room shifted. The heavy tension that had hung between us for weeks seemed to dissipate, leaving something lighter in its place.

"Alright," I said, straightening up. "Now that the mushy stuff is out of the way, we've got more pressing business. Steg—who's this girl you're meeting tonight?"

Kylo's ears perked up, her arms crossing. "Yeah. Name, address, social insurance number, and date of birth, please. I'm running a full background check this time. We don't need another Carlos situation."

I groaned. "Thanks, Kylo. Subtle as always. But... probably not wrong."

Steg waved his good arm dramatically. "Hey, not much to tell. My old roommate introduced us. She works at Mapleview Bank."

"Really?" Kylo interjected, her tone dripping with mischief. "So, she handles your deposits, huh?"

Steg's laugh boomed through the room. "No comment."

We all burst into laughter, the tension completely broken.

Steg turned to me, his grin fading slightly. "Speaking of the asshole—Carlos— have you heard from him?"

I shook my head, my jaw tightening as I clenched my fists without realizing it. "No. And honestly? I'd prefer it stay that way."

Kylo clapped a hand on my shoulder, her grin sharp. "Just say the word, and we'll teach him a lesson."

"Thanks," I said, my tail wagging faintly. "Good friends who'd commit battery for me—what more could I ask for? Now, enough about me. Steg, stop deflecting. We need details."

Laughter filled the room again, Steg's grin and Kylo's biting wit bringing a rare sense of normalcy. Victor was still out there, but that is a problem for another day, but for that moment, I let myself savour it.

Chapter 20:
CUTTING TAILS

Ah, closure! The precious closure. The dictionary defines it as... *ugh*, this is boring. *Who the fuck cares?*

But for real—closure is part of human (and, Aniform, I guess) nature. Our brains crave it. Sometimes, you even have to trick yourself into believing things ended the way they were meant to, just to feel that sense of finality.

I wanted things to be different. I wanted Victor gone—completely out of the picture. But I made myself believe (or at least tried to, and kinda failed) that we got the best outcome we could.

At the very least, what we got was enough to make me grin when I spotted Tyrann's figure coming into view, his tail swishing behind him as he strode through GUIP's sliding glass doors.

A cheer went up from our little welcoming party, and I caught sight of his surprised expression just before it melted into that familiar warm smile.

"Welcome back, boss!" I called out, stepping forward to clasp his shoulder.

Tyrann's eyes twinkled as he looked down at me. "Miss me that much, Nyx?" he said.

I snorted, about to fire back a snarky retort when Kylo appeared, carrying an oversized cake. The frosting was a garish shade of orange—Tyrann's favourite colour—and scrawled across it in wobbly letters were the words: *Welcome Back, Work Dad!*

Tyrann's ears twitched, and I swear I saw the hint of a blush. "Work Dad, huh?" He said, turning to me with a knowing smirk. "I should've known this was your idea, you little troublemaker."

I held up my hands in mock surrender. "Whoa there, big guy. Don't go pinning this on me. This masterpiece," I said, gesturing to the cake with a flourish, "was all Kylo's doing."

Kylo's tail wagged as she set down the cake, her grey, and white fur ruffling slightly in pride. "Guilty as charged," she said with a wolfish grin, waving her ankle monitor.

Tyrann chuckled, shaking his head. "Aren't you only what? Five years younger than me? Practically a work sibling."

"Six, I'm 39, still in my 30s," Kylo quipped, grinning as she crossed her arms.

Tyrann shook his head with an amused chuckle. "Oh, forgive me, *youngster*."

Steg appeared from behind, his golden fur perfectly ruffled. Of course, since he was still recovering, he hadn't passed up the opportunity to show up at the office in sweatpants and a sweatshirt. A card rested on his bandaged arm, secured in a sling.

With a dramatic wag of his tail, he handed it over to Tyrann. "Here you go, boss," he said. "We all signed it."

Tyrann took the card, his ears twitch as he opened it. His expression softened as he scanned the scrawled signatures and heartfelt notes. "I can't believe you all did this," he said, his voice warm. "You really didn't have to."

"Of course we did," I said, stepping closer. "Your family, Ty. And we don't let family go without obnoxious cakes and over-the-top celebrations."

Kylo nodded. "Besides, if we didn't do this," she said. "Nyx probably would've thrown you some embarrassing solo party with balloons and confetti."

"Not true," I retorted, my tail flicking. "Well... maybe. But that's not the point."

Tyrann looked around at all of us. "Thanks, everyone. It's good to be back. And for the record," he said, his gaze flicked to me, a hint of mischief in his eyes, "I did miss you, son."

I rolled my eyes, trying to hide my grin. "Yeah, yeah. Let's not make this weird. Dad."

Tyrann's expression shifted, his usual no-nonsense demeanour taking over. "Alright, team," he said, his voice commanding. "Let's get back to work."

I straightened automatically, snapping me back into focus. As much as I enjoyed our lighter moments, we still had a job to do.

We filed into the briefing room, our hands full with plates of half-eaten cake.

"What we got?" Tyrann asked, leaning forward in his chair.

Kylo's tail swished as she pulled up a presentation. "Not much, unfortunately. The good news is, Chasing Tails digital trail has gone dark since Victor's disappearance. And the bad news? There's still no sign of him."

"So, we're back to chasing our own tails?" Tyrann asked.

"For now," I said, my ears flicking back. "But we're not giving up. Victor's out there somewhere, and we *will* find him."

"And what about double agents?"

"So far, a dozen agents have been uncovered," Kylo said. "They're facing charges for obstruction of justice and espionage. But... It's not over. We all are being audited, from top to bottom. There could be more."

"A dozen?" Tyrann said. "I was hoping it wouldn't be that many."

"And counting,"

"So," I said, crossing my arms, "can we even trust our own anymore?"

"Trust isn't something we can assume," Tyrann said, his tail still flicking, his expression hardening. "We need to rebuild, vet everyone from the ground up. And those who've stayed loyal? We give them the tools they need to succeed."

"And how about a pay raise?" I teased, my tail wagging.

Tyrann's lips twitched into a small smirk. "Someday, rookie,"

We continued the briefing for a while, catching Tyrann up on everything we'd been working on.

A gentle knock at the door made us all jump.

A lynx administrative assistant rolled in slightly, stopping just at the threshold, her expression apologetic.

"Excuse me, Agent Baryonyx?" she said, her voice low. "You have a visitor in Conference Room 2."

I tilted my head, confused. I never received visitors—not here, not anywhere. It made me uneasy, and I was half-inclined to refuse, but then my gaze shifted to Tyrann.

"It's okay, go," Tyrann said, with a subtle nod.

I hesitated, then stood, masking my unease with a cocky grin. "Don't do anything fun without me, eh?"

Kylo rolled her eyes, and Steg chucked. "Oh, you bet we will," Steg said.

I forced a laugh and followed the assistant, my tail flicking nervously.

As I made my way down the corridor, I couldn't shake the sense of nervousness. My eyes drifted to the faint wheel tracks left in the carpet ahead of me, and I followed them as I walked.

I took a deep breath to steady myself. My paw hesitated on the door handle for just a moment before I pushed it open. What greeted me made my blood boil.

"You!" I growled, my voice rising. "Please do me a favour. Get the fuck out of here before I throw you out through that window." I said. Gesturing to the floor-to-ceiling glass behind him. "Don't worry, you'll survive—I have experienced it."

Carlos stood in the room, his hyena ears twitching nervously. That stupidly adorable grin of his faltered as he took in my rigid posture and the fury in my eyes.

Carlos flinched. "Stud, please, hear me out—"

"No!" I snapped. The anger I'd been suppressing for months finally coming out. The betrayal. The lies. It all rushed back, sharper and more cutting than I'd prepared for.

"You don't get to crawl back and expect me to listen." I said. "You lied to me. You betrayed me. And your actions got people hurt. So, unless you're here to beg for a prison cell, my fist in your face, or both, we're done talking."

His ears drooped, and maybe were my feelings for him, but, I swear I saw a flicker of remorse in his expression. A part of me wanted to hug him, and to tell him everything could somehow be okay. But the memories of what he had done—the pain caused—pulled me away.

"Please," he pleaded, his voice cracking. "I know I messed up. But I want to make things right."

I scoffed, crossing my arms and stepping back to put more distance between us. "There's nothing you can do to fix this,"

"I didn't mean for any of it to happen." He said. "I thought I could control it, that no one would get hurt. That they just wanted to—" He exhaled sharply, shaking his head. "To restore what we lost. But then you... you showed me how to be okay with what I am. And when I saw what they were really capable of— what they did to you—I couldn't... I couldn't live with myself."

"That makes two of us," I shot back

Carlos's shoulders sagged, and he looked at me with puppy eyes. "I'm not asking for forgiveness, Stud. I don't deserve it. But I can help you take Victor down. Let me help."

I stared at him, my claws digging into my palms as I tried to process his words. The room felt suffocating, the weight of his betrayal clashing with the temptation of using his knowledge against Victor.

"I don't trust you," I said finally. "And I don't know if I ever will."

Carlos nodded, his gaze steady despite the pain in his expression. "I don't blame you. I'll do whatever it takes to make this right. Even if it kills me."

"That can be arranged." I said, letting out a sharp breath, crossing my arms. It came out harsher than I meant, but I didn't take it back. A petty, bitter part of me wanted him to feel just a fraction of the pain he'd put me through.

"I'm serious," Carlos insisted, stepping toward me. I instinctively backed away. "I have information—Victor's location. It's yours."

My ears twitched involuntarily at the mention of Victor. Damn it. Even as suspicion gnawed at my gut, I couldn't ignore the lead. "And why should I believe you?" I asked, narrowing my eyes.

Carlos' shoulders slumped. "Because... because I still care about you, Spencer." His voice was quiet, almost hesitant. "I know I don't deserve your forgiveness, but I thought maybe... if I shared this, we could start over."

I wanted to believe him. Wanted to close the distance between us, pretend none of this had happened. But my instincts screamed otherwise.

I exhaled sharply. "Doing the right thing shouldn't be conditional," I said coldly, holding out my hand. "Want to make amends? Give me the info and get out."

Carlos hesitated, visibly crushed by my dismissal. Slowly, he reached into his pocket and pulled out a USB drive, placing it in my paw—but held it tight for a moment longer.

"Spence, I—"

"Save it," I cut him off, yanking my arm away. "You should leave. Now. Before I punch you or decide to have you arrested."

His tail drooped as he turned to go, lingering for half a second before stepping through the door.

I let out a slow breath, my grip tightening around the drive.

For a while, I just stood there, staring down at it. My tail curled between my legs. For the first time in months, I let a few tears fall.

Taking a deep breath, I plugged the drive into the room terminal. The screen lit up with a wealth of data—documents, invoices, letters, emails, and copied text messages. All of it pointed to a hideout in the heart of Montreal's Centre-Ville.

Adrenaline coursed through me as I compiled the information into a mission briefing. Forty-five minutes later, I left the room, freshly printed documents in hand. By then, the briefing meeting was over, so I bursted into Tyrann's office, my tail wagging with excitement.

I slammed the papers onto his desk with a satisfying *thwack*. I scattered a few loose files. "What do you think, partner?" I grinned, baring my sharp canines. "Ready to come and kick some ass?"

Tyrann leaned back in his chair, a faint smirk tugging at his lips. "Do you know I'm still your boss, right?" he said.

"Yeah, yeah. For now," I fired back, my grin widening. "So, are you coming or what?"

He grabbed the document and started reading it, his eyes scanning each page. My heart raced as I waited for his response.

This was it—our chance to finally nail Victor. After everything that had happened, I needed this win.

"And where did you get this?"

"Carlos gave it to me," I said, my voice tight with annoyance as I said his name.

"Carlos? And you think it's real?"

"He said he wanted to make things right. I didn't want to believe him, but he seemed genuinely remorseful. Anyway, I did some digging, and the property is being leased by a foreign corporation registered as *CT Rising Holdings*. I mean, come on—could they make it more obvious?"

Tyrann stood, his powerful frame casting a shadow across the desk. "Road trip, then," he quipped, already heading for the door. "Come on. Let's gear up."

As we prepped for the mission, I couldn't shake the mix of emotions swirling in me. Excitement, sure, but also a gnawing uncertainty. *What if this was another dead end? What if I screwed up again?*

But as I caught Tyrann's steady gaze, I felt my doubts start to fade. We were a team. And together, we were going to bring Victor down.

The sleek GUIP vehicle purred beneath us as we sped down the highway, the familiar skyline of Mapleview fading in the rearview mirror. My tail twitched nervously against the leather seat.

Tyrann's eyes flicked toward me, his feline features unreadable. "Have you ever been to Montreal before?" he asked.

I snorted, my ears twitching. "Yeah. I was born there, actually. Moved to Mapleview when I was still in diapers. Been back a few times—to visit family and stuff."

Tyrann's tail swished in amusement. "I didn't know that."

"Really?" I shot back. "I would've bet the great Riley had all our files memorized."

"Okay, fine. I might have seen it there," he admitted, his tone light. "But it feels weird bringing up personal stuff before someone shares it themselves."

"Fair enough," I muttered, my grin widening. "Wait, did you know my name before I told you?"

Tyrann gave me a pointed look. "Oh, Spence. Do you really think we recruit people without a full background check? Although I knew it before we met."

"What? How? Was my name in some kind of prophecy or some magical shit like that?" I tilted my head.

Tyrann chuckled. "Not quite. Your name was in the Munch Munchy Bites app."

"Oh yeah. Forgot about that."

The tension in the car eased a bit, and I relaxed into the banter. For a moment, it was almost easy to forget we were racing toward another potentially life-threatening confrontation.

"You know," I said, a mischievous look on my face, "I'm actually the reason my parents got married in the first place."

Tyrann raised an eyebrow. "Really?"

"Yep! They never actually told me, but I did the math. Married in March, and I was born in July. Quite the scandalous origin story, right?"

Tyrann's laugh filled the car. "Somehow, that explains a lot about you."

"Hey!" I feigned offense, but his laughter was contagious.

The skyline of Montreal started to come into view. The sight should've brought some kind of comfort, but instead, it amplified the doubts in my mind.

"Hey," Tyrann's voice pull me back to the present. His sharp gaze flicked toward me. "You good?"

"Yeah, just enjoying the road," I replied, my tone light, even though I wasn't sure if I believed myself.

Tyrann nodded, but I could tell he wasn't entirely convinced. He didn't press further, though, and for that, I was grateful.

We parked in front of the building, the tinted windows of the unmarked vehicle shielding us from prying eyes. The quiet hum of the city outside was a stark contrast to the tension in the car.

Using binoculars, Tyrann and I took turns scanning the building for any sign of Victor.

Bursting in without knowing if he was actually there, would've been a rookie move—one we couldn't afford.

Three long, painfully boring hours later, there he was. Walking down the street toward the building, his casual stride making my fur bristle.

"There he is," Tyrann said, his voice low.

I followed his gaze and froze as Victor's eyes swept in our direction. For a split second, it felt like he was looking directly at us.

"Do you think he knows we're here?" I muttered, my tail twitching.

Tyrann shrugged. "I don't think so."

Victor entered the building, his pace unhurried—casual, like he had all the time in the world.

As we prepped to head inside, the parking garage door rumbled open. A sleek black SUV rolled out.

Inside, Victor sat comfortably, his smug grin aimed right at us as he passed—flipping us the finger.

"Yeah. He knows," I muttered, grabbing the radio. "Target spotted on Rue Notre-Dame. Black SUV, Ontario plate FCK AFRM, heading east. In pursuit."

"Hold your tail," Tyrann growled, slamming the accelerator.

The vehicle roared forward, and the siren shattered what little stealth we had left.

My heart raced as we tore through the streets, weaving between cars with a recklessness that would've made my dear old driving instructor faint. I gripped the dashboard, my claws digging tiny indentations into the plastic.

Victor swerved wildly, clearly trying to shake us off. "He's heading toward the Victoria Bridge!" I yelled, my ears flat against my head.

"Not for long," Tyrann said, his eyes locked on the target. He made a sharp turn, tires screeching as we cut through a side street to intercept.

"There!" I shouted, pointing as Victor's vehicle swerved around a corner two blocks ahead.

"He's heading for the rail yard!" Tyrann barked, his hands tight on the wheel as he made the turn.

The chase ended abruptly as Victor crashed and abandoned his vehicle at the edge of Pointe-Saint-Charles. The smell of burnt rubber filled my nose as Tyrann slammed on the brakes.

"Let's split up," Tyrann said, already moving toward the shadows of the train cars. "We can cover more ground until reinforcements arrive."

"Copy," I said, adrenaline pumping as I prepared to dash into the maze of rusted shipping containers.

But before I could move, Tyrann's hand clamped down on my shoulder, stopping me. "Wait," he said, his voice quieter now, almost hesitant.

"What?" I asked, confused by the sudden pause.

"You know what day it is?"

"Uh... yes, it's Tuesday... why?" I said. Confused.

Tyrann's whiskers twitched, and his lips curved into a rare, amused smile. "Well, yes. But also, tomorrow marks one year since we met."

An entire year since I'd stumbled into GUIP, a lost fox doing the bare minimum to exist. A year of battles, of growth, of discovering who I could be. And through it all, Tyrann had been there—first as a mentor, and now a friend.

"Wow," I managed, my voice thick with emotion. "Time flies when you're constantly on the edge of dying, eh?"

Tyrann chuckled. "True. Let's catch this bastard. Ready?"

"Let's go," I said.

Tyrann gave a sharp nod and disappeared into the shadows, and I followed, our footsteps fading into the clatter of the rail yard. *The hunt was on.*

I crept through the maze of train cars, ears swiveling to catch any hint of movement. The sharp scent of oil and metal mingled with the tang of my own nervous musk. Every shadow seemed to shift and writhe, each one hiding a potential threat.

"Vic, Vic, come out from wherever you are," I said, in a mocking tone. "Can you just give up already?"

A flicker of movement caught my eye. I spun around, but before I could react—a sharp pain exploded across my muzzle as something solid slammed into my face. I staggered back, my gun clattering away into the darkness. A massive weight crashed into me, knocking the air from my lungs as I hit the ground hard.

Victor's snarling face loomed above me. "Thought you could corner me, you mangy pet?" he growled.

Through the pain, I managed a wheezing laugh. "Well, what's the fun of a hunt without a chase?" I rasped, the copper tang of blood coating my tongue.

Summoning every bit of strength I had left, I drove my knee up into his crotch. He grunted, his grip loosening just enough for me to twist free. We scrambled to our feet, circling each other warily.

My mind raced as I sized him up. Victor's massive build was all muscle and fury, a stark contrast to my smaller, leaner frame. But I was quicker, more agile. *If I could keep him off balance, I might have a shot.*

"You know," I panted, dodging a wild swing, "for someone who hates Aniforms so much, you really rock the whole 'angry bear' aesthetic."

Victor's eyes flashed dangerously, his lips curling back in a snarl. "I'll tear you apart, you freak!"

He lunged, but I ducked under his arm, landing a solid punch to his kidney. Victor howled in pain and frustration, his fury driving him into another reckless charge.

Gritting my teeth against the burning in my muscles, I taunted, "How does it feel that a `dorky fox` is about to kick your ass?"

I feinted left, then darted right, using my speed to my advantage. Victor's massive fist swung through empty air as I slipped past him, shoving him hard from behind. He stumbled forward, crashing into the open door of a nearby train container marked with a volatile contents warning.

"Time for your nap, big guy?" I muttered, seizing the opportunity.

With a burst of adrenaline, I charged forward, ramming into Victor's back with everything I had. He tumbled into the container, the metallic clang of his impact echoing in the confined space.

"End of the line, Victor," I growled as I climbed back to my feet, fists clenched. "Your little hate group is done. And you're next."

Victor's eyes darted around wildly, searching for an escape. "You don't understand," he snarled. "Aniforms are an abomination. We have to—"

I rolled my eyes and cut him off with a fake yawn. "Yeah, yeah, yeah. Same tired speech. I've heard enough of your speciesist bullshit."

As the adrenaline began to fade, I sucked in deep breaths, trying to steady myself. *Just need to keep him contained until Tyrann gets here.*

Victor's breath came in ragged pants, but his smirk never wavered. His eyes gleamed with something dark.

"You should've shot me when you had the chance," he said, his voice dripping with malice.

My ears flicked forward as Victor's hand went behind his back. A glint of metal caught my eye. His fingers closed around a weapon.

I was too close. Too damn tired to move in time.

"Nyx!" Tyrann shouted behind me.

Victor raised the weapon, his grin triumphant. "Unlike you, I do know when to take the opportunity." He said.

Fuck me.

I flinched, squeezing my eyes shut—bracing for the pain. A gunshot rang out. But the pain never came.

Instead, the air itself seemed to rip apart. A shockwave slammed into my chest, crushing the breath from my lungs as a wave of heat rolled over me, scorching everything in its path.

The force sent me flying. My stomach lurched as the ground vanished beneath me. For a bit, there was nothing but weightlessness—then impact. Pain exploded through my spine as I hit the ground.

A split second later, a deafening boom shook the air, drowning out everything else.

My ears rang. *Loud. Too loud.*

Through the noise, a faint but familiar voice— "Spencer!"

A firm grip latched onto my arm, yanking me upright. My legs buckled, barely cooperating, but Tyrann didn't let go.

I stumbled forward, half-dragged, feet catching on debris. Behind us, flames roared. Sirens wailed in the distance. But all I focused on was the solid presence at my side, grounding me, pulling me toward safety.

The wreckage burned behind us, flames swallowing everything in their path. "That was too close." I said, my voice cracking. "Can't believe I let him get the drop on me."

Tyrann chuckled, low and unexpected, cutting through the tension.

"Don't beat yourself up," he said, casting me a smirk. "You did good. We made it out alive, didn't we?"

As we put distance between us and the explosion, my breath finally evened out. The heat still licked at my back, but the weight of what we'd just survived made my legs shaky.

"Victor didn't," I muttered, staring back at the twisted wreckage of the container.

"Ty holy fuck!". I exhaled sharply, leaning against a stack of crates for support. "I almost died back there."

Tyrann's face was a mix of concern and amusement. His ears twitched as he eyed me. "Welcome to fieldwork, kid," he said with a hint of dry humour. "How's it feel?"

I let out a shaky laugh, running a paw through my soot-streaked fur. "Honestly? Terrifying. I think I might throw up."

"Do it over there," Tyrann said, already pulling out his phone. "And try not to get it on my boots. We need to call this in and get a cleanup crew here ASAP."

As Tyrann made the call, I surveyed the surrounding destruction. The container was a mangled, smoldering wreck, flames licking at its edges. Somewhere inside that inferno was Victor—or what was left of him. A small, guilty part of me whispered that this wasn't how I'd wanted it to end. But mostly, I was just relieved it was over.

The sirens of approaching emergency vehicles echoed faintly in the distance, growing louder with each passing second. I turned back to Tyrann as he pocketed his phone, his expression more relaxed now that reinforcements were on the way.

"Hey, Tyrann?" I said softly.

He looked up, his sharp eyes meeting mine. "What's up?"

"Thanks for having my back at there,"

Tyrann clapped a firm hand on my shoulder. His tail swished behind him. "Always, partner. That's what teams are for."

The sirens wailed louder, red and blue lights slicing through the smoke that clung to the charred train cars. I stood still for a moment, taking it all in—the fire crews scrambling to contain the blaze, agents weaving through the wreckage, barking orders as they secured the site.

Amidst the destruction, a strange sense of clarity settled over me. For the first time in months, I knew exactly what needed to come next.

"I wonder what the Zenitharians are up to," I said, breaking the moment of calm with a playful grin. "They've been quiet lately, haven't they?"

Tyrann groaned, raising a hand dramatically. "God damn it, Spence. Why did you have to jinx it?"

"Sorry, bud," I replied with a smirk, the tension in my chest easing. "I'm worried about them. Think we should pay them a visit?"

Tyrann's expression softened, but his eyes remained sharp. "Let's focus on this victory first. Whatever they're planning... we'll be ready."

I nodded, letting his words settle over me like a comforting blanket. Tyrann was right. We'd won this battle, but the war wasn't over.

I allowed myself a small, weary smile as I surveyed the aftermath. This job wasn't easy. It was messy, dangerous, and sometimes felt impossible. But in that moment—standing beside Tyrann, the wreckage behind us and the unknown future ahead—I realized something important: *I was made for this.*

By the time I got home, the adrenaline had faded, leaving me bone-tired but restless. I found myself outside Steg's room, hesitating for just a second before knocking.

"Come in—unless you're here to give me more painkillers. In which case, definitely come in!" Steg's cheerful voice called out.

I couldn't help but grin as I pushed open the door. There he was, propped up in bed, his injured arm in a sling but his tail wagging furiously.

"How're you holding up, Mini-Coop?" I asked, leaning against the door-frame.

Steg's eyes twinkled with mischief. "Oh, you know, just hanging out. Getting shot is fantastic, highly recommend it."

I winced. "Oh yeah. You make it seem so nice."

"Ah, come on," Steg chuckled. "If I can't joke about it, what's the point?"

I rolled my eyes, but couldn't suppress a smile. Trust Steg to find the good side in a bullet wound.

His persistent optimism was contagious, gradually easing the guilt I felt after the raid.

"Listen, Steg," I started, ears flattening slightly. "I wanted to apologize again. If I hadn't been so reckless—"

Steg held up his good paw, cutting me off. "Nope. None of that. We're a team, remember? We watch each other's backs. And last I checked, you didn't pull the trigger."

I sighed, sinking into the chair beside his bed. "I know, but—"

"But nothing," he insisted, his tail thumping against the mattress. "We signed up for this. SJ. Danger comes with the job. And hey, it's getting me some matches on Tinder."

I snorted. "You're incorrigible, you know that?"

"It's part of my charm," Steg said with a wink. "Now, are you gonna keep moping, or are you gonna help me plan my *Welcome Back to Active Duty* party? I'm thinking streamers. Lots of streamers. Maybe balloons shaped like foxes and golden retrievers."

"Balloons? What are we, five?"

"Hey, balloons are universally loved. Like me."

I shook my head. "You're sure something, Coop."

As we bantered about increasingly ridiculous party ideas—including a suggestion involving glitter cannons that I firmly vetoed—I felt a warmth settle in my chest.

This was what it meant to have a team. A family. People who had your back in the field and knew how to pull you out of your own head when you started sinking under the weight of it all.

The next day, I stood in the conference room, taking a deep breath as I looked around at the faces of my newfound family.

Tyrann's steady, stoic gaze. Kylo's sharp focus. Steg's ever-present smirk, despite the bandage on his arm.

Memories flashed through my mind—the confusion of my transformation, the thrill of my first mission, the heartbreak, and betrayal. Through it all, these people had stood by me, even when I wasn't sure I could stand on my own.

My eyes flicked to the window, catching my reflection. Fox ears twitching slightly. Tail swishing behind me. The Spencer staring back wasn't the same one who stumbled into GUIP headquarters a year prior, clueless, afraid and just trying to survive.

I wasn't perfect. *Fuck*. Not even close. But I was stronger. Ready for anything.

Whatever lay ahead—Chasing Tails wannabes, Zenitharian schemes, the messy reality of this new world—I wasn't facing it alone.

Straightening my shoulders, I let a determined grin spread across my muzzle.

Time to show the world what this *dorky fox* was really made of.

ONE MORE THING

"Seriously, if you'd told me a year ago I'd trade my awful delivery gig for a GUIP badge, I'd have flipped you off and told you to quit whatever you were smoking. And yet... here I am. And honestly, I can't see myself doing anything else. This job has changed me, left its marks—like this raised line on my arm. What is it? Just a little souvenir from my rogue agent days."

"Days? Ha! wasn't even 24 hours." A snort cut through the room.

"Still counts, Steg!" I barked back, grinning. The room erupted in laughter, and for the first time in a while, it felt like everything might just be okay.

That little snippet was part of my toast during our victory party—a celebration we definitely deserved. Though, calling it a "party" might oversell it.

It was really just the usual gang: Kylo, Alex (Kylo's date—or hookup? Honestly, I'm not sure what they were), Steg, Jessica (Steg's girlfriend), Tyrann, Allo, and someone I assume was Allo's husband (though I don't think I heard him speak all night). Andy and my parents were there too, along with a few other agents. I should probably talk more about them at some point.

Instead of going somewhere fancy, we kept it simple: takeout from a fancy place, a ridiculous amount of drinks, and full control of the 10th floor at GUIP's headquarters. Our grand plan was to bitch about the year we'd survived. All taxpayer-funded! (Okay, not really—we all chipped in. But hey, our pay cheques *come* from taxes, so... thanks?)

Anyway, I wish I could say things got easier after that year. I'd be lying if I did. If anything, life found new and creative ways to throw shit our way.

Would I change anything? My life's been a rollercoaster of ups and downs. If I had the chance to redo it all... well, yeah, I'd probably change one thing. Okay, *definitely* a few things.

But even with all the mistakes, the close calls, and the pain, I wouldn't trade the life I've had so far for anything. Not the people I've met, not the bonds I've formed, and not the lessons I've learned—some of them the hard way.

I'm glad I've had the chance to share a bit of my story with you. But before I wrap up this, there's one last thing I think you'll like to know: how that party ended.

After my toast—and a few snarky remarks from Steg, who was definitely making the most of the open bar—the night carried on like only our weird little group could.

"So, Mr. Baez, any plans for the summer?" Tyrann asked my dad, casually swirling his drink.

"Oh, please, call me Enrique," Dad replied with a smile, taking another sip of his beer. "Mr. Baez is my father."

Tyrann nodded, his ears twitching slightly as he tried to get it right. "Okay, Enr-Enriq—Enrique."

Dad laughed warmly. "Not bad! Rick works too. As for plans, this one,"—he gestured toward me with his bottle— "keeps talking about heading south for a while. I wanted to visit my mother, so maybe we'll make it happen. And how about you?"

Tyrann tail flicking. "I don't know. I haven't taken any time off in five years. So, I might just visit my fiancée, if our schedules align."

Steg, who was in tipsy territory, barked from across the table, "Tyrann, don't you fucking dare get married without inviting us! Or—or Tyrann will be *piiiiiiissed*!" He started laughing at his own joke, then added, "Okay, maybe it's time to stop with the drinks."

We all burst out laughing. Even the Chief cracked a rare smile from her corner of the room. For a night, the weight of the world felt a little lighter. It wasn't perfect, but it was ours, and in that moment, that was enough.

At the corner, my brother leaned back against the wall, finishing a beer with a small grin, like he was taking it all in. I wandered over, handing him another bottle. "Hey, Andy, you figured out what you're doing after college?" I asked, leaning casually beside him.

"Actually, yeah," he said, his voice steady in a way that caught me off guard. "I recently got into a job I'm really excited about."

My ears perked up. "Oh? Do tell. Where is it?"

Andy hesitated for a moment, then looked me in the eye with that same determined grin he used to have as a kid when he was about to do something bold. "A little place called GUIP."

I stared at him. "GUIP? As in *this* GUIP?"

He nodded. "Yeah. I figured... after everything I've seen you do, everything you've fought for—it's where I need to be. Plus, this place could use some Norforms, you know?."

My tail swished. "That's awesome, dude!" I gave him a small bump on the arm. "Wait, does that make you the *first human in the field*? Or one of the first?"

"That's the plan," he said, his grin growing wider. "Someone has to start, right?"

I let out a low whistle, my ears twitching. "You're really sure about this? You've seen what this job is like. I know you can do it, but I just want to make sure you're ready for it."

Andy shrugged. "I'm sure. I want to do my part. And I'm not going in blind. I know what I'm signing up for."

I rubbed the back of my neck, trying not to let the pride swell too obviously on my face. "Alright, but... uh, are you even allowed to? You know, the whole 'nepotism' thing? Like, wouldn't be an issue if we end up working together."

Andy laughed, shaking his head. "Relax, Spence. I already disclosed everything. And signed like a thousand things. They know we're brothers. Besides..." He shot me a teasing look. "Maybe if you checked your emails once in a while, you'd already know."

"Ugh," I groaned, rolling my eyes. "I'll check them on a day when nobody's shooting at me, okay?"

Andy chuckled and clinked his beer bottle against mine. "Deal."

I looked at him for a bit, letting it sink in. I didn't just see my little brother— I saw someone ready to stand alongside me, ready to fight for something bigger than both of us. My tail wagged faintly, and I couldn't help but smile.

"Welcome to the mess, Andy," I said, shaking my head. "You're gonna love it."

"Yeah, but Mom? Not so much," he shot back with a smirk.

"Don't worry about her," I said, lowering my voice. "Just leave out the near-death experiences, and you'll be fine."

We both laughed.

"My training starts in two weeks," he said, taking another sip of his beer. "Got any tips?"

"Oh, plenty," I replied, leaning in conspiratorially. "Come over this weekend. Steg and I will run you through some pre-training. Deal?"

"Deal."

The party was still in full swing, laughter and clinking glasses filling the air. We'd even improvised a little dance floor by shoving some furniture aside. Steg was reenacting some over-the-top action scene—complete with sound effects— while Tyrann halfheartedly tried to keep him from knocking anything over.

It was chaotic, but the good kind—the kind that reminded you what it felt like to be alive.

"Another bottle down?" I asked, eyeing the increasingly empty table. "Do we even have more left?"

"I think there's a couple of wine bottles in Agent Sello's fridge," Steg said, his tail wagging mischievously. "We can... borrow them."

"Oh Steg. You are a bad influence, you know that?," I muttered, shaking my head.

"I'm a bad boy.," Steg said with a dramatic wave of his paw. "I'll bring you to the dark side soon enough."

I sighed. "Alright, alright, I'll grab them. Just... try not to burn the place down while I'm gone."

"No promises!" Steg shouted after me, earning a round of laughter.

My worries had slipped away, fading like a distant memory. The only thing that mattered was the people I was with—their laughter, their camaraderie, their presence. For one night, we could forget the problems and just be... normal.

The late hour had triggered the automatic lights, which dimmed when no motion was detected, leaving long stretches of darkness along the hallways. The party's hum was still audible in the distance, a soft and comforting reminder that the others were nearby, as I made my way toward Sello's fridge.

I didn't come to this side of the office often, so I barely noticed the faint glow of lights still on in some of the offices. *Maybe the motion sensors here were slower,* I thought. *Or maybe they hadn't upgraded the fixtures in this part of the building yet.* Either way, it wasn't worth thinking about.

Reaching the fridge, I scrawled a quick note on a post-it:

"I borrowed your bottles. -Tyrann."

He could handle the fallout better than I could, and honestly, it felt like the perfect move. I grabbed the bottles, feeling the cool glass against my paw, and turned back toward the party.

On my way back, I passed Conference Room 2 and couldn't help but stop. The floor-to-ceiling windows offered a stunning view of Mapleview's skyline. It was a breathtaking moment of stillness.

I pulled out my phone and snapped a picture, lingering for a moment longer than I'd planned.

I shook the thought away, muttering to myself, "Oh yeah. Corkscrew."

With a sigh, I made a quick detour to the kitchen, still carrying the warm buzz of contentment from the party. The sounds of laughter and music faded as I stepped into the kitchen, leaving me wrapped in an unsettling silence.

My paw hovered over the light switch, but I froze mid-motion. In the shadows, a figure loomed—ominous, familiar, yet with something I couldn't quite place.

A Calm, polite, and unmistakably smug voice broke the silence.

"Hello, Bary."

My heart stopped. My paws went slack, the bottles slipped from my grip and shattering on the floor with a deafening crash.

"Did you miss me?"

The voice was smooth, calculated, dripping with the kind of confidence that came from knowing you held all the cards.

Victor stood there, alive—and looking at me like he wanted to tear me apart.

The air felt too thick to breathe. My mind scrambled for something—anything—to say, to do.

But all I managed was a dry throat and two words that summed up everything.

"Oh, fuck."

A NOTE FROM THE AUTHOR

Hey there! Taylor here—but please, call me Tay. I hope you've enjoyed stepping into this world as much as I've enjoyed creating it. Which I believe you did If you've made it this far—unless, of course, you skipped ahead. In that case, hey no cheating! Go back to where you left off... I'll wait... Back again? Good.

This book results from a decade of daydreaming. Writing these silly stories has been my little escape during tough times, and I'm so glad I finally got to share them with you.

"My Dinosaur Life" was born from my dream of creating an animated show. But as it turns out, breaking into the animation industry is nearly impossible unless you know the right people (which, spoiler alert, I do not). Still, I'm relentless (or, as Nyx would say, 'Relentless... annoying... I've been called worse'). I had this story I wanted to be told, so I said, 'fuck it,' and turned it into a book.

Honestly, it still blows my mind. If you'd told me a year ago, I'd be writing a book, I would've said, 'Me? A book? Nah... That'll never happen.' Well, what a way to prove myself wrong. Kinda rude of me to me, don't you think?

The world of Nyx and the gang is close to my heart, and I wanted to make it feel real and personal.

At its core, I wanted to tell a story about acceptance, with characters like myself—people who feel alien in a world that doesn't seem to have a place for us—discovering their true potential. But I wanted to do it in a way that's thought-provoking without being preachy.

Did I make it work? Well, that's for you to decide.

There are still so many stories I want to tell in this universe, and I hope I'll get the chance to share them with you someday (maybe I can finally do it in an animated form... *wink wink* Netflix, Disney Plus, Amazon, Apple TV+—operators are waiting by the phone).

Now, just in case—after more than 200 pages—you're still wondering why a story about anthropomorphic animals, aliens, and wannabe police drama is called My Dinosaur Life.

The name started as a metaphor. It was originally called *Walking with Giants*—meant to reflect how the characters deal with oversized problems in a world that's changed beyond recognition. That feeling of being small, overwhelmed, or out of place? Yeah, that.

But the clever twist (if I can say so myself) is that it's also a direct reference to the plot, since the story follows Nyx's and his journey in GUIP's dinosaur division. So the title isn't just symbolic—it's literal too. And also, dinosaurs are coo, so.. Yeah.

Oh, and hey... if you really liked it, share it with your friends. Or If you hated it, share it with your enemies. Either way, spread the word!

From the bottom of my heart, thank you.

Wishing you all the best,

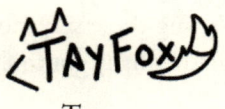

Tay.

ABOUT THE AUTHOR

Taylor Jay Fox is a creative guy with a passion for storytelling and a knack for crafting unique worlds. With an extensive career in web development and design. Now, you might wonder: What's a web developer doing writing about animal people and aliens? Great question! You see, I'm—I mean, he's—always been... well, let's call it imaginative.

Storytelling has always been a part of who I am (yeah, I dropped the whole third-person thing—it felt weird), right next to caffeine addiction and late-night overthinking. Writing lets me dive into the "what ifs" of life—a little escapism that's helped me navigate its more challenging parts.

I currently live somewhere between reality and my next idea, fuelled by a love of storytelling, connecting with others, and the occasional existential crisis. Oh, and also in Ottawa, Canada (the inspiration behind Mapleview).

MORE FROM TAY

Well, this is my first book. But I can assure you, it won't be my last. If you're hungry for more, here's a sneak peek at what's coming next from THE EMERGENCE UNIVERSE catchy name, right?

Emerging Tails.
A collection of stories that dive into the raw depths of the Aniform experience. These tales explore themes of identity, resilience, and self-discovery, showing how ordinary lives adapt, survive, and thrive in the face of extraordinary challenges.

Rory's Guide to Writing Fiction.
Rory's an aspiring writer, working on his debut novel and eager to share his totally ordinary creative process. Or so he thought.
As he struggles to find the perfect story, reality slips in ways he can't explain. Maybe his life isn't as normal as he believed—especially when he questions what's real... and what isn't. This isn't a sci-fi story... probably. Maybe.

And, of course, continuing Nyx's story.
Nyx's story is far from over. There's so much more to come (some hints are already out there), and I can't wait to share their next adventures with you.

Neat, right? If you want to stay updated on my latest projects and other shenanigans, head over to tayfox.ca, or don't... but that's rude.

TAY WAS HERE

www.ingramcontent.com/pod-product-compliance
Lightning Source LLC
LaVergne TN
LVHW040420210525
811744LV00006B/497